THE FINAL PLEASURE

When the vines coiled around him they were the arms of a lover that he embraced, his skin on fire and unable to feel the tiny needles piercing his flesh, the tiny mouths commencing to feast. A music blossomed nearby, a brilliant flute chased by falsetto voice, and everything within and without felt like magic.

He opened his eyes and found an empty skull the size of a small child's staring back—even this was beautiful. Overhead the stars danced to the music, a harmony to the melody of his death.

His death, he thought. *They were killing him!*

A
SECOND
INFINITY

MICHAEL D. WEAVER

AVON BOOKS • NEW YORK

A SECOND INFINITY is an original publication of Avon Books. This
work has never before appeared in book form. This work is a novel. Any
similarity to actual persons or events is purely coincidental.

AVON BOOKS
A division of
The Hearst Corporation
1350 Avenue of the Americas
New York, New York 10019

Copyright © 1996 by Michael D. Weaver
Cover art by Romas Kukalis
Published by arrangement with the author
Library of Congress Catalog Card Number: 95-96051
ISBN: 0-380-76101-7

First AvoNova Printing: June 1996

AVONOVA TRADEMARK REG. U.S. PAT. OFF. AND IN OTHER COUNTRIES,
MARCA REGISTRADA, HECHO EN U.S.A.

Printed in the U.S.A.

RA   10 9 8 7 6 5 4 3 2 1

I

IN THE BLUE LIGHT OF THE PHILADELPHIA MORNING, Derek Soul opted to walk to work. He needed time to think, not that he expected it to matter much; Secretary Collier rarely changed his mind. But in that case, Derek reasoned, Collier could damn well wait.

Overhead, official government flyers roared by in packs of twos and threes, making peaceful thought difficult but not entirely impossible. Now and then, the chirps of birds nesting in the trees along the empty sidewalks cut through the cacophony of the city, the capital of the United States of America, at least what was left of it. Derek had a sudden, ominous thought that he might never see any of this again. His future was Moscow; beyond that, he couldn't bring himself to imagine anything. The tunnels of the devastated Sov city spread out before him, a horrible hydra with all mouths open, dark jaws competing for the right to swallow him whole. He tried to laugh at the melodramatic imagery but failed; however overstated, the picture came too easily to his mind, too close to the nightmarish memories of his marriage. Collier could pontificate on the positive aspects of the mission all he liked; he'd never been to Moscow, but Derek had. It amazed him that they'd even consider him for the job—they being the RD personnel systems—much less insist he was the only qualified candidate. It made absolutely no sense at all, but the secretary's faith in artificial intelligence was complete, so Derek was faced with taking the job or, as his boss had so succinctly put it, else.

With the sun beginning to break through the buildings and touch the street, he could almost put a good face on it. Almost . . . After all, the travel orders had come attached to a permanent promotion to inspector general—wasn't there something positive in that? No—ten years before it might have made a difference, might have given him enough lift to pull himself up from the melancholic mire that had been the bed of his adulthood. Now he was too old to care. It occurred to him that his depression had begun here—not figuratively but literally—here on this very street. He stopped to ponder the thought, facing east where he could see the mighty towers of American government, just as they'd been that day, only now they marked a landscape of white, silver, and gray-black edges. Then they'd been orange—defiant, fiery monoliths against the black and bloody sky. He'd been walking, just as he was now. . . . An old woman had been coming by (he could picture the gnarled hand on her cane as vividly as if it all had happened only yesterday), then a flash high above had betrayed the arrival of the first bomb, and they'd stopped together to watch.

Derek smiled sadly at the thought of the old woman. Not a single word had passed between them the entire ten minutes they'd stood side by side, fixed to the sidewalk, while the world beyond the city had melted and burned. Protected by the Japanese peace shield, Philadelphia had survived, but elsewhere, the devastating nuclear barrage had rained down unopposed, and those in the city had witnessed the most terrifying display of fireworks ever seen by man.

When it had finished, he'd helped her along her way for a while before they'd parted. Still, they'd never let a word pass between them; with one look into her eyes, he'd learned all he'd needed to know. He wondered where she was now—whether she was still alive; he'd like to think so, but he knew in his heart she'd likely died that year, when the food had run low and the solar power reserves had been rationed in the long, sunless winter. He'd nearly died himself.

The renewed morning sunlight on the buildings was beautiful; it only pained him that there were so few left alive to see it. His father and the rest of his relatives in the Midwest had died that day, along with much of the rest of the world. If he'd found living since then a generally depressing endeavor, not even a psychtech could fault him.

So now he was going back to Moscow. . . . The Philadelphia sun could bring little light to his darkened heart; within him, mankind had never emerged from the bleak shadows of the nuclear night, each day but a borrowed nugget of time that could be neither invested nor repaid. And he was one of them, the last tenants in nature's crumbling house.

A brisk breeze came, and Derek pulled his jacket tight and hurried along. When he reached his office, Collier was waiting for him. "Where the *hell* have you been?" the old man spit impatiently. Derek shrugged; something in the morning had curbed his appetite for argument.

"Well," Collier said, opening up a portaterm on the desk between them, "this is your data link for the trip. Say hello to Dr. Soul, Juliet."

"Hello, Dr. Soul," came a soft, feminine voice from the machine.

"I think you'll find her more than adequate," Collier said with a smile. "She's absolutely the best we have."

"I'm sure she is."

The secretary talked on for a while, but Derek only half listened. When the meeting finally ended, he folded up the portaterm and went home to pack for the journey.

And so was the first beginning, but there are beginnings and there are endings and there are things in between— Derek Soul was but the richness of soil to the seed of Orfei Agamon's time.

In the palace of Linn at N'Gaia Fall, a gossamer sculpture rises up from the marble floor—a web of jade fibers, a beehive of cells within cells, cells touching and breaking away. From a distance, it appears but a plain, androgenous human form: This was Orfei Agamon's final work, and he called it Novyraj, the end of Earth and the last great society. And so was Novyraj in truth, a honeycombed society whose cells split away, yet remained connected by the threads of the whole, the filaments of The One, and the laws of remembering.

Orfei was the first rememberer, and until N'Gaia demands her next testament, he shall remain the greatest. Yet he was not born a rememberer; he was born, simply, son of Agamon, at the center of rememberer's time.

Ages past, that time was. This, then, is the tale of the worlds divided, and it begins truly with Orfei.

II

AT HIS FEET GREW GRASS, REAL GRASS WARMED BY A synthetic sun in the high vaulted ceiling, a roof of clouds and blue sky, holoimages of life before the great descent. On the grass were flowers, a path of white petals that led to the Door of Transition. The son of Agamon squinted into the sunlight flashing off the door's golden arch. Carved in the gold were words as ancient as Novyraj itself: *Novyraj is the heart of the beast.*

Lysis, the head of the Fourth Council, stood next to him; she followed his gaze and laughed. "Soul meant man," she said. "Novyraj is the heart of man, and man is the beast. It was to remind us."

Orfei glanced at her but said nothing; words felt wrong here. She stood tall, smiling. The rest of the Fourth Council ringed the walls of the initiation place, white-robed ghosts wavering at the edges of his vision. Somewhere above would be lenses, eyeing him, transferring these images through the vidwork to all of Novyraj. All sects, the weak and the mighty, watched him now as he stood on the precipice of ascension. Through that golden gate, all the children of Soul would watch him pass.

A crystal shimmering teased the air next to the gate, and new light joined the sun to batter his eyelids shut; Orfei fought; the shimmering pranced and fell; towering holographic mountains sprang up from the bed of grass, and from between the center peaks, a crystal dragon emerged, soaring serenely, wise eyes meeting Orfei's, then moving on, lighting on Lysis, on the rest of the council, breaking free of the holographic alpine cage to fly up toward the sun. Orfei finally smiled; that was *his* dragon, his creation, the entire light-opera was his. It was why he was there. "Beautiful," Lysis sighed next to him. "We have muted the audio here, but they hear it on the 'work. You must go now."

On their own, Orfei's bare feet moved him across the grass, the golden arch over the Door of Transition glowing more brightly with each step. *The heart of the beast*, he thought. The door itself was black and hard like stone, but when he pushed against it with his fingertips, it swung inward.

Communion with the beast was sacred, both an honor and a terror—the last step in ascension to the Fourth Council, the most elite order to which a man or woman of Novyraj might belong. The mark of this communion remained forever present in the gazes of those who had known it—some distant spark, a fragmented moment taken root in the impressionable soil of human mind and memory. To the people of Novyraj, the fourths were mystics, those who had known, mysterious guardians of wisdom to be admired from a distance, to be partaken of in times of dire need but otherwise to be avoided. The mark of the beast was permanent and palpable, a vast presence cast in shadows and in the footfalls of those who bore it. They had absorbed it, but to those below them who had not it evoked disturbing visions, time-enshrouded racial memories, the bloodlust of the hunter and the desperate alarm of the hunted, dreams in which time turned back and long-dead animals howled and called out for revenge, as if life itself had taken shape and manifested in the hearts of the initiated fourths, as if it churned and flailed the air with primal fury, chaotic, terrible, full of unspeakable majesty.

It was said that fourths were all but immortal.

The Door of Transition closed behind Orfei, the darkness within growing gray as swarming pinpoints of light filled the air around his head. He heard whispering, a vague murmuring from the lights in a language beyond his understanding.

The lights—the mind-bytes of Goliath—floated closer, licking his eyes and tickling his skin, then nestling into his ears like moths seeking further shelter from the darkness. For a moment, a blackness returned, then a world of color exploded inside his head. "Goliath," he gasped weakly, but no answer came, and his words slipped away into the shadows of a lost reality, Novyraj itself growing distant within the mind of its first rememberer.

Time melted, and Orfei Agamon *became* someone else; he became the founder of Novyraj, Derek Soul, in the year 2107 by Old Earth's reckoning, and this is what that was like:

III

METALLIC SCREAMING FILLED THE NIGHT, STROBE-LIT memory flashing dim, stop-action images of a London tube station back when he was a boy. A precise, mechanical voice admonished all: "Mind the gap. . . . Mind the gap. . . ."

Masses of people obeyed, like ants there in the underground visiting this platform of newsstands and street minstrels before boarding their trains and disappearing into tunnels swamped by darkness. By dust, rock, and unnameable horrors now—if anything existed at all under the radioactive, rotting carcass of London.

Inspector General Derek Soul bolted awake, shaking off the fatigue of his jet lag and the childhood memory it had summoned up, unbidden into his dreams. "London," he chuckled grimly. *Who would have ever thought . . .* He blinked his eyes; his watch told him he'd slept through most of the morning and half of the afternoon. Around him, the old-fashioned German hotel room created an illusion of idle comfort—it was what he'd wanted, better than the sumptuous, sanitized, underground quarters that were his due at the main viaduct complex, but now the old, tattered cotton curtains and wooden, antique wardrobes all but glared at him, as if he were to blame for their decay. With his tired eyes, he glared back, rising unsteadily, grabbing for the soap-spotted glass on his nightstand and filling it from a bucket of nu-ice.

After finding his way to the toilet, he filled a pitcher with distilled water and went to look out his window. His room was on the second story of the *Der Spinner* hotel. The day outside was hazy, the eastern horizon streaked with columns of blue and malevolent purple where heavy high tides of deadly gases smashed up against Thurman's Wall. Derek stood on his toes a moment, trying to see the McDonald Viaduct snaking off into eastern Europe. No luck—half of Berlin was in his way. Absently, he poured the distilled water and looked down to the street, which was full of what passed in Berlin as midday commerce: drab, rag-covered transients shuffling with absent purpose toward this or that Refugee Aid center; street urchins asking for anything at any price from even the most modestly dressed American; and, of course, the swift, silent passage of government officials and criminals in their armored hovercars.

One of the groundcraft, a late-model Mantis disturbingly reminiscent of its namesake, screeched to a halt a block to the east. Two Japanese got out, looked around briefly, then retreated inside the vehicle, which shot away as quickly as it had arrived. Derek wondered who they were—the unofficial officiators over all this? No wonder they didn't want complete control—the street people reminded him of the android populations of the Midwest industrial centers stateside, except these were men and women unfortunate enough to have been born with all organs more or less intact. Doomed to short, painful lives—no hair by age twenty, no teeth by thirty, nerves, thankfully, all dead by then.

From around the necks of those few pedestrians not wearing hoods, thin, fluorescent collars shouted out morbidly happy colors—the marks of the New Legislature in Philadelphia. Derek sipped his water, then added a shot of whiskey as he remembered faces back home, cheering demoniacally, with the president crying, "Purify the gene pool!'' Faces twisted—belligerent, too lost in the tattered American dream to feel even the much-publicized Amsterdam Documentary and its vidfootage of a pair of bright-eyed kids—fourteen, fifteen, maybe, with hair just starting to thin and lose luster—coupled in mortal passion, jerking spasmodically as Humanity Force bullets punched ragged holes in their inferior flesh. . . . All to prevent the birth of another who had less than one chance in ten of entering the world alive anyway. Europe had died a truly slow and painful death.

A piercing squeal erupted from the east, clattering the nu-ice against the side of Derek's glass. Breach of the Old Wall? he wondered. Several spats of machine gun fire answered him coldly.

He thought that Stalin might look upon this American Berlin and approve.

Against his will, Derek found himself moving—setting down his drink, dressing, donning a thin overcoat, and heading for the door. So he was here, wasn't he? Just on his way to Moscow—did that make sense? No. . . . And he'd asked for this room so he could see the city, if only briefly—might as well get out and explore while he had the chance, danger or no danger. If he couldn't make some sort of sense out of it, he wasn't really sure he wanted to call himself human much longer.

Downstairs, scenic holos decorated the hotel lobby while a six-inch-thick gate of smoky plexi dominated the streetside wall. A few RD transients lounging near the robo-bar choked off their rambling conversation and shifted uncomfortably as Derek descended the stairs; at the bottom he paused, glancing at the holos and wondering vaguely which landscapes were real and which were reconstructions. After a moment he rubbed his eyes and smiled wryly: Fucking computer artists were too good anymore.

One of the RD men—a psychtech by his insignia—called out to him as he pressed his palm against the gatekeep and muttered his access code. The translucent slab swung out and the man called again. ''Inspector! You can't—'' The rest was lost as Derek slipped through the opening and walked rapidly away down the sidewalk.

Outside, the desperate undercurrents of the street struck him in waves. The radiation-sick destitutes were uglier because they were closer—near him, around him. Unnameable smells hung in invisible clouds at every turn. And always, the distant, midrange hum of Thurman's Wall played its gut-shattering sound track; the ebb and flow of its energies, so Derek had heard, could dislodge fillings from human teeth at a range of five hundred yards. And beyond the wall was certain death. Farther beyond was Linda, her lover, and Moscow, the final end to his journey through this madness.

A neon sign with broken bulbs creaked on its rusty wire hangings as Derek passed beneath it. Hollow eyes fell on him from all directions, their owners keeping distant as if empathetically eyeing the yawning emptiness within him that yearned to be filled.

It didn't make sense. . . . Three weeks before, Derek had been a minor aide to the secretary of reconstruction, but one man on a staff of nearly a hundred before Secretary Collier had promoted him and packed him off under near-paranoid secrecy to Europe to inspect the Moscow installation now run by Linda Kramer, Derek's ex-wife, and Paul, her new husband. In Derek's opinion, he was the worst man for this job. Aside from Linda, he had the Viaduct with which to contend; he'd ridden it during the death throes of his marriage two and a half years before—plummeting, trapped in a claustrophobic capsule, through a black-gray void as featureless and constricting as the belly of a snake. The psychtechs had nearly disqualified him for admittance at the receiving terminal, and the return trip had been worse. Even as he thought about it now, there was something horrible about that thin line of life snaking across the wastelands of a half-dead planet. He'd told the secretary as much and he'd still gotten the job. "The techs have cleaned it up," the old man had said. "You weren't the only one, you know. Even the strongest suffered hot flashes, fainting, general unease. We have more than a few

documented cases of aggravated schizophrenic trauma
nearly identical to your own.

"Doesn't happen anymore. TravelDoc has been fully im-
plemented in each capsule, and the holotechs have inte-
grated a scenery control system that'll fly you through an
asteroid belt or over the old Swiss Alps, and make you
believe it. Don't worry about it, Soul. You survived far
worse during the Tortilla Wars."

Why me?

Don't worry about it, Soul. . . .

The Tortilla Wars—what could the secretary know about
that? Derek had spent most of his life as a clerk in the
Department of Culture, denying nine out of ten Hispanic
applicants for immigration. Then when the revolution had
finally toppled Mexico City, they'd reclassified him an intelligence specialist, so south he'd gone with a pat on the
back from dear old Dad. After laying waste to half of Central America, the United States had overcome. . . . Now, in
the wake of the Big One, Mexico's left had risen anew; he
wished it could end during his lifetime.

In Topeka they'd said the Sovs were the cause of it,
killing people, stealing freedom with their lies. Even his
father: "Drak," he'd said, "the problem with the world is
that half of it's still Communist. Ain't much you can do
about it. It's like a disease; once someone's got it, the best
you can do for the poor, misled soul is shoot him. Like a
horse with a broken leg."

Death had finally come to cleanse the Earth of the per-
sistent stains of Marxism. But it still went on with the enemy dead. Here, it came in a fashion older, uglier because
it was more personal.

Steel girders rose toward the limpid, purple-gray sky,
supporting nothing, the ghosts of buildings. Piled within the
empty frames, mounds of masonry waited for a forgiving
hand to lift and suspend them again above the street. The
nearest extant structure was two blocks back; beyond it,
Derek could see just a corner of his hotel.

He walked on, seeking some overlooked clue to the

city's unique, cosmopolitan past. The occasional rubble-cleared street and sidewalk granted an illusion of hope, yet even the former natures of most buildings were lost. Was this one a bank, or just offices? A furniture store, a warehouse, or condominiums where children had once played, lovers once loved? These ancient, silent specters looked down upon him stoically; he could almost feel the weight of their eyes, and then a sound turned his head toward a flash of motion that stabilized into a pale little girl. She ducked to hide in the rubble and peer at him with remarkably innocent blue eyes. Her collar, also, was a glowing blue.

Another sound came then—a sound he felt he should know but all his conscious attention had locked on the girl. He smiled at her; she scrambled over the rock onto the sidewalk. The sound came again—closer: a hovercar streaking around the nearest corner, its pilot kicking in his front jets so violently they knocked Derek down to the concrete. He flailed his arms about and felt one smack lightly against feeble flesh. When his vision cleared, it filled with blue. The girl crouched next to him—rising from the flat position she'd taken at the hovercar's approach. She smiled shyly, grotesquely; half of her upper lip was pulpy, twisted flesh, and yet that vast, sunny blue still shone from her eyes. Derek rose, taking her arm and pulling her to her feet. Her smile blossomed nearly into beauty and her eyes glowed softly. Little fingers dug into Derek's arm.

Somewhere in the distance a hydraulic door hissed open and slammed shut. The girl opened her mouth and emitted an inquisitive, soprano purr. Derek noticed she had no tongue.

Boots clacked on pavement. "Inspector? . . . Get away from him, you little bitch!"

As he started to turn, a thin black blur split the air, a slender club cracking against the girl's forearm, tearing her fingers from his flesh, but not before he felt the impact, a nerve-numbing shock like electricity stabbing up his arm. The girl fell away from him, racing away into the rubble jungle.

"Inspector General Soul?"

Derek spun toward the voice; an RD pol eyed him suspiciously, his grip still tight on the shaft of his club.

"With respect, sir," the pol said, "you shouldn't be out here. Come with me. I'll take you back to the hotel."

He nodded dumbly, unable to find words he cared to speak to the man. Stepping into the hovercar, one thought screamed over and over again in his mind—*You broke her arm, you bastard! She wasn't whole to start with, and you had to break her arm!*

IV

SUCH WAS THE CONFUSION OF THE DYING OLD EARTH, before Novyraj—what the wiggly mind-bytes fed wholesale into Orfei's brain, their laser talons latching onto neurons like rabid lice. In the lib-banks at N'Gaia Fall, one might find an account of the end in Soul's own hand, presented here as a reference, the esoteric names left intact for the interpretation of the more inquisitive scholars:

Slow was the Earth's end, progressive but sure. The War happened in 2092, between 0300 and 0400 GMT on the third of April, and afterward there was nothing left of Sov Confederation or China, while about an eighth to a half of America remained radiation-free, depending on the day and the prevailing winds. Protected by the Heiwa Shield at the request of the U.S. government, Philadelphia came through relatively unscathed. All other large American cities were destroyed; Heiwa saved mostly farmlands.

Japan herself went untouched, proving those who'd refused to believe she'd already won the space defense race dead wrong (literally). Excepting the nu-

*clear winter, the closest the Japanese came to the war
were their vidscreens where sat-scanned mushroom
clouds played to record, generally inebriated audi-
ences as the state distributed twenty years worth of
surplus sake for the occasion. Yes—secure in their
self-sufficient economy—the Japanese celebrated, for
they had, once and for all, proven their genetic su-
periority to the rest of mankind. . . . The main event
began when Australia, the upstart pit bull of the socialist bloc, invaded New Zealand on the Kremlin's
behalf. The Australians, being relatively new devotees
of The Book by Marx, held high The Book during
their early victories, and the Japanese, accepting the
gambit, blew it out of Aussie hands with about a thousand megatons of nuclear firepower. For good luck,
they dropped a few thousand more megatons around
Moscow, and the Americans—who'd engaged the
Sovs nearly constantly over the past century in some
form or another of low-intensity warfare—followed
suit, but even they couldn't understand precisely why
their Asian allies had flown off the handle.*

*No one will ever really know, unless the blame be
placed on books and their strange powers to drive
history: The Bible, The Koran, The Communist Man-
ifesto, Mein Kampf . . . The Japanese had their own
books: Miyamoto Musashi's Book of Five Rings, detailing the samurai frame of mind, and the more recent, popular doctrines of Yukio Mishima, the
twentieth-century writer who'd strived to embody
Japanese ideals and committed hara-kiri in the end
to prove his point. When Australia took Japan's New
Zealand, shouting out phrases from its book all the
while, perhaps it had been just too much for the Japanese spirit to handle honorably. And since their
books had tended to hold actions above words, they'd
acted.*

*Death followed death: Third world bombs began
to pop off like firecrackers around the globe, syste-
matically eliminating the last patches of green. Then
the United States obliterated Brazil, the last signifi-*

cant socialist survivor, while Japanese technology erected Thurman's Wall across the small section of Europe that remained livable, and America began to expend its remaining GNP on the theoretically humanitarian Reconstruction Department whose first and last major manifestation was the McDonald Viaduct constructed for excursions to Moscow. . . .

All this the mind-bytes planted like bedrock in Orfei's mind. To the first rememberer, it was a giddy understanding: Future and past converged around Derek Soul's present of 2107 in the center of the last dark bright years when civilization hung on tenaciously like a wounded wolf intent on ripping its prey—itself—to shreds.

V

BACK AT *DER SPINNER*, HOLLY LINN GREETED DEREK brusquely, sending the pol back out to the streets with a slight nod. She glared at Derek, a quivering lip and rigid stance betraying her nervous uncertainty about the whole affair. A few RD men looked on silently; Derek turned his attention to a holo of the old White House on its sprawling green lawn.

"We must talk, Inspector General," Holly said.

"Got to be fake," Derek mumbled. *By the time holo-technology came into its own, that place was a fortress.*

"Excuse me, sir?"

"Nothing, Doctor. Lead on." He glanced at the others in the lobby. "You obviously don't want to give your little speech here."

Walking behind Holly, his eyes fell involuntarily to her swaying hips. For a moment, he almost desired her, then a memory of Linda unexpectedly superimposed itself over Holly's back, and he felt slightly ill. Just as well—sex didn't belong in this place, so close to death.

*　　*　　*

Most of the makeshift first floor offices were empty, barren. When opening the Viaduct complex, the secretary had ordered all central administrative workers from around the city to the newer—more hospitable if less varied—installations. A few programmers and mechanics still supported a small under-over hover terminal in the basement; otherwise *Der Spinner* could have almost been a civilian establishment, except that no one from east of the English Channel could get through the plexicast gate to the reception desk.

Holly stopped before entering the drop shaft and slipped into the old offices of the Coordinating Systems Safety Director. Derek followed her hesitantly; he'd hoped to have the chance of conversing with her within earshot of her aides. Inside, she spun on him, faint creases above her eyes betraying her irritation.

"Linda tried to warn me about you," she said after a moment.

"What has she got to do with anything?" He tried to conceal the sudden shock of hearing his ex-wife's name so unexpectedly. Inside, he felt as if Holly had jabbed a knife into his heart.

"Not much," she said, looking down from Derek's accusing stare. "She's just a friend. We occasionally spend time together when she gets away from Moscow."

Slowly, Derek sat behind the Coordinating Systems Safety Director's abandoned desk, trying to clear his head. "I want that cop fired."

"Why?"

"Brutality. There's a little girl out there who won't live another week because that Nazi smashed her forearm to splinters."

"What was she doing?"

"Touching me," he said. "Just touching me."

Holly sighed. "I'm sure you know, Derek, that our laws don't protect these people. Any moment, Congress might bow to domestic pressure and unleash Humanity Force here in Berlin."

"Fuck that!" He spit, smashing his knuckles against the old wood. "The Nunn Mandate implies citizenship for all," he continued, glancing up at her. "At least in my book. If that cop has any problems with being unemployed, let him take it to the courts. Maybe then I'll get the chance to run my mouth and have people listen."

"At the expense of your job?"

"You worry about your job, Doctor."

"And you'll worry about yours? Very well, Inspector Soul. I'm not arguing with you by the way. I enjoy seeing a little old-fashioned compassion in this place, but I'm a realist by necessity. I have to be to stay sane enough to monitor the mental health of everyone here. That's my job."

He laughed—it sounded rough, unnatural to his own ears. "So what sort of abnormal behavior have I displayed? Will you disqualify me for the Viaduct? Please do. And clue me in if I'm on the borderline, so I can cook up a way to step over it."

"You don't *want* to go?"

"Hell no!"

His words erupted like palpable venom; he felt the sudden expulsion of his anger and recoiled from it, feeling like a rebellious kid. Where was the sense in this? He looked at Holly and still saw Linda—is that what bothered him, his mental transformation of this woman into an old enemy, a soured love? He could still hear that club cracking against the girl's arm, and meanwhile another part of his mind kept replaying the sound of his ex-wife's name rolling off this woman's lips—hell, she kept repeating it of her own accord! Or was it just his imagination? He hadn't anticipated this sort of situation—here, trying to deal with some antagonistic friend of his ex-wife's, demanding from her justice for a little girl he didn't even know, whom he'd met on an assignment he didn't want, much less understand. He glared at her, trying to keep his anger subdued, or at least within some frame of reference which made sense, and then the woman across from him smiled.

Derek felt the claws within him ease their grip; he knew smiles. There were happy smiles, ironic smiles, condescending smiles, and smiles that rejuvenated childhood, that held back tears, that forced joy into a world of sadness.

Sincere smiles, and knowing smiles—Holly's was a smile of compassion, of sudden, unexpected understanding, almost like the smile of an old friend. . . . "Linda told me you wouldn't want to come," she said. "I couldn't bring myself to believe her until now. I imagined you wanted revenge."

"So you're not that close to her," he said, relieved to feel the conversation shift gears, resigning himself for the moment to the sudden, odd familiarity. Still, his disorientation persisted. . . . *What more does she know of me? Everything? Linda's version of our marriage from beginning to end?* In Holly's eyes, he imagined he could see everything, from how he'd met Linda on her first liberty in Philadelphia after her initial assignment to Moscow, to their divorce six months later. He'd never been sure how he'd won Linda's heart; how would she have described it to Holly? Truthfully, the story merely laced with her particular brand of feminine machismo? Hell, Holly probably knew everything about him from his sexual dimensions to the color of his underwear! Who knew what women discussed among themselves?

So what sort of confidential version of the marriage had Holly really heard? If he knew Linda, whatever fond memories she might have retained from their happier days would have been colored black by her spite. But Holly couldn't have believed too much, else Linda's misogyny would reveal itself in her eyes. Wouldn't it? Maybe he was overly concerned; all this rested on the assumption that his ex-wife cared enough to make him a subject of casual conversation. He should be so lucky that she'd even remember his face.

"Close enough," Holly said abruptly. "We're friends, you might say by professional necessity. We don't have many others to choose from." She dusted off a corner of the desk and sat on it, hiking up one leg to keep her balance.

But what *did* she know of him? He found his gaze wandering again and had to fight a sudden impulse to ask her about lovers. . . . This was crazy! Granted, he didn't want this assignment, but he had to at least attempt to keep his

mind on it. He forced his eyes away from the bared calf
and grunted, looking at her blankly. After all, this wasn't
a social visit, no matter that it had almost started to sound
like one. And visions of this woman's thighs he didn't need
lingering in his mind.

She smiled again, though this time uncertainly as Derek's
unease grew contagious. "Then I don't understand anything," she said at last. "When we heard you were coming,
I assumed you'd engineered it, that you'd pulled whatever
strings necessary to get the assignment. You know, I hon-
estly thought you might have come to murder her."

Derek chuckled distantly; there was Linda's propaganda
surfacing unblemished by tact. "She's the one with the
temper. When I told her I was leaving her, I thought she
was going to kill me." He did his best to keep his gaze
steady. "If you want to know the truth, Doctor Linn, I
fought this assignment from the beginning. I made them
run the selection programs at least ten times, but every time
I won. I still haven't decided what to make of it. Maybe
they actually suspect Linda. . . . I can't manage to believe
it."

"Maybe there's another reason."

"Yeah—well tell me then."

"I don't really know. . . . I don't know exactly what
caused them to send you, but strange things happen right
here, Derek—not only in Moscow." She looked up nervously. "You don't mind if I call you that, do you? It's
difficult; since I've known Linda, you've been Derek or
Drak. Inspector general just doesn't roll off the tongue very
well."

"Derek's fine," he said. "I've never liked Drak; it has
a sort of evil aura about it."

"Yeah . . ." Her voice trailed off a moment before she
continued. "They're dying out there, you know? They're
starting to call excavation duty the suicide shift."

"I thought they were just disappearing."

"Sure—but what do you suppose disappearance in a
place like that means? And it's crazy *right here*," she continued distantly. "Computers go down without warning;

classified terminal displays scramble themselves before your eyes sometimes.''

"Sounds like some sort of magnetic pulse."

"Maybe," she said, "but there's no regularity to it, no clue to its origin."

"Thurman's Wall?"

"That's what all the techs thought at first, but the wall is thoroughly grounded. If it weren't, we'd know it, but even so, they've mapped all possible transient energy fluxes, and the data doesn't match the net abnormalities."

Derek frowned; Holly continued to speak: "You know," she said, "sometimes I think I'm going paranoid, thinking these terminal problems single me out more than anyone else, and since the techs gave the system a clean bill of health, I've been kinda terrified of talking about it."

"Then why are you telling me?"

"I'm not sure," she answered, her voice almost vulnerable. "I'm really not sure. Maybe because my gut's starting to tell me to trust you, maybe because you're not at all what I expected. I want to understand what happens to the data while I'm looking at it; I can't shake the feeling that it might mean something."

"What? The scrambled data?"

"Yeah—I've even been saving it and trying to figure out how to analyze it."

"No luck?"

"Some. I identified a couple of patterns just this morning, just before they called me in on your escape."

He smiled. "My escape, was it? I thought I had authority to go where I please."

"You do," she said. "But there are limits, the main being you don't do it alone, without support. Christ, Derek, you haven't even been here a day yet! What was I supposed to make of your unscheduled adventure? It was crazy enough your wanting to stay here rather than in the main viaduct complex."

"Credit that last one to nostalgia," he said. "This was a great city once; I wanted to get the feel of it, and I never got half a chance to look at it the last couple of times I passed through."

"So did you satisfy yourself?"

As he looked up at her, he could feel the desperation of the street again, the destruction, the architectural ghosts. His arm tingled where the girl with the glowing blue eyes had grabbed him. . . . "If you want to call it that," he said at last. He stood slowly, trying to shake off the memories. "Your room or mine?" he asked abruptly, attempting a joke to regain a semblance of internal equilibrium. The cliché reflected oddly off Holly's eyes; he recovered before allowing her the grace to react: "I mean for your data—I want to see it. We might do better at my terminal; it's got some net access authorities built in that I may not be able to get at your workstation, even if we overlay your key with mine."

He stumbled over these words, and at the end Holly smiled again, this time a smile that disturbed him a little, a smile of almost-spoken consent, to the question he had not intended to pose, but had asked nevertheless.

VI

BEHIND THE DOOR OF TRANSITION, IN THE ROOM OF THE Fourth, Orfei's own eyes opened, the consciousness of Derek Soul blazing behind them, the mind-bytes tickling neurons and filling his head. He'd eaten nothing that morning in order to remain pure, yet he felt ill. His field of vision pulsated gold—the door lighting up, calling him out of the room. But the mind-bytes hadn't left him! He staggered, realizing with amazement that he still stood, and as he fell against the door, as it opened outward, Derek Soul seemed to step with him (and he with Derek Soul, leading Holly Linn up creaking wooden stairs to the portaterm in his hotel room . . .). Orfei, however, stepped into the presence of Lysis, chair of the Fourth Council.

Lysis was tall, a woman taller even than Orfei. For a moment, Orfei saw her more clearly than before: She wore white, as did all of the council, a sensual, pale white skin-wrap flex-coat, transparent around her crotch, up her sides, and over her breasts. His vision blurred again, and the life of Derek Soul blazed and erupted, planting Holly Linn's face and eyes between Lysis's breasts. He began to fall forward, and the woman caught him.

"Do not fear," she whispered, her lips tickling his ear, her voice an electric buzz, a soft-wet burst of alien sound. He could feel her; in one world, he held a whiskey glass in his hand; in another, he discovered it was a breast. He pulled his hand quickly away, attempting to regain his feet.

"It is like this for some," came the whisper, a sound which melted into the high-pitched electrostatic hum of Derek's portaterm as he powered it on. Holly sat before him. "The Room knows," Lysis whispered. "It knows and shows to all what must be shown. It did not harm you, as it did not harm me. It showed me the beating of my own heart, the pulsing life of the rock of the earth. It showed me my lovers and my fears, and how to love the people of Novyraj so that I might rule. It was in the Room that I was chosen, Orfei."

That was true; Lysis had ascended almost a century past. ... How did Orfei suddenly know this? How could he know she spoke truly? Yet he knew this as surely as he knew his own name. What more did he now know, and was it *his* knowledge, or the knowledge of someone— something—else? What had happened to him? Why had the mind-bytes not left him, and why did the life of Derek Soul still blaze so strongly?

"What did you see?" came the wet-soft, inquisitive purr of Lysis. Didn't she know that he knew what he knew, had seen what he'd seen? What he was still seeing?

He tried to answer her, but could not. He gave up his struggles and went limp, helpless, in her arms.

VII

HOLLY'S SAVED DATA ROLLED OVER DEREK'S SCREEN, pausing where she'd programmed the match recognition stops. Derek frowned at it, then reached over Holly's shoulder and placed his thumb against the user keypad. "Combine user keys or override?" the portaterm asked.

"Combine with override," he answered.

"Done. Hello, Dr. Soul."

Holly turned to look at him, raising an eyebrow. "Dr. Soul?"

He shrugged. "I've been called overeducated—Juliet, run this file against the highest level linguistic/decrypt system you can get into."

"Reconstruction? Defense?" the portaterm asked.

"Everything, RD, DD, CIA—I want an answer. If our systems can't cut into it, get into the commercial knowledge banks, put in a request to Tokyo, do whatever it takes and keep doing it until you've run out of everything everywhere. Use your imagination."

"That may take some time, Dr. Soul."

"We've got time," he said. He turned away from the screen and moved to his window, drawn for some reason

to look down, to the streets where life withered and ago-
nized before his eyes. After a time, Holly came to him and
drew him away, and they sat and drank, awaiting Juliet's
answer.

*Lysis whispered, her lips velvet shackles, soft red cuffs,
but like a fly, Orfei escaped, into a dark night of real stars
and the seductive moon, crater-pocked behind purple
clouds beyond the window, the cage of Soul's essence. His
hand felt wet, the sweat of hotel glass and the uncertainty
of the moment. Holly, like Lysis, whispered, and he strained
to hear, twisting toward her through rock, through water,
the heart of the earth.*

"Does it have holo projection?"

"I'm sure it does," Derek answered, glancing at the portaterm. "They didn't reconfigure her hardware for me until
just before I left the States. . . . Juliet?"

"Affirmative, Dr. Soul."

Holly stood, smoothing down her dress. "Then there's
something else I want to show you."

Derek rose, gazing absently at the window for a moment
before turning to face their chairs toward the computer.
"Where is it?"

"Public access."

"Local?" he asked, sitting again.

"Of course," she answered, smiling unexpectedly. "Despite first impressions, those aren't thorough primitives out
there."

"As long as this is relevant," he said, pouring himself
another drink.

Holly smiled; as she sat, Derek noticed her hands trem-
bling slightly and began to feel guilty for attempting to
place some distance between them since they'd entered his
room. She hardly deserved it, but he couldn't shake the
thought that Linda still lurked deep in the shadows behind
her eyes; the idea of this woman's friendship with his wife
continued to unnerve him.

And he still had little idea of what really was going on.
Could Holly—like him—simply be confused, or could she

be a part of the puzzle? These scrambled files of hers were a new mystery; he'd certainly had no mention of them from the secretary. Maybe Holly was crazy; he might learn soon enough, once Juliet finished her raid through the datanets.

Holly shifted next to him; he ordered Juliet's holofield activated, and the screen of the portaterm thrust suddenly out from behind its glass to hover like a pristine, crystal cube in the air. Derek glanced at her. "Well?"

"Berlin pub-ax bank three," she said. "It's called *The Shining Wall.*" Derek rephrased this for Juliet, and the holocube immediately began to fill with black, inky clouds of fog.

The smoky mass rolled, to an aud-track that sounded like whalesong. Derek abruptly felt as if he moved into it; at his feet he sensed stone—cobblestones as the fog grew patchy. The street was wet, and he moved forward, suddenly gripped by terror. He could see nothing but blackness and street; the vidholo was conceptually simple but intensely engrossing, each step forward a temporary catharsis relieving a throbbing, terrible anticipation—an effect precisely the opposite from what he would expect as he felt no threat of danger from behind, but only from ahead. And yet he didn't fear anything real; not monsters that might emerge from the fog, not the terrors of night and blackness, the haze of blindness; not even what destination might await his walk. He feared, rather, something in the deepening unreality of it all, of the black fog—it oozed like liquid, shimmered like a desert mirage, curled up in swirling pirouettes like breath exhaled through the cobbled spaces. And yet the street compelled him forward, until something else pulled him violently, physically backward and he fell.

He lay on his back on the stones, looking up. The banks of black rolled away, dispersing, and he began to sink into the street, his tension fading, his eyes filling with the brilliant blue of the sky emerging high overhead.

As the holocube cleared, Derek stared fixedly into the now-empty space, watching dust dance lazily in the holocube's passive glow.

"It isn't empathy," Holly said, breaking his trance.

He shook his head and turned to her. "Emotive keys in the sound track?" he asked, his voice a distant thing, like the voice of someone else.

"That's what I thought at first." She smiled, reaching out for his hand, her touch luring him back slowly into the room. "Subliminals, Derek. Subconscious probes about every two or three seconds, each lasting maybe five or ten milliseconds."

"That's illegal."

"Of course! That's how I found this—the psych monitor systems picked it up and queued it to me for review the day before yesterday."

"So what were they?"

"The subliminals? All pretty much the same: Shots of the wall, pulsating—people throwing themselves against it from the other side, killing themselves. . . . Would you like to see stills?"

"No." He stopped her. "I'll take your word for it." He stood and yawned; the sky outside was dark—somehow night had fallen without his noticing it. What was it like out there now, engulfed by the darkness?

Holly yawned reflexively, then smiled sleepily. "I hate that," she said.

"What?"

"That subconscious impulse—you yawn, and I can't help but do the same. It's part of the mental substructure of language; I'm sometimes surprised that it never breaks out into a chain reaction, an incurable epidemic of yawns." She raised her arm and stretched, then relaxed and let her head fall against the chair's back. "Actually, I'm quite tired. Haven't had much sleep lately with all this going on."

"Go lie down if you like. I'll wait up for Juliet."

"Do you mind?" She looked up at him, her eyes a deep, gray-green. The way she did it made him feel tall; her head almost tilted downward—the uncertain posture of a child eyeing an adult as if the latter lorded over lofty, treacherous heights. This was a shy, unprofessional gesture, but so was his offer that she rest in his room. She'd let down her guard completely; perhaps because she felt relieved of the strange events with which she'd been burdened, now that she'd pawned them off on him. . . . "But you haven't asked yet, Derek—why I showed you that vid." She rose, drawing his eyes into the motion; she wore some sort of synth-cotton dress, black flecked with silver and gray. It hung loose from her shoulders, except now when the body within tested its fabric.

"I didn't assume there had to be a reason," he said, wrenching his gaze away. Within, he felt as if the black clouds still roiled and swirled. The aftermath of the experience had a definite effect: He felt listless, depressed, as if suddenly deprived of a drug. The clouds nagged at him to replay the vidholo, for the release of the blue sky at its end. Its comforting warmth had faded all too quickly.

"Didn't you find it odd? I mean the title, *The Shining Wall*—it only really applies to the subliminals."

"Where did it come from?"

"Ah," she said. "That's the question you were supposed to ask. It showed up in the banks three days ago, artist unknown. The psych monitors tracked it back, and—" She hesitated, forcing her eyes to level on his. "I'm sorry," she continued. "I feel it too—more each time I watch it except that the feelings of terror lessen each time, and the release at the end grows. I feel strange, that's for sure—the pace of the subliminals seems to induce a sort of self-suppression, and it always takes a while to get your mind back on track. Anyway, Derek, this is really important, and scary because it's so important, or at least it seems that way to me. That vid didn't originate here in Berlin."

"So?"

"It came from Moscow; you might want to let that sink in." She started to reach for his hand, then nervously drew back. "I really do need that rest," she said. "Will you wake me if Juliet comes back with an answer?"

He nodded; she started to turn away, but he stopped her. "Who there has the time for such things?" he asked.

"The same question I first asked, and the answer is no-body—oh, they've got a vid facility, but nobody knows anything about this. Neither does Linda—I called her. The next questions are how, then, did it get here, and why is it the way that it is? There's no story to it, yet it's as engrossing as any full-blown production, and addictive at that. And who's watching it? Virtually everybody out there with a vidsystem. . . . The first day, we wiped the banks clean of it four or five times, but someone kept putting it back.''

"From Moscow?"

"No, from here—who knows how many copies they've made by now? The damned thing's like a drug! We could shut it out completely, but that takes authorization from Philadelphia, and I decided to wait for you before moving ahead.''

He looked at her, realizing after a moment that his fingers had bitten deeply into her shoulder. He drew his hand away and forced a weak smile. "Go get some rest, Holly.''

VIII

THE NIGHT GREW LONGER, AND DEREK SAT, DRINKING AND gazing at the empty holocube. More than once, he felt an urge to replay the vid as its consumptive substance diminished, an alcoholic blur taking its place. In a moment of strength, he ordered the holoextension canceled, and the cube disappeared, taking with it some part of his internal tension, making the room feel more real, though no less full of questions. All Holly had said and asked recurred again and again in his mind; he kept her sleeping form behind him in an attempt to escape the question of Holly herself, and for a time he was successful in that.

He thought mostly about the mystery of the vid and Moscow—two and a half years had passed since he'd been there. Of the city itself, there was nothing left; all the Reconstruction Department's efforts had focused on the labyrinthine warrens belowground. Before they'd completed the McDonald Viaduct, most of the early, flyer-based expeditions to the city had ended tragically; the land was too wild, the few survivors of the holocaust too desperate and in most cases armed and ready to shoot anything at all out of the sky. Faced with this threat, as well as that of surface

radiation, the Wilson administration had made a decision
to construct the Viaduct under a protective umbrella based
on the Thurman's Wall technology of destructive repulsion.
All during the 2090s the work had gone on, the McDonald
Viaduct inching slowly toward its destination like a huge
technological mole. Once they'd reached the Soviet capital
and its underground complexes, they'd put an energy bub-
ble over the city and proceeded to sterilize the surface of
the last traces of life.

Underground, they'd found surprisingly few survivors.
Philadelphia had supported the initial invasion of the labyrinths with fifteen Marine Flyer squadrons, so paranoid
had it been of a still-strong, intact, and belligerent core of
survivors. Derek supposed they'd still felt their defeat of
the Sovs impossible, yet in the labyrinths, the survivors
they'd found had been without exception insane, and stacks
of uniformed corpses had proven themselves much more
common. And so America (and a few Japanese advisors)
had stepped unchallenged into the heart of its most feared
enemy's power. That had been the undeclared mission of
the so-called Reconstruction Department all along, and internal secrecy had plagued it from the start. Derek, however, knew its general plan, mainly due to his marriage to
Linda, head of the Moscow project since its inception.

Early in the twenty-first century, geosat scans had revealed excavated caverns below the Kremlin and Red
Square as well as deeper tunnels, ones running far beneath
the city's metropolitan subway system. Over the years,
they'd watched the tunnels grow, and the CIA had managed
occasionally to substantiate widely traveled rumors of various ultrasecret research projects conducted in subsurface
labs, mostly in the fields of bioengineering and receptor
control, fields heavily regulated—virtually banned—in the
United States in the 2050s by Jeffrey Night-Wilmington's
first New Socialist administration. The wildest rumors, of
course, went far beyond this; for instance, an unmanned
Sov probe had returned in 2045 from Alpha Centauri with
a brace of sentient extraterrestrial creatures, all but two of
which it had left on the moon—it seemed they could thrive
only in a vacuum, and rumor had it they drew all their

sustenance from background cosmic radiation through a sort of silicic photosynthesis.

For one year, the Sovs had kept the earthbound pair—star elves as they'd become known through the media—in an artificial vacuum, more or less on display to the world in the Moscow Zoo. After that, they'd taken them underground in 2046. . . . NASA had quickly sent a couple of secret missions to the moon in attempts to capture one or more of those left behind, but the agile star elves proved themselves elusive and unwilling, and the U.S. Space Defense Department's lunar satellites had lost track of all of them, one by one, over the ensuing ten years. In the end, the earthbound pair perished, their corpses put on display for the whole world to mourn.

Further detailed knowledge of the Alpha Centaurans had been among the primary motivations behind the Moscow project. After 2046, the Sovs had published absolutely nothing concerning them, and what knowledge mankind had left of non-Terran life remained indelibly tainted by Soviet propagandizing. Yet even with its army of linguistics specialists, translator programs, and scientists, the Moscow project had found no records of them as yet, though it had found, indeed, laboratories by the tens and hundreds.

IX

IN NOVYRAJ, LYSIS SMOTHERED ORFEI; HE STRUGGLED AND broke free, a flock of butterflies fleeing the female fire, the dawn of lust, the presence of she and Goliath and the council and now something else—mind probes injected into his brain by some new force. . . . Mind probes—slithering, snaking worms punching microscopically through his skull. His mental butterflies scattered, pasting trees of memory in pastel wings, collages of repatterned childhood behind which the mind-bytes of Goliath gathered in ranked formation before swarming against the mind probes in protective fury, bright lights dancing menacing steps, forcing the invaders back over the borders until Orfei forgot them and fell back, into the past.

He was Orfei, and he was Soul. He was the heart of them all—the heart now of the Fourth Council, of Novyraj itself, and yet his fellow fourths wished him less, wished him small and helpless and revealing.

Clystra, the Keeper of History, the Fourth Council's second in command, moved to gaze down at the new ascendant. Lysis glanced at him and shook her head.

"He remains in the Room?" Clystra asked.

"Completely."

"And you've learned—"

"Nothing," she said.

Clystra grimaced, ruffling his robes. "This is too important—we need him; the Fest is but cycles away. Goliath must be preparing him for *something*—perhaps your job, Lysis."

"I know," she said, reaching down with her long arm, wiping the sweat from Orfei's brow.

"Goliath tells nothing?"

"He says he cannot find him."

"That is a lie! Completely without precedent—"

"Holly," whispered Orfei.

Clystra jumped back, stunned by the word. "What is that—what is Holly, Goliath?"

"An ancient plant substance," the computer returned, its voice coming from the air itself. "Ancient Christians bestowed upon it ceremonial significance."

"Then you and the room show him the ancient Christian legends?"

"Insufficient data—I know nothing of that aspect of myself which resides in the Room of the Fourth."

Lysis knelt next to the flotation bed, taking Orfei's hand in her own. "I think it's someone's name," she said distantly. "Orfei," she whispered into his ear. "Orfei—tell us more! What lies beyond the here and now?"

The soft-wet whisper stung his ears. Orfei was no longer his name; Orfei sank deep, and he was Derek Soul, vigilant and full of whiskey, awaiting Juliet's return.

X

"TRANSLATION SUCCESSFUL, DR. SOUL."

The hotel room had dimmed its lights, and Derek nearly slept, his closed eyes assailed by shadowy dream images of black fog and clacking cobblestones. Thurman's Wall ebbed and flowed; he half dreamed the subliminal suicides of the mutants trapped in the hell of the East. Juliet had to repeat herself before he acknowledged her.

He blinked his eyes at the newly ordered lines on the portaterm's screen, reaching back with one hand to shake the flotation bed on which Holly snored softly. "Wake up, Dr. Linn," he mumbled before bending forward, bringing the plasma display into focus.

Black clouds swam in and out again like a tide within his mind, a fog of unreality, a subliminal addiction, the blur of his awakening meshing uncertainly with the light as his eyes scanned over the data, restarting several times before he was sure he truly comprehended what he read:

CIS ACTION SUMMARY, 10Mar05
CTL:A91-0224-9-1309

SUBJECT: Derek Steven Soul, 562-99-091, b. 13Mar65, KC, MO, posted Moscow 19Sep04

FATHER :   Rupert Murdoch Soul, 723-15-8723

MOTHER :   Margaret Walker (nmn), 444-03-9277

SumHist:

10Jun79:	grad P. Schroeder HS, Denver, CO
02Jun82:	BS, Comp Mgmt, Yale Univ
03Jun82–13May84:	unemployed, St. Louis, MO, minor left-wing activity, vol for Thad Kennedy in NS primaries
14May84:	Entered government service, Department of Culture, grade GS-7, posted Wash, D.C., Immigration Spec
18Nov85:	Promoted GS-8
20Dec86:	Promoted GS-9, transfer Philadelphia
09May88:	MS, PSPhil, S. Nunn Univ.
15Jul88:	Promoted GS-10
17Mar89:	Promoted GS-12, transfer to Cultural Intelligence (CIA), posted Acapulco, Hispanic Intel Spec
23Aug91:	Reassigned Philadelphia
05Jun92:	Transfer Reconstruction Department, Administrative Spec
01Jun95:	PhD CultrPhil, S. Nunn Univ.
15Jul95:	Promoted GS-13
02Jan99:	Promoted GS-14, assigned Secretary RD
15Jul03:	Promoted GS-15
15Sep04:	Married Linda Webb (523-19-4901, GS-21, RD Moscow)
19Sep04:	Transfer Moscow, Logistics Spec

PsycSum: Career tendencies evince maverick behavior; resisted Mex-Am War assignment on pacifist grounds; voting record consistently liberal; outspoken politics, not recommended for high security posts.

Cnclusn: Security breaches feared during Moscow assignment, 2104–2105. Emotionally unstable, though normally competent. Unpredictable reactions to stress situations. Recommend early forced retirement nlt 01Aug05. May require exile or PD.

Derek read and reread, scrolling the file up and down, shaking his head. Cobblestones and fog lurked invitingly in the recesses of his consciousness; he wished he could summon again the black swirls to blow through him, to strengthen his sense of dream, make what he was reading an illusion, a piece of reality he could detach from himself and cast aside on waking. Holly Linn, psychtech (and confidante of his wife . . .), intruded brashly; "What's CIS?" she asked behind him. "Central Intelligence Systems?"

He nodded, feeling her hand on his shoulder; he could smell her perfume, a light, almost–baby powder scent—the same scent Linda had used during their last few, futile attempts to make love, as if she'd felt convinced that the innocence of her odor could mask the sins of her afternoons. And Holly's breath tickled his ear, warm and wet; this wasn't a dream, no matter how much he wanted it to be, no matter how little sense it made.

"What's PD?" Her mouth was so close to his ear, her voice so soft it could have been a proposition.

"Physical discontinuation," he answered numbly. "I can't believe this; it looks authentic—the CI date codes and abbreviations are unmistakable—but this can't be! Look at that date—it's almost two years old! Nobody ever confronted me with anything like this. . . . Juliet, have you run a trace on that CIS control number?"

"Affirmative, Dr. Soul—it was acquired by Europe HQ, Berlin on March 9, 2105. The master file in Philadelphia shows a blank record entry, verified and voided by Security Specialist William Burgess March 12."

"It was assigned but never entered?"

"No, it was entered—blank, considered an error. Requests for reentry from Berlin received null responses. The systems here show no record of the original, nor any receipt of the responses logged in the tracking systems in Philadelphia."

"Jesus Christ! Someone here was suggesting they kill me!"

"Correction," Juliet countered. "That was simply one of several recommendations by the Berlin subsystem. To assume human initiation is also faulty; the parameters governing such recommendations are set by human managers, but the recommendations themselves come from AI decision subsystems."

"Is it authentic?"

"Speculation? I have insufficient data for definitive proof."

"Yes, yes," he said, irritated. "Speculation."

"Yes, it's authentic. The format conforms exactly to standard CIS action reports, and its control number is unique and traceable, with a history to suggest that it originated here but was intercepted on transmission."

"By what?"

"Speculation?"

"Yes!"

Juliet went silent a moment; Derek's hand moved up, instinctively, over Holly's. Whoever she was, wherever her true allegiances lay, he needed her humanity, at least as far as he could accept it. After an interminable wait, Juliet broke her silence. "Insufficient data," the machine said.

"That's enough," he told her. "Power down."

"You do not wish to save this data?"

"What for? So someone else might find it and have it acted upon? Kill it, Juliet!"

"Done. Good-night, Dr. Soul."

He poured himself another drink and stood, moving again to his window. Overhead, the moon wavered beyond the haze over the city; it was a bluish orange tonight; the night before, in Philadelphia, it had been red.

Holly slumped in his chair. "I'm sorry," she said.

"About what?" Again, his voice seemed distant, not his own.

"That—I never suspected . . ."

"If I didn't trust you—"

"That's not my idea of a joke," she said, looking up at him defiantly.

He sighed, the dam of his patience slowly crumbling under the weight of the only fact at his command: Holly, after all, had given him this data to decrypt—"Then what was it? If that thing was real, then some gremlin snatched it from the system two years ago! Where were you?"

"In Philadelphia! I've been here barely a year!" She stood, approaching him cautiously. "Listen, Derek. Did anything strange happen to you here before? Out of the ordinary?"

"Like what? I've never even spent a night before in this godforsaken city!"

"I don't know. But if you could remember something, then we might make sense of this."

"There isn't any sense to be made of it! Here's a recommendation to retire me—physically, no less—materializing encrypted on your terminal just conveniently enough to coincide with my arrival here! You tell me how we can make sense of it."

"I can't," she said. "But I know one thing now—whatever explanation this thing has is tied to the rest of the strange events, possibly including even that vid. There's intelligence behind all this."

"Certainly," he said, turning on her.

"I didn't make this up, Derek!"

"I'm not in the mood for games, Doctor." He turned away then; a moment later, he heard her leave the room.

He gazed long out his window before collapsing on his bed and falling into a fitful sleep, full of dreams of Holly, the banks of black fog, Linda, and the dark constriction of the McDonald Viaduct and the gloomy world of uncertainty that awaited him at its other end.

His sleep didn't last; when he wakened, he tossed restlessly for half an hour before looking at his watch. It wasn't even ten yet, local time. He closed his eyes again, trying unsuccessfully to think of something pleasant, like the night long before in Topeka when Cheryl Green had finally given in to his advances and they'd spent a wonderful evening chatting over beer at the local pizza parlor for hours—But what had they talked about?

It was no good, and it really didn't make any difference. Memories of a long-lost, adolescent girlfriend were not going to save him here. Grumbling, he rolled off his bed, dressed, and found himself heading back out into Berlin, into the night.

XI

ORFEI WOKE SUDDENLY, THE MIND-BYTES BUZZING IN HIS ear; they were still there, he could feel them inside his head, gyrating, moving, clawing—waiting to take him again; Soul faded in the distance—Orfei felt he could almost see the back of him, descending the stairs of that ancient hotel.

He stood cautiously; he was alone, but as soon as he stepped onto the floor, Lysis entered—he had the sudden inexplicable perception that this was her room. It was not right: This was not ascension as he'd understood it to be.

The chair of the Fourth Council approached Orfei, her white skin-wrap flex-coat rippling and shimmering and secreting pheromonal aromas; he backed away as he felt the aphrodisiacal bite; he had been not himself for too long— Soul's repressed lusts surged in his newly revitalized body, and he screamed within to maintain control. He didn't have time for this—he didn't understand what was happening to himself. Why was he here? Why was it, every time he opened his eyes, he found Lysis there? He looked at her critically, seeking out the blemishes in her skin, trying to focus his mind on thoughts of her defecating—anything to avoid losing himself further to the forces surging within him, anything to preserve what he had left of his own self-control. His art demanded control; he'd vowed long past never to succumb to seduction, never to enslave himself to the capricious bitch-heat of a woman unless she be a woman chosen of his own accord.

"Don't be afraid," Lysis said. "I've come only to hear you speak."

"Of what?" He had backed away against the wall; he grew aware of his fearful posture and pushed off, standing straight and defiant.

"Of your ascension."

"But surely you know," he said scathingly. "You've been with me since the Room."

"Not inside your mind. All ascendants experience the Room differently. There are tales among us, tales of trust."

He remembered the needling mind probes and the way the mind-bytes had battled them. . . . Those probes had been hers; he *knew* it! She'd tried to force entrance into his mind. In his ears now, the mind-bytes buzzed threateningly; did she even know he still bore them? What was it she'd told him of her own ascension, when he'd first left the room? *It showed me the beating of my own heart, the pulsing life of the rock of the earth. It showed me my lovers and my fears.* . . . "It was nothing," he said, trying to think of how to shape his reply to mesh with her memories of her own ascension, feeling a desperate, almost-primal need to hide the truth from her. "Dark disturbances within me," he continued. "Disturbances that are mine alone to bear."

"In Novyraj, only the unseens are alone." It was a saying for children she offered him. He did not waver; he stood strong in silence. "You do not find me attractive?"

She began to look vulnerable, despite the fact she was taller than he; he thought back again to that moment outside the Door of Transition: The tickle of her lips at his ear replayed itself against his flesh; she might have licked free the mind-bytes then had she known to try. . . . Her hair was white and long, full and fresh against pale skin and flex-coat. She had long arms and long legs—an Amazon, his father would have said. Darth Agamon would have pined for days over the thought of canvassing her form for the eyes of the future. "You are not unattractive," he answered, "but I have sated my lusts long past."

"So I understand," she said, smiling disturbingly. "You like boys?"

"No." Now he smiled. "You know so much of me— you should surely know that."

She looked him up and down a while and frowned. "Why do you treat me so? You know I head the Council, as I've told you. Have you no respect for my authority?"

He frowned, remaining silent.

"You are special, Orfei. The Fourth Masters of Light fear you even now. They fear you will surpass them, become the Picasso of this age."

"That is flattery," he retorted, though the tides of pride swelled within him.

"Is it? Say to me the same when *Dragon Dance* shows in the blue circle at Beltene Fest."

"I still feel it is undeserving—it is a simple piece of work. You should have honored my father so," he continued more loudly. "He was a much greater artist than I!"

"You are blind." She smiled, relishing his open burst of emotion.

"I don't believe you," he said, catching himself, framing his internal state, pushing down the anger and the pride. Should he lose his temper fully, she would have him then.

"You will." She smiled again and turned away.

"Lysis!"

"Yes?"

She twisted her hips, shifting her weight; only her head turned back toward him.

"Are all fourths not equal?"

"Of course—it is the law."

"Then I require solitary chambers."

"They are prepared, Orfei. You have but to ask Goliath."

Her skin-wrap flex-coat rippled seductively, flowing out of the room, leaving an uneasy void in its absence. Orfei shook and clasped his hands together, closing his eyes a moment in an attempt to learn how soon Soul might return to him. . . . The mind-bytes seemed nearly silent; Orfei sighed, then asked Goliath directions to his new home.

In the halls of the fourths, he walked cautiously. New faces smiled at him; he returned the smiles with stares. This wasn't right! He had ascended into tension; Lysis lusted after that which he sheltered in his mind. Had the Room not shown another the heart of Derek Soul? (No, he knew—this had never happened before . . .) She had lied to him, pretending benevolence with murky distrust hidden behind her skillful eyes. What was so important? Had she not come so eagerly to devour his thoughts, he might have told her. Had she not fallen on him, her wet-soft whispers and mind-probes intruding into the shadow life of Derek Soul, he might have accepted her, honored her. Now he had gained the enmity of the Fourth Council's chair, and for what?

With such thoughts he couldn't suffer the smiles. He reached his new chambers and escaped within, finding his vidsonic boards intact and installed before a hundred-cubic-meter holofield, more space than he'd ever dreamed of having to himself as a third. In his absence, his collection of holostats had been arranged artfully on his walls: Beside his door loomed a static print of *The Petals of Pauline*, his father's greatest work, and over his bed hung a horizontal panorama of the city they'd once called San Francisco. Elsewhere were holostat reproductions of the great ancients: Redon's *Roger and Angelica* holoprinted by Arsans, the Picasso of the first age of Novyraj; a reproduction of an untitled Brueghel; a Dada nostalgia series by Cato, the leader of the thirty-first century New Expressionist Revival; and Arsans's multifaceted holocompression of the works of Egon Schiele.

Orfei walked around, examining each piece, touching each lightly, feeling himself at home. Here was his haven; Goliath had shaded the lights correctly in all corners of the room, and when he neared his vidsonic boards they powered on, inviting his exploration; when he moved away, they moaned discordantly in sorrow. His bed was in a recess, and there were two flap-doors leading to attached

rooms; one proved to be a bath, the other a cushioned view-
ing room with a lateral view of his holofield. He entered
and found more holostats on the walls, ones he hadn't col-
lected himself: There were two Dali reproductions flanking
a large, pale, animated vidframe with nothing but a small
windmill in the artificial depths, its wheel spinning slowly,
detached under a featureless sky. As he peered closely into
it, the pallor grew darker, then black boiling banks of fog
began rolling in from either side, and the lower quarter
grew shiny and squared—a near-perfect duplication of that
which he'd seen through Derek Soul's eyes. . . . Orfei
jumped quickly away from the piece, turning his head to
the side to avoid even another glimpse of the vid he had
already experienced earlier that day—the vid seen through
Soul's eyes. "Goliath!" he shouted. "Put it back!"

"It is done."

Only after a long moment did Orfei turn back, hesitantly,
to look at the wall; once again, the windmill turned in the
distance, a speck of detail in the white center supported by
melting clocks and other symbols displaced in time.
"Where did this come from?"

"It is your room."

"What?"

"It is the room of Orfei, Fourth Holomage, son of Agamon."

"I mean who did this—the artist's name."

"That is unknown."

"From what period?"

"That is also unknown."

Orfei backed away, out of the room. His ascension yet
haunted him though he had nearly forgotten the mind-bytes
still hiding in his head. It had not yet ended. . . .

As he had this thought, the mind-bytes' talons dug deep,
and ancient rooms flickered before his eyes. He stumbled
for his bed. "Goliath!" he shouted. "I am a fourth?"

"Yes, Orfei."

"Then seal my chambers and files—" He fell forward;
it was a long way down. "I invoke sanctuary."

"It is done."

XII

ON THE GROUND FLOOR OF *DER SPINNER*, DEREK CON-
fronted the same RD pol who'd tracked him down on the
streets earlier that day. He pushed past the man on his way
to the gate, only to discover the portal failed to respond to
his handprint.

"I'm sorry, sir," the pol said behind him. "You're not
permitted out alone."

Derek grunted; he started to turn, then a thick arm passed
over his shoulder, a hairy hand pressing against the access
plate. The gate swung open, letting in the musky, sour
breath of the Berlin night. "I'll come with you," the pol
said.

"I don't need you," Derek protested.

"Nevertheless . . ." The man left the sentence incomplete. "All vehicles are to your left."

With slow deliberation, Derek turned right. They walked
for a while in silence, Derek wondering whether Holly had
actually taken his demand for this man's job seriously, or
whether she'd purposefully ignored it. His anger churned
slowly—anger at Holly, but also anger at himself, at the
stubborn, paranoia-tinged obstinacy with which his mind

seemed engaged. Intransigence—a quality he'd always hated in others. And yet he felt his obstinacy justified, and that made matters worse, *de facto* proof that he accepted in himself something he disdained.

The pol walked behind him, leaving him with the uneasy sensation that he was being followed. The fact that he was and he knew by whom didn't help. The sounds of boots clacking softly on the pavement, in time with his own footfalls, had a sinister timbre, like the low thrumming of a drum in a suspense vidholo. In the end it was Derek who broke the silence. "Where am I going, anyway?"

"Nowhere," the pol answered. "That's all there is around here. A lot of nothing."

"Not enough little girls to beat on, Sergeant?"

"I'm a captain, sir. Shaw, if you'd care to know my name."

"I didn't ask."

"Well I thought you might like to include it in your report. Dr. Linn told me I made something of an impression." Shaw's boots clacked a little less timidly now. "Let me tell you a story," he said. "It shouldn't stretch your imagination to suppose that a lot of the people in this city are hungry. Well, starting about a year ago, we began to find bodies—uh, carved up is the polite way to put it. Been happening once or twice a week ever since, always in some remote place, kind of like where I found you this afternoon. Usually it's their own kind, but once it was an American, and another time it was a Japanese." He paused a moment, but Derek stayed silent. "Coroners tell us they always find some kind of animal tranquilizer in the victims' blood, though there's never been enough left of a body to determine whether it was ingested voluntarily or gotten into the system some other way—one guy I know thinks they use blow darts like, what were they called? Pygmies?"

"That's no reason to maim a little girl."

"Depends on how you look at it. I left out one part of the story—the bloody handprints. Seems to be ten or more individuals involved in the murders, or at least the disposal of the evidence. All have hands less than four inches from wrist to fingertip, that means the oldest might be about ten years old. Or very small women, take your pick.''

Derek shuddered involuntarily. *I'm sorry*, he tried to say, but the words wouldn't come; they twisted up in his mouth like foul-tasting wads of cotton. He wanted to apologize, even though he still couldn't condone the day's violence. What was worse, he wanted to *apologize for the children*; cannibalism was all too easy to envision in this man-wrought hell. Images played before his eyes, blood and sharpened teeth, good and evil meshed into a homogenous blend. That was the way of nature, of the wild—the hunter stalking prey, being stalked from behind and on into infinity. If men were treated as animals, as they were here, could they be expected to conduct their lives as other men?

Thurman's Wall stained the horizon with grotesque, earthbound northern lights. Derek imagined he heard popping sounds—of people surging into the wall's overpowering bands of energy, sounds like those made by the old insect zappers, the things men once used to keep the air free of pests when there were enough pests to worry about. Men dropping like fried flies, human moths exploded to bits during final, desperate acts of futile glory. He wished he'd let Holly show him those stills of the subliminals in *The Shining Wall*; they couldn't possibly surpass what he now imagined. Then, gradually, over the hum of the wall he began to hear music—he followed it, Captain Shaw always close behind.

They reached a low, stone building, one of a minority of still-extant structures. The music came from within, and Derek pushed through the door. "Not wise," Shaw said behind him, but he ignored the warning.

Those in the bar eyed them with unmasked hostility. Resolutely, Derek smiled at them and took a seat. It was painfully obvious they were the only outsiders who'd dared to enter the place in quite some time (and quite possibly the only outsiders crazy enough to have braved these particular streets). A young woman stopped at their table, a scratch-pad held limply in her hand.

"Whiskey," Derek said gruffly. The pol sat and shook his head. Derek noticed Shaw's hand firmly on the butt of his blaster; the only other weapons he could see in the place were hidden deep in the eyes of the other patrons. He couldn't bring himself to blame them.

The whiskey, when it finally came, was horrible. As he drank, Derek fought back fears of drugged liquor with only moderate success. Children hid in the corners of the bar to all sides—hell, most of those there were little more than kids—survival of adolescence meant approaching death. He almost felt glad Shaw had come with him, now the pol wasn't drinking. The animosity in the air was beyond his talent to dispel. He could jump up on the table and try to talk to them, but what then could he say? We come in peace? We bearers of radiation and death? Mutaters of life? Gods of technology?

Servants of death, more like. He could more easily forgive them than they him.

The music he'd heard outside came from a woman on stage playing a rotting piano patched into a bank of electronics she adjusted with an occasionally free hand. Ominous chords preceded bursts of synthetic pulses against which she added vocal harmonies full of weird accidentals, like an animal crying in sorrow. Her only accompaniment came from a pair of youngsters near the stage who slapped theirs hands rhythmically against the old wood of their table. Derek tried to focus on the woman, but her very features seemed elusive and malleable. She, he finally noticed, was like the little girl in the afternoon. She had no tongue.

Resolutely, Derek drank and listened, the woman's warbling riding scales of angst few human ears could comprehend.

XIII

Night came in Novyraj (when Goliath dimmed the lights), and Orfei awoke. Soul seemed less real; it was the music of the murky past that held him this time, flowing through his head like a burning river. The woman before Soul's eyes. . . . Her voice stabbed at his nerves, resolved into near-beauty, then tore away into madness, throbbing webs of chaotic harmonies. Over the millennia, mankind's first dark death reached out to speak to him—Orfei, and Orfei alone.

He rolled off his bed to his boards, the holofield lighting up dimly, the boards purring in anticipation of his touch. He activated the mind-link and filled the field with mist, then he closed his eyes and summoned up the past, the woman at the ancient piano taking slow shape, features solidifying as he saw them through Soul's eyes. Detail by detail, from the coarse stone walls of the bar to the hair on the back of Shaw's hands, Orfei reconstructed the past in the holofield, the ancients reincarnated in light, their ruddy complexions massaged into view by Orfei's mental touch. When he was finished the scene before him was complete— he'd brought the past in his mind into the present. As the

woman sang, so her lips moved before him. The imagery
resonated, heightening his sense of being, and he began to
listen to the low droning sounds she urged from her key-
board with long, gnarled fingers. Slowly, he touched his
fingers to his own boards, following her leads, chasing her
harmonies with sympathetic chords. As he played, he began
to cry, wishing more than anything that she could hear him,
that she could play off him as he did her. Wishing he could,
through his music, resolve her pain.

Into the holofield, he conjured snow—almost without
thinking. Snow—he imagined it might cleanse her with its
whiteness, the flakes large and fluffy, coating her hair, her
instrument, her tortured song coming forth now on frosted
breath.

So he played until the echoes of Soul in his mind diminished and faded, leaving him alone in his solitude.

"*Dragon Dance*," said Orfei when the silence enclosed
him in its gray, featureless prison. The holofield responded,
his carefully crafted mountains growing up from misty
nothingness, his creature emerging to fly. An orchestra
came alive, urging the dragon to new heights—the music
shocked him with its clean chords and unmuddied lines. It
began to swell, and he ordered it off. He couldn't bear to
listen to it—his best work, they called it. In the aftermath
of the music of the past, of the woman's song of despair
and death, it grew sterile, insignificant. Learned, but possessing nothing.

He tried to compose something new, but each fresh note
fell away into the unforgiving silence. He wanted *her*
back—he closed his eyes to cast about for Soul, but the
past, for now, eluded him. "Goliath," he said at last, "did
you record that?"

"Your improvisation?"

"No—I mean, yes. My improvisation."

"Certainly. Unless you instruct me, I record everything."

"Then bring it back."

Quickly, the mist in the holofield returned and the
woman began to take shape. Her voice, though, was miss-

ing; it had all been in his mind. He watched until his own playing began, then he stopped the piece and started it over. Concentrating until sweat beaded on his forehead, he painstakingly reconstructed her voice, note for note. Until exhaustion overcame him and Soul called him back, he rebuilt her song, with all its pain and longing, to the best of his ability to remember.

XIV

IT TOOK A WHILE FOR THE HAZE OF SLEEP TO CLEAR, BUT when it did Derek was back at *Der Spinner*, in his bed. The nightclub seemed a fleeting dream—but for the dull pain at the back of his skull he might have believed it. And his throat felt raw, tainted with fire—aftereffects of the whiskey. The pol must have carried him to bed; he couldn't remember walking.

His morning exercise in reality adjustment proceeded at snail's pace; only slowly did it recur to him where he really was and where he was going. The previous day's time spent with Holly Linn floated in and out of perspective, the CIS memo and *The Shining Wall* vidholo vying for his attention, liquor-tortured nerves striving to cope with the overload. Nevertheless his return to the waking world demanded, as awakening did of all men, that he readjust his sights outward and take stock of his corporeal existence, whatever disjointed life he might have conducted in dream sleep irretrievably lost. Whatever whispery dream life he'd known. . . . The hard reality facing him could be only arguably less fantastic.

* * *

In the cool morning Derek refreshed himself and gathered his few unpacked belongings. Holly knocked on his door as he powered down Juliet and readied her for travel; the woman entered without waiting for an invitation. "I'm going with you," she said.

Derek didn't answer, or rather, barely heard. He looked up at her and managed a nod.

"You're not stable, Derek," she said. "I heard about last night."

"Is that why you're coming with me?"

"No. The orders came from Philadelphia about two hours ago."

Derek stood up straight and stretched, the new tension in his back muscles aggravating his headache momentarily but providing some relief in the end, when he finally relaxed. His sleepy eyes fell on Holly—she wore a dark blue dress, pleated, with gray-and-white trim, the official formal attire for a civil servant of her status. On most women the outfit created an air of stuffy authority, but dammit if Holly didn't make it seem natural! Perhaps she'd dressed too hastily; she'd left two buttons undone below her neck, the dress's collar fallen slightly askew. Or perhaps she'd left them undone on purpose. . . . Linda used to snap the damned thing so tightly he'd been surprised she could eat with it on.

But Holly's eyes were shadows now. In their depths he recalled the mournful song of the woman the night before. He wanted to say something gentle, but he couldn't make the words come, not with part of him screaming inside to remain wary—nothing at all was predictable anymore. *Before the jaws of the dragon*, he thought, *I stand alone*. Now who'd written that one?

"Don't you care?"

"About what?"

"My orders! It doesn't seem strange to you they'd come on such short notice."

"Everything seems strange to me, Holly. You could tell me Jesus Christ was sighted in the southwest quarter last night performing miracles, and I'd be inclined to believe you."

"That's hardly applicable to the present state of affairs."

"Well," Derek said, "*if* it happened, I think you'd find it applicable if not quite significant."

"With that attitude, Inspector General, your presence on this assignment makes even less sense."

"I quite agree," he returned curtly. He finished packing his bags and handed them over to the escorts Holly had waiting outside the door. "Let's go, Dr. Linn."

Soon, Berlin became memory. In the viaduct terminal, smelling as it did of disinfectant and electricity, he could have been back in the States. Not a native in sight—if the accommodation scheduling program had gotten its way, this would have been all he'd seen of the old German capital: White walls and white tech coveralls—modern man bereft of nature. . . . He felt some vindication for staying at *Der Spinner* and braving the Berlin streets; however gray and despairing and dangerous they'd been, they'd been infinitely more alive than this place. And, he thought with sinking spirits, the place he was going. It wasn't as if he hadn't been there before.

Most movement in sight was that of machines. Vac-bots scoured the floors and the walls, and miniature, spiderlike automatons crawled in and out of access ports on the two bullet cars waiting at the boarding platform. As Derek looked around, only Holly seemed alive. Two faceless white-coats were packing their luggage into the cars. That done, they guided him to the first vehicle, then left him alone. Holly would be following him in the second car. As soon as he pulled down the door and locked it in place, his car lurched forward into darkness.

So much for America's New Berlin.

The bullet-shaped vehicle had three windows, one directly in front and one to each side of the passenger. At first they showed only the bleak inner surface of the McDonald Viaduct, a cold, black-gray streaked with dull yellow lights—just as it had been before, the last time. He felt his heartbeat quicken again with the realization that all that separated him from the irradiated wastes were the car and the viaduct's walls—twenty feet beyond in all directions lurked certain death; he was as dependent on his artificial environment as an astronaut. Then, just as he felt the first beads of sweat on his skin, the windows went white and a light pinprick teased the back of his hand. "Hello, Dr. Soul," said a voice in the car.

A feeling of well-being breezed through him as the drug took quick effect. "Are you human or machine?" His voice felt elastic, as if he could toss it any direction and listen to it bounce back.

"Machine."

"Then identify yourself—have you forgotten your programming?"

"No, Doctor. I am TravelDoc Version 7. My programming no longer requires nonresponsive statement of identity owing to the demands of my job. I am human interactive level 1."

"The demands of your job?"

"Different biochemical reactions to the viaduct journey require different responses, Doctor. My primary purpose is to maintain the mental well-being of my passengers."

"You sound like Holly," he said dreamily.

"Irrelevant. Continuing—you must understand that some humans retain latent metaphysical resistance to the idea of machine intelligence, and in such cases I am programmed to conceal my identity. For human benefit."

"That's illegal."

"Incorrect. Reference Article Sixteen, Paragraph Three of the Non-Comprehensive Special Systems Authorization Act of 2102—quote, any maintenance system positioned beyond civilian public access, particularly those systems designed to human preservation specifications but not including standard—"

"Enough, I believe you."

". . . not including standard—"

"For human interactive level 1, you sure are boring."

". . . not including standard—st—s—stan—"

Derek laughed silently at his joke as the computer's stammering grew more erratic. "Shut up, dammit!"

The machine's voice began to fade. Whatever drug it had

given him made him feel almost weightless—he tried to get up but found himself held down by straps. The white sheen over the car's windows grew milky and insubstantial; he reached out to the one on his left and his hand went through it. He tried to stand again and succeeded this time; the straps had disappeared. His head passed through the roof of the car as if breaking the surface of a pool after a deep dive, and the air that welcomed him was light and smelled of roses.

Derek Soul was no longer moving, and he'd all but forgotten he was supposed to be. He'd emerged from the viaduct into some sort of night—late summer somewhere; the roses were real, their deep red blossoms catching elusive moonlight so that they shone like fading lanterns along either side of his path. He walked and a large white building came into view ahead, its gold-inlaid doors preceded by a series of wide steps built up in tiers.

He was back in Philadelphia; this was the Armenian Embassy. A groundcar—an antique limousine—rolled to a stately halt at the curb ahead, discharging a trio of passengers: a middle-aged woman in evening dress wearing a mask and a headdress of peacock feathers; a younger woman in a translucent, erotic outfit in the French style of the 2020s; and a large man who no doubt was supposed to be Henry VIII of England—appropriate, perhaps, but certainly unoriginal. Derek expected he'd find three or four more identical costumes inside. He glanced down at his own dress, a simple, loose-fitting suit of the type popular in the mid–twentieth century. He tilted back the brim of his hat and practiced a Cagney snarl; he doubted he'd be any more unique than Henry, but at the very least he looked good and retained some dignity. Only women and younger men were supposed to make spectacles of themselves at these affairs.

It had been a long time since he'd attended a formal party, and he wouldn't have bothered with this one if the secretary hadn't implied his attendance was mandatory and not a matter of convenience. Some special project team had just returned from Moscow, and to his boss that made it an important night for the department. So Derek had made a promise he'd try to have fun. Inside the embassy he learned that might not be too difficult. The lighting in the main hall was subdued and the crowd remarkably sedate, gathered in small groups and conversing softly if at all. Over the quiet voices came the melancholy strains of a dodouk playing some traditional Armenian melody—the embassy had brought in what looked to be a mostly acoustic band; if nothing else he'd have an enjoyable evening just watching the musicians.

Secretary Collier noticed his entrance and waved him over. Derek joined his small group and soon had a drink in one hand and a cigarette in the other. His companions were all dressed in the white-wigged, waistcoated garb of America's founding fathers. A robot rolled by offering hydroponically cultivated marijuana, but Derek passed on it, at least for the moment. "Don't know what you're missing, my boy," Collier said, taking a small pipe from the robot and lighting it. "By the way, this is Saunders from Energy—a very important man."

"We've met," said an aging man across from Derek. "Bet he doesn't remember though."

Derek nodded in agreement; he didn't remember. Saunders took the pipe from Collier, inhaled the smoke deeply, and passed it on. "Guess you weren't even twenty last time I saw you, Drak. Me and your old man used to be real tight; you used to worry the hell out of him back then with all your crazy liberal ideas—he was sure you'd end up a pansy."

Derek raised an eyebrow but said nothing. He remembered why he habitually avoided large gatherings of bureaucrats; his father's ghost always tended to rear its ugly head.

Saunders cast his gaze about from side to side, brushing back a shock of synthetic white hair. "Jesus, but this stuff makes some of these old bitches look twenty years younger!" Laughter rippled slowly through the group of old men; Derek waited for it to subside before he excused himself.

* * *

He found a seat at a table midway between an old-fashioned bar with real wooden stools and the wide platform that functioned as a stage for the musicians. He expected Collier would have something to say about his behavior the next morning, but he *was* there, and as far as he knew that was all his boss had required; he certainly didn't need his hand held to get through the evening. He nursed a tall bourbon and absorbed himself in the music; when the woman sat down across from him, he didn't even notice until she gasped, and he looked up into a strange face, made stranger by an expression of complete bewilderment.

"I *know* you," she said breathlessly.

"I don't think so," he countered.

"No, really," she said, her voice growing excited. "I'm not crazy; I've seen you before! What's your name?"

"Derek. Derek Soul."

She looked disappointed for a moment. "Well that doesn't ring any bells. . . . Never mind—my name's Linda. So tell me, Derek—tell me."

"What?"

"Everything. You have to tell me everything about yourself so we can solve this mystery and be done with it."

He looked at her closely, growing even more certain he'd never seen her before; she had an Oriental slant to her eyes, very slight, but it was the sort of feature he didn't usually forget. Her face had otherwise strong lines—large lips; when she smiled they made her beautiful. Most of her hair was black, but she'd done nothing to hide the shocks of gray brushed back from her temples. When he asked, she admitted she was almost forty.

For the rest of the evening they talked, Derek giving up his history, Linda listening raptly and shaking her head as his story failed time and again to reveal where their pasts had converged.

The next morning, Collier summoned him and offered congratulations while Derek stood stupidly expecting a reprimand. The secretary laughed at his confusion. "You mean she didn't tell you, son? That was Moscow you charmed

last night—she runs the whole banana! Damned if I know
how you did it, though. She really didn't tell you?"

"No, sir."

"Well I'll be damned." Collier sighed.

Linda met him later for lunch; she looked different by
daylight—a little less clearly defined, softer, Derek thought.
As they dined at a small Indian restaurant he found himself
noticing her perfume, a blend of jasmine and something he
couldn't quite identify. She apologized for her appearance
and said she'd had trouble sleeping. "But I figured it out,
Derek," she said. "I figured it all out this morning."

"What?"

"Where we met." She lowered her silverware and wiped
a small spot of curry from her lip with her napkin. "You're
going to think I'm crazy."

He smiled; he was thinking of how gracefully self-aware
she was, especially in contrast to her girlish exuberance at
the embassy. He could tell she wanted to impress him, that
she feared making an offending move. He'd resisted marriage when he was younger and had involved himself in so
few serious relationships in recent years that the fact this
woman was attracted to him excited him in a way he hadn't
pondered the night before. Now she seemed vulnerable—
open to him; that required a measure of trust he found refreshing, and he almost didn't care about what she was
actually saying. "No I won't," he responded. "Go ahead."

"Well, okay," she said, dropping eye contact. "I've had
this recurring dream lately; it's pretty weird, but I'll try to
describe it. Somehow, you see, I start out in this palace
where there are all these people who are, well, deformed.
I get scared and try to run, but I can't and I look down and
my legs are fused together—nothing erotic or anything like
a mermaid, just fused together from my knees to my ankles.
It's hellish; I said dream, but I really meant nightmare.
Everybody's writhing around on the floor, some with no
arms, others no faces; nearly everyone's crying. This goes
on for—I don't know, seems like forever; then this man
comes in the far side of the room; he's tall and whole and
that's about all I can see. He starts touching people; some

of them get up and shout for joy, but others scream and burst into flame, get burned to cinders. So he moves through the crowd, getting closer and closer to me, and I don't know whether to weep for joy or feel terrified. That's when I usually wake up.''

She paused a moment and looked up. "Last night he reached me. He touched me and my legs came unglued and I jumped up and kissed him and finally saw him clearly. He was you, Derek.''

He frowned, feeling he'd missed something. "Uh—I don't see where . . . I mean, I don't know much about recurrent dreams, but if you didn't see this person clearly until last night, what does that have to do with your thinking you knew me before then?''

"I thought about that—it must have been subconscious. I couldn't remember your face when I woke up, but I must have seen enough of it to recognize you at the party.''

"Sounds more like a metaphor for Christianity to me.''

"Well you think what you want,'' she said, smiling now. "I'm not much for religion.''

He smiled back at her. "You know, I couldn't figure out last night whether you were just using an elaborate line.''

"Oh,'' she said, "that hurts! I made a rule years ago never to pick up strange men, nor get picked up by them. That's probably why I've stayed single; it's hard to fall in love with someone you've known for a while—all the mystery is gone by then.''

He chuckled, resisting the easy temptation to ask which category he fell into. Whether or not he believed it, her dream had a definite romantic edge; the idea that she'd told a story in which she'd been saved by him flattered him a great deal, no matter whether it was some subconscious gyration on her part or just a story she'd made up to resolve a pretense fabricated the night before. Either way she was growing more attractive by the moment, and that feeling appeared mutual.

When she finished eating she again dabbed her lips and smiled. "I think you should take the afternoon off, Derek,'' she said. "I think I'd like to take you back to my hotel room—we can work off some of this lunch." To his later regret, he happily agreed.

If nothing else, Linda Webb was a true wonder in bed, and over the next week that's where they stayed. After a few days she began to have despondent moments—at first she fended off his gentle questioning, but she eventually admitted the source of her despair: She had only two weeks leave from her duties in Moscow; their affair would soon come to an end. By the time the scene repeated a third time, he'd fashioned his reply: "Let's get married," he said. "I'm sure the department can post me to Moscow; must be something I can do there."

"Do you mean it, darling?"

"Does that mean yes?"

"Of course!"

"Then I mean it."

For a while then, all their problems were solved. They married, Linda left when her leave expired, and Derek followed her a few days later after taking care of what little unfinished work he had left at the office. He flew to Berlin and from there rode the McDonald Viaduct on to Moscow. The journey left him with lingering claustrophobic fears that Moscow itself did nothing to relieve; the place was little more than a warren of tunnels, its living quarters cramped and overly ascetic. Still, Linda was there, and the evenings were all that mattered. By day, Derek held the post of co-administrator of logistics management—a pointless job that demanded only that he review the output of the logistics management programs which were seldom, if ever, wrong during his entire tenure. For the first time in his career he knew genuine boredom.

On the other hand, the department was working his new wife to the point of exhaustion; their sexual interludes lessened in frequency, duration, and intensity, and the stony walls of Moscow began to close in. Derek had never actually *hated* a place before. One day he received an anonymous message on the local net suggesting he surprise his wife with an unannounced visit to her office. He did, and found her there with her uniform on the floor and she, naked, next to it. With her was Paul Kramer, her second-in-command.

Derek pulled strings and got out that same night—before his wife even knew he was leaving. Once stateside he filed for divorce while his wife seemed to spend most of her time writing him, pleading that he return. He rarely bothered to read her messages and never answered; they eventually grew vindictive and hateful, then stopped. A year later he learned she'd actually married the bastard he'd found her with.

XV

A COLD CHILL RAN THROUGH DEREK AS THE IMAGES OF Moscow dissolved and shriveled up, leaving him back in the bullet car. He felt nauseous, completely disoriented— the illusion had been complete; he'd *relived* the entire sordid affair. Now he was back in his body; he could feel the car's vibrations as it sped through the viaduct. The side windows had misted over, undoubtedly the result of his own perspiration; his clothes were soaked from it. His heart thumped violently in his chest; he closed his eyes, trying to slow it down. "Goddamn it, computer! Is that what you call making my journey pleasant?"

TravelDoc Version 7 failed to respond; instead, an audio speaker crackled somewhere behind his head. "Dr. Soul, is that you? Shit! I was afraid you were dead!"

"Who's this?"

"Tech Specialist Willis, sir, from Viaduct Control. You lost your intelligent systems just outside Berlin. I've been trying to hail you for the past hour; didn't you hear me?"

Derek took a moment to digest the words. "No, Mr. Willis, I didn't."

"Shit!"

"How much longer do I have to endure this?"

"Not long—are you okay, sir?"

He swallowed hard, feeling sweat beading on his brow. The sides of the car seemed to pulsate at the edges of his vision; the drug he'd been administered hadn't completely worn off. "I'm trying," he answered.

"Well, hold on. I'm here if you need to talk, okay?"

"Sure—oh, how's Holly, I mean Dr. Linn?"

"She's fine. Guess you just drew the wrong straw, sir."

The crackle shut down abruptly, leaving Derek alone. The pulsating rhythm of his vision grew stronger, so he shut his eyes tight and clenched his teeth. He remembered Collier's assurances about the viaduct journey and tried to sort out an appropriately graphic comment for his return to Philadelphia. But what the hell had really happened? The kid on the radio had said he'd lost his systems before he'd barely started—had his own mind dragged him through the business with Linda all over again? Was the drug itself that powerful, without computer assistance? Shit kept getting weirder; with his eyes closed his vision swam with colors and ghostly images—one part of the hallucination went into a loop: that meal with Linda at the Indian restaurant, where she'd told him about her dream. He opened his eyes and saw the roof of the car crashing down on him; he closed them and saw a distorted image of his ex-wife licking curry off her lips. He couldn't decide which was worse.

XVI

Orfei wakened in a sweat of his own, his room like a blue, twilit prison. Within him, Soul had relived the horror called Moscow and now the terribly constricting viaduct—all underground, like Novyraj itself. Soul's claustrophobic fears gripped him—a terrifying, alien experience as Orfei had known life without walls only in his dreams, his imagination, his art. Walls were his reality, yet now they closed in on him, made it difficult to breathe. They menaced and seemed alive. Something within demanded he be free.

He tried to get up, but Soul wouldn't let him go—he kept Orfei trapped, on his bed beneath the towers of ancient San Francisco, which legend said burned and collapsed before following Atlantis into the sea. Orfei gazed longingly at the picture, the high towers and the bridge beneath the open sky; before Soul they'd seemed strange, but now they looked right, only the frame around them unreal as if reality was reversing, changing up to down, inside to outside, safety to danger, and danger to freedom. It was Novyraj that felt wrong. Orfei wanted those old dark streets of Berlin as Soul had wanted them; he wanted that rose-bordered path before the party, when the moon shone down through a murky night. Though Soul hadn't looked up then—hadn't shown Orfei the stars he knew must be there—Orfei wished he'd go back where perhaps he could will Soul's eyes skyward.

He wanted space, and in doing so grew horrified of the morbid desire. Space meant the surface world, and the surface world meant death—how could he contemplate it otherwise? From childhood, all in Novyraj knew the terrible perils of the surface, the mutants with nine eyes and finger-length fangs, the walls of flying, burning sand, the places where all life stopped, where all life that entered was doomed to die. What of the expeditions of the past? None had ever returned. And what punishment did all in Novyraj fear the most—what punishment deterred the horrible crimes that plagued humanity's old history? Not death, but expulsion—forced ejection into the central lift shaft. The surface world. The very fear of it helped them live in peace!

Now Orfei wanted it, and the longer he thought of it, the harder he fought, the wilder his desire became.

XVII

THE DOOR OF THE BULLET CAR PEELED AWAY LIKE THE
shell of an insect preparing for flight, Derek's stale air ex-
pelled into the recycled atmosphere of the Moscow terminal, which smelled strongly of ozone and steel. A figure
stood above him, made a silhouette against the artificial
glow filling the chamber. Its small hand reached toward
him, and twin beacons of blue seemed to flicker in the
shadows; Derek peered into the depths and thought he saw
the little girl's tongueless smile, but when he took the hand
it had a firmer grip, and when he stood the figure grew
taller until it attained a height nearly level with his own.
Linda's face emerged from the shadows. "Hello, darling,"
she said. "I'm so glad you're all right."

His reply was little more than a grunt—he might have
found something to say were it not for the vertigo that
seized him once standing. He searched her eyes, feeling
helpless but surprisingly unafraid, as if he'd fallen back into
dream, this scene a mere footnote to the past he'd so recently relived, something unreal that he didn't have to believe.

"You'll feel much better after a rest," she said, putting

her arm around his shoulder to steady him. "Let's get to your quarters; the bio systems can monitor you there to make sure you recover okay."

Now he was walking, Linda holding him up. Before they left the terminal he heard the roar of the second car's arrival and had a sudden desire to run back and greet Holly, but his body failed to obey; its every step kept time with his ex-wife's methodical pace. For a short stretch outside the terminal they walked in the open, under the big dome, separated from the devastated city by only a thin energy shield. Clouds bubbled and writhed overhead, but sparse shafts of sunlight broke through. Derek saw what he thought must be the rim of a crater in the near distance, its sides littered with large chunks of masonry and the roof of something that might once have been a cathedral. The sunlight granted it all a sort of wounded, tragic beauty with bits of cracked granite sparkling like lost gems amid the wreckage. He squinted and noticed—yes, there was a large crucifix planted at a slant a short distance from the fallen roof; beneath it he could just make out the shape of a hand reaching up from the rubble. In their wrath they'd blasted Christ from the cross, freed him from a torture endured for centuries to atone for their sins—sins they could no longer explain, at least not here. Funny: They were all supposed to be atheists. . . .

The corridors returned, growing dark, then light—gray-walled cousins of corridors he knew in the government complex in Philadelphia—lighting courtesy of luminous strips in the upper joints that, if you half closed your eyes and quickened your step, could make you feel like an old-time airplane flying upside down and coming in for a landing. It seemed ages before they stopped, and when they did it was only to change direction; they took a short elevator ride down into a herd of t-bugs, one of which Linda promptly commandeered, and then they were moving again, only now they rode.

The t-bug (*tunnel-bug* shortened—Derek couldn't even remember the official name for the thing) glided lightly over the occasionally uneven surface of the passageways—it was a popular vehicle for this sort of work, owing its existence to the demands of the prewar deep mining industry. On first inspection it resembled the bumper-hovers of old amusement parks, low-riding hovercraft cushioned with thick layers of shock-absorbing rubber to withstand collisions. Engineers had added retractable wheels stored in the undercarriage to enable hoverless use and provide support during cave-ins; this feature, combined with the inertia-negative shielding over the passenger area, had saved many a miner's life. Now, with commercial mining at a worldwide standstill, the government possessed them all.

Linda voice-fed sector data into the t-bug's navigator, placing one hand over Derek's. "It's a bit of a ride these days," she said. "We moved HQ closer in to the work about two months ago, hoping to improve morale."

Cool air gusted against his skin and quickly dried his perspiration, matting his hair against his forehead; he hoped it would clear his mind, but his sense of balance failed to return, Linda's voice seeming to phase-shift and fluctuate in volume. He had to struggle to find his tongue. "Did it work?"

"I think so. There's a sense of safety in numbers."

"So tell me what you think is happening." His mouth worked automatically, and he felt almost like a spectator, outside himself and looking in. Linda, next to him, appeared a ghost—he seriously began to question whether he'd left the bullet car, whether the viaduct still held him in its grip.

"They just disappear—over fifty of them now. Never found any bodies." Her shape began to twist into wraith-like strands—Derek felt as if he were falling. "I'm sure they're okay," came her voice from a great distance. "He promised me."

He? Derek thought, then his world went black.

XVIII

ORFEI SAT GROGGILY AS SOUL FELL INTO THE EMBRACE of deep, dreamless sleep. The tendrils of the past peeled away, taking with them the oneiric shroud that had enveloped him since entering the Room of the Fourth. The mind-bytes went completely still, and the void they left crashed down in merciless silence.

He felt suddenly free; he held his head in his hands and sobbed, not knowing whether to rejoice or mourn.

He stood, and the silence intensified. Had the mind-bytes truly released him? *Is it done?* he proposed with great focus. The buzzing—the sense of two worlds—had abandoned him.

"What do I do now?" he asked aloud. "Goliath?"

"Sensors suggest you wash and take nourishment," came the ubiquitous voice. "Neglect of proper human maintenance is incorrect living."

He frowned, wanting to rephrase the question but not knowing what to ask. A part of him—the deep part rooted in Novyraj that knew Goliath as trusted friend and confidant—wished to externalize all, to voice Soul's tale and torments as puzzles to be solved and interpreted together, with Goliath's help. After all, were the mind-bytes themselves not Goliath's? "Do you know what I have seen?"

"Your eyes are your own, Orfei."

"I mean since the Room—my ascension."

"That is closed to me."

"Should I tell you?"

A pregnant silence chased his voice, redirecting his thoughts inward. Goliath's answer would be meaningless. He couldn't speak yet; it was too soon, and the past might yet lurk in dark corners—if not the mind-bytes themselves, then pieces of the past they'd left behind. *If* they'd in fact left at all.

No, he realized, the puzzle was his alone. He had communed with powers he did not understand, perhaps looked into the eye of God. . . . What artist could betray such a vision by giving it away misunderstood?

"I think not," Goliath answered at last.

Slowly, Orfei nodded.

Time passed and the deep silence thickened and grew dense. Orfei took an air-bath, drank a gallon of water, and ate three full portions of food-cakes before his hunger was sated. Though he ate, his mind never stopped, for what could it *mean*? Derek Soul was legend, the father of all, that much everybody knew, and yet the world through Soul's eyes was not Novyraj. Had Orfei merely been the vessel through which a portion of Soul's life might be relearned—remembered? With the mind-bytes silent, had it really come to an end?

If so perhaps he *should* tell Lysis and everybody else— he should sit before his holofield and rebuild it, detail for detail as he had the scene in the ancient bar—all in Novyraj might then know what he'd seen. As art he could make it a great work. If only that felt right; but it didn't.

Though he'd seen more than he could have dreamed, he had no answers, only mysteries demanding but evading solutions. What could he show people? That Soul was a man? That he drank alcohol as those in the hedonist sects worshiped? That he'd practiced the dubious custom of marriage? That his world was one of desolation and confusion?

The first and last were well-known and the rest often guessed at—what was the point? The images themselves? Soul's face in a mirror? The man hadn't even looked into one.

The more Orfei thought back, the less he found of value. He was no scholar, but surface images from Soul's time were surely in Goliath's vidbanks for those who wished to find them. Even of Berlin—perhaps not of the McDonald Viaduct and Moscow, but again, what was the point? "With his first children, Derek Soul built Novyraj and Goliath and their building was vast and full of hope and it preserved the race from itself, a new world prospering beneath the fires of Armageddon." *That* was the legend—the history. He hadn't experienced the building of anything— and of other parts of the legend? Of Soul's presidency of the United Free Nations? Of his brave battles against the toxic tides adrift on the seas? Of his great speeches—his futile pleas to mankind to unite against the terrible bloody traditions of the past?

Where was all that in the Soul he'd relived? He'd been but a small man—well, a man with authority but no great power—in fact a Soul enslaved to other powers against which he seemed in constant rebellion. His Soul was real, but it was no match for the one Novyraj revered. The legend lied, but suppose he did reconstruct all he'd seen in holo and give it to his people—would they even believe him?

He asked the question of himself and the answer was no—there had to be something more. With his eyes tightly shut he attempted to turn his mind inward, to seek out the dark pockets and learn whether they lived, and if the mind-bytes hid within them. He felt free, but only as Soul slept— a very deep sleep perhaps. In time Soul might waken; Orfei would have to wait.

"The chair of the Fourth Council has requested an audience," said Goliath.

He'd finished eating—only contemplated the silence now. Lysis, he thought. From the dream life of Soul she came back to him. He'd confronted her how many times?

Never fully himself then—had she really attempted to penetrate his mind? With the immediacy of his initiation diminishing by the moment, every part of it came back like snatches of elusive dream, his own moments of partial self-awareness as well as his vicarious experience of Soul. In fact, after all that, life now felt too lucid and clean, too rational, as if Soul's departure had stripped away his artistry, leaving a mind too clean to create and capable only of thinking. He felt a void in the place of the muddiness and vertigo, the way Soul had felt after that projection vid with the cobblestones and blue sky. (*There had to be more!* He'd seen that same vid in this room—"artist unknown". . . . His mind had been mangled, stretched into unfathomable dimensions—how could he expect to understand through reason split-lives he'd lived in which reason had played no known role?)

"Will you see her now?" Goliath pressed him.

More easily now than before, he thought. On the one hand he craved solitude, on the other he felt caged, and Lysis might hold the key, or at least a portion of it. Excepting recent events which he'd perhaps interpreted wrongly, he had no reason to mistrust her. But for her attempt to penetrate his mind. . . . "Yes, Goliath," he said. "I think I must."

Lysis came, Clystra with her. *Almost Immortal*, Orfei recalled—he could picture her young, a century past—knowledge out of nowhere. . . . *There had to be more!*

"Orfei," she said smiling. "You have returned to us!"

"Yes," he answered flatly.

She approached, crossing to his chamber with the pictures where he awaited them. Her flex-coat was gone, replaced by amorphous robes more befitting her station. "We must speak of important things, Orfei."

"My ascension?"

"That is past—" Clystra said.

Lysis silenced him with a gesture. "We did not mean to pressure you—you may tell us in time if you wish. These are critical times, and my prime concern was for your return; the Room lingered with you, and that has never hap-

pened before. We feared you might be lost, just when we
need you the most."

"Why?" Her words made little sense. *Critical times?*

"Clystra is Chief Sage of the Fourths—he will explain."

The other man cleared his throat; Orfei recognized him
but couldn't recall from where. "Novyraj keeps deep secrets, holomage. Those who have searched our passageways have found no end to them, and Goliath is
everywhere. Have you ever questioned this?"

He shook his head; what Clystra described—that was
life. Accepted.

"Well I am sage," the other continued. "To question is
my purpose, and the purpose of all who have gone before
me, just as you and your father have perceived your purpose to be the creation of art. In Novyraj we have a good
life. The system of sects nourishes us, and Goliath sustains
us. We have space and follow the customs established by
Soul—when we conflict, we separate and make peace, else
risk the perils of the surface, thus neo-Christians may worship in one set of halls while hedonists enjoy their pleasures
in another, and throughout their lives they may never meet.
This is how it should be; when new conflict arises, new
sects are formed, and Novyraj and Goliath give new space
and comfort whenever asked. Because of this the old conflicts known on the surface—over land for growing, over
fertile fields—we are free of them.

"Though the surface is denied us, we have paradise.
Novyraj is limitless, a world within the world."

Orfei nodded. He knew all this.

"This was Soul's gift," Lysis said, "but what technology made it—what built Novyraj and Goliath—none but
Soul has ever known. Over millennia sages have pondered
and explored the depths of Goliath's knowledge, but none
until Clystra has even cracked the mystery—this is a great
man who stands before you, holomage."

"I am lucky," Clystra insisted, though he beamed with
pride. "But yes," he said, "I have learned secrets—code
commands to Goliath that he himself is blocked from
knowing. At Goliath's heart hides a true machine; no one
has ever found it, but it must be true. Witness this." The

sage turned his eyes upward. "Goliath, when the monkeys reproduced Shakespeare, which play came first?"

"*Hamlet.*"

"Incorrect."

The voice that was everywhere seemed to sigh, then another broke through, a grating, synthetic voice: "Support documents not found, recovery in progress." A long pause followed before Goliath's normal voice returned. "Rephrase your question, please. I misunderstood."

"That's okay," Clystra said. He looked at Orfei. "Do you see? The sage Alexander discovered that aberration two centuries ago. There are others—some that probe more deeply and can be quite dangerous. The sage's work is very delicate—for instance, what if Goliath is injured? It has never happened, but it must be possible. What if Novyraj ceases to produce new oxygen, new food-cakes? Care is the first tenet of my craft, so we have learned very slowly. Only by luck did I learn what I now know, but I have learned something beyond the guarded codes to build new halls—something much more."

"You command Goliath?"

Clystra laughed. "Hardly—but I have scratched beneath the surface. We hold the key now—"

Lysis again interrupted. "Of all that's good in Novyraj, Orfei, what do we not have?"

"I don't know."

"The surface world, holomage—we are denied it."

"I thought we didn't want it."

"We don't," she agreed impatiently. "But what if, instead of new halls in Novyraj, we could give the sects new worlds? Entire landscapes with grass and trees and buildings and a sky overhead—much more than just these walls we now know," she concluded. "Fantastic worlds, limited only by your imagination."

"What if," Clystra added excitedly, "we could build a world like your *Dragon Dance*, step into it, and it be real? Not just light, but real—an entire reality! With a vision as clear as yours in your art, we need not be satisfied with halls. We *can* build worlds!"

Lysis again silenced the sage. "Do you follow, Orfei?"

He nodded cautiously. Not that he truly believed what he heard. . . .

"Tomorrow," Lysis went on slowly, "is the feast of Beltene—of particular importance to several sects including the First Chivalrous Order and the Legion of White Sorcery." She leveled her gaze firmly on Orfei. "I want to give it to them, holomage. I want to give them *Dragon Dance* as their own world, separate from ours. Clystra assures me it will work."

"Ninety percent chance," the other said.

"Together we can change Novyraj—make it grow. After *Dragon Dance* you and other mages can build more worlds in light, and Clystra will make them real. Through the secrets we possess, we'll regain for our people all that humanity has lost."

His art made real?

Orfei looked at them, stunned. Their words worked his imagination like old clay—could what they said be true? *Dragon Dance* a world unto itself? It would be a dangerous place—one with death very real. "I—" he began, then a soft buzzing grew up from the nape of his neck. . . . The mind-bytes hadn't left him after all, and in the distant past Soul stirred. "Give me time," he said in quick desperation. He needed solitude, but he couldn't let them see. Not after all he'd heard.

"You must stand with us tomorrow, Orfei," Lysis insisted. "You are a hero, and your presence will win their trust."

What if they die? he wanted to ask, but instead he nodded. *Go away!* he screamed in his mind. Deep within, Soul was rising up from oblivion, and the walls about Orfei closed in.

"Tomorrow then," Lysis said, smiling curiously. She turned, and Clystra followed her out of the room.

XIX

A COOL HAND BRUSHED OVER DEREK'S BROW LIKE A GEN-
tle breeze, and he opened his eyes slowly. The lights in the
room were subdued, but they still hurt. It took him a while
to focus and find Holly's concerned gaze between him and
the biomonitoring systems which hovered higher up.

"You're okay?" she said. He thought he saw the wet
remains of a tear near her eye.

"I think so," he said, finding his voice. "Where's
Linda?"

"Haven't seen her; she contacted me once through voice
comm to say she hasn't got time for us until you're ready.
Must've sent her five messages since then in protest, but
no luck yet."

"What—she brought me here. . . . In a t-bug."

"I don't think so," she corrected him gently. "When I
arrived you were leaving the terminal on your back, on a
med-hover. What happened?"

He tried to sit up, but a sharp pain in his forehead
knocked him back. "Who knows?" he whispered.
"TravelDoc malfunctioned. Been through pure hell. . . ."

"Well you're back now. What's this about Linda?"

He blinked his eyes, trying to clear his mind. "Could've sworn she helped me here—pretty much carried me. Said something about the missing people, that they're safe."

"You were hallucinating; some woman was directing the med-hover, but I've never seen her before. That viaduct drug's a bit unpredictable when left uncontrolled. You're lucky that's all you saw."

"So what happened to you—on the trip?"

"Had a wonderful, breathtaking tour of Australia."

"Lucky you!"

"Yeah," she said distantly. "Listen, Derek—mine's two rooms over; we've got a work lounge in between. Got access to all local systems as far as I can tell, so I don't know why I can't raise your ex-wife unless she's purposefully ignoring me. If you need me, I'll be there. You look like you still need a lot of rest."

"Feel that way, too."

She nodded and backed away, doing something with the biosystem hovering above. A thin arm extended from the mass of metal and sensors and brushed against his skin— another drug that took effect quickly, washing away his headache, placing a fuzzy sheen over the external world until it went dark and sleep came again.

XX

ORFEI STAGGERED TO HIS FEET AS THE MIND-BYTES EASED their grip—how long since Lysis had left? He'd lost all sense of time—mere seconds or centuries might have passed. This time, Soul's sleep was gentle; deep in Orfei's mind his dreams progressed like shadow-plays. When he concentrated he could find and follow them, but he hadn't the time. He *had* to think for himself, as impossible as that might be. . . .

Lysis and Clystra were serious—either that or reality itself had betrayed him. They'd tapped the power of Goliath. . . . It all sounded crazy, and he couldn't decide what it meant. Soul tugged at him, the ancient's fear of walls feeding the same sense in Orfei, walls gaining metaphysical substance, possessing a dark, oppressive will—walls in opposition to man, providing only illusory protection.

Did Lysis and Clystra not offer worlds without walls, only a sky high above? Wasn't that a *good* thing? Some undefinable, menacing cloud hung over what they'd introduced to his mind; he couldn't tell if it came from within, from Soul or from somewhere else. His nerves felt steeled for action—but to do what? To move—if he stayed, Soul would sooner or later overcome him again, leaving him physically helpless. What would they do if they learned of his state? Let him go on peacefully, excusing him from the festival and all their plans to live the life of a mystic? Or pry again into his mind, perhaps with more powerful tools, perhaps breaking through? If he told them all of his own volition, would they believe him? He couldn't shake the thought they would not.

And what if he left? In Novyraj there was nowhere to hide. Not from one with the power of Lysis—they'd surely locate him through Goliath.

It had to be the lift shaft. The surface.

He donned a thick blue robe and asked Goliath for pants and boots, making a supreme effort to follow the thought through and not dwell on the consequences. He had to try, even if it might kill him. When Soul again made him helpless he had to be safe, far from the intrigues developing around him. After stuffing several days' worth of food into his robe's inner pockets, he ran his fingers sadly over the keys of his vidsonic board, then abandoned his haven.

He met no resistance before the lift shaft—it plunged through the core of Novyraj like the central stalk of a tree, its lower currents much used conveyors for those traveling from one depth to another. He stepped out onto the air, the shaft's mass reduction technology granting near weightlessness, a steady breeze from below lifting him quickly and easily. Colored streamers delimited the currents; he avoided the central updraft at first, preferring to zigzag up to successive levels only to glide past the entrance ports and continue his ascent. Once he'd passed the last port into a main hall, he entered the updraft and kicked his feet to pick up speed. Directly above was the safety net, Novyraj's final defense against uncontrolled upward drift; it slowed him only a moment; in a burst of strength he opened the mesh of the fabric and wiggled through to the sound of surprised shouts from below.

As he climbed the air grew warmer. The surface itself was still far above, no more than a pinprick of darkness against the ambient light of the shaft. Below, a single distant figure squeezed through the hole to follow him up. He kicked faster to increase his speed, but the figure came faster, propelled by auxiliary air jets—it wore the red-caped garb of the League of New Order, a disciplinarian sect the council used to keep peace at large gatherings. Despite all his efforts, he stood no chance of his escape; his pursuer—a woman—quickly gained his side.

"Quick," she said, while adjusting a device at her belt to control the air jets strapped to her back. "Grab me under the arms—I can guide us back down."

Her features were hidden under a thick shock of nut brown hair; she hadn't even looked up at him yet. He backpedaled away from her. "No," he said.

Now she eyed him—she appeared quite young. "You're Orfei Agamon!" she exclaimed with surprise.

He felt some internal relief, realizing nobody had purposefully sent her after him; he supposed her sect maintained surveillance on the shaft as a matter of practice. "Yes," he said. "You'd better go back by yourself."

"What do you think you're doing?"

"Going up," he answered plainly.

"To the surface? You'll die!"

He didn't respond; they hit an unexpected eddy in the updraft, boosting their ascent. A loud sucking sound erupted as a panel opened in the side of the shaft and pulled in air—as if Novyraj, far below, was breathing. Orfei knew a moment of fear as the eddy whipped him toward the opening, but the panel closed after a few seconds, the resulting currents sending him spiraling ever more rapidly upward. The girl from New Order lagged behind; from beneath him she simply watched now, her hands on her belt and her air jets holding her constant. In a short time she diminished, becoming a featureless, red speck.

The column of rising air terminated beneath a circular structure and spilled slowly to the sides like a graceful fountain. Orfei rode the current as it deposited him on a wide ledge that ran about the circumference of the shaft. There, he stood, looking beneath him. There was no way down, and no turning back. Through thin slats in the dome above him, Orfei saw the blue hues of a distant sky. One of the slats came down to meet the ledge—just wide enough for him to squeeze through.

XXI

*Beyond Novyraj loomed the world of past ages, gifted man
and forsaken, wiped clean by fire and rain so even the
blood was gone. What survived the twilight was, as the
Earth, wounded and known to tragedy, like lost stars tra-
versing a void free of the hand of gravity that both holds
and protects.*

—PRIESTESS KALI,
The Book of Lost Migrations

Soul came again, a gentle wipe behind Orfei's eyes as
the holomage stepped out into the light of the yellow sun.
The ancient stirred in dream as if to hold his rememberer
and guide the future from the past.

A dusty brown landscape spread out in all directions,
broken only by low craggy hills and dark patches of low,
creeping vegetation. Orfei moved forward, and all transformed behind his eyes; Soul's dreaming superimposed—
here, Orfei saw, was the ridge after the viaduct, the crater
at the heart of Moscow flanked by dead buildings and
speared by the cross of the man the ancients called Christ.
The ghostly images wrapped about the contours of the land
as if memories themselves alive, heedless of the weathered
shapes and buried features they overlaid. They slowed his
progress as he stepped gingerly over rubble that wasn't

there, skirted structures now but low, wind-beaten mounds. "Here," he whispered. Beneath here Soul had built Novyraj. . . . The mystery had commenced to demystify itself.

Orfei reached the ridge of the crater and dropped to his knees, brushing away at the ground. There had stood the cross, here the fallen statue. He sought proof—anything, if only a shattered brick, to assure him Soul's dream did not lie. Time, it seemed, had banished all traces of the past. Still, he brushed away the dust, then scratched at harder ground until he hit rock—small pieces in a mound; these he moved, and he found what he looked for, a fragment of something that felt equally like rock, yet its surface retained faint traces of paint, and when he brushed away the dirt he found the curve of a cheek and a depression cut in the shape of a closed eye. He cupped the object in his hands and rose. Soul's dream faded, the fallen city of the past giving way to the desolation of the present. Orfei looked up at the sun and began to wander.

The patches of green smelled rancid, of death. He approached one cautiously to examine the tangled mass of weeds—nothing like the subsurface gardens some sects of Novyraj maintained. These plants were tough and fibrous, leaves mottled but persevering, stalks deformed and knotted, but alive. A few feet in from the edge lay the skeletal remains of some small animal; when Orfei looked closely he noticed tendrils of green wrapped tightly about the creature's bony legs. He picked up a small rock and tossed it into the center of the vegetation; the plants moved then, stalks raking over the ground toward the point of impact. The rustling quickly subsided, the plants seeming to sigh their disappointment upon discovering the inedible nature of the invader.

Orfei moved a short distance away and lay down on the earth; now that he'd reached the surface, he'd also attained a goal, and no purpose beyond the moment had made itself apparent. Soul's touch among the ruins had been gentle, as if the mind-bytes had metamorphosed, retracted their talons, enhancing Orfei's reality instead of dragging him into another. When Soul finally wakened—what then? Would the mind-bytes keep it as distant? Something within him felt different, as if he'd crossed a bridge, as if he'd *pleased* whatever power held sway over his senses and had now been rewarded. He took the fragment of Christ from within his robe and caressed it—everything had changed. In the ruins above Novyraj he'd been handed an answer, his remembering had connected with the present—Soul's life within him had suddenly gained new meaning, not anything he could yet explain, but something that had been *applied*, something that made it real. In the smooth cheek broken away from a statue, old mysteries were answered and new, deeper ones laid bare. He knew beyond doubt he had a purpose, though its details remained elusive.

He gazed at the sky as white tufts of cloud moved slowly from one horizon to the next. This now—the surface in all its desolate splendor—was his home. Over time he felt all tension flow from his body as he joined Soul in sleep.

XXII

". . . WHERE YOU WANT TO GO? TAKE YOU—I KNOW where—"

The rusty voice paused as Orfei opened his eyes. Above him hovered a server droid—the type Soul had known in his day, the same type still used in Novyraj to provide assistance that Goliath could not.

"Take you where you go," it repeated. One of its extensors flapped uselessly against its dirty casing; the other reached down and motioned Orfei to stand.

"Where?" he asked.

"Where you go—take you—I know where."

He rolled to the side and stood while the droid made clacking sounds and spun around on its internal bearings several times. "You malfunction," he told it.

"Take you, lost man. Where you go?" The machine began to move away.

"I don't know where I'm going."

"Take you then. I know where."

"Where?"

"I know where," the droid insisted.

He regarded the strange machine and scratched his head.

His hand brushed against the rough side of his cheek, posing the unanticipated question of how he would shave without Goliath to do it for him. Or how he would bathe or expel biological waste—the true barren nature of the surface became ironically apparent; he'd indeed radically altered his life.

The droid continued to move away, seemingly heedless of whether or not Orfei followed. He knew it might pose danger—how could it know where he wanted to go? It could lead him, perhaps, to a drop shaft and a forced descent back to that which he'd left—it could even assume that was his desire.

Or maybe it *did* know what he wanted. . . . *What are the rules of this surface world?* He needed to learn but hadn't pondered how; as he reflected, his most persuasive thought directed him away from his present location, to increase the distance between himself and access to Novyraj in case Lysis came after him. And then he couldn't expect to stay where he was anyway—there was nothing there. The droid indeed moved away; Orfei decided to follow cautiously, letting his guide stay far ahead.

The sun moved low in the sky, casting shadows to bury the droid in pools of darkness for long minutes at a time. Orfei increased his pace to catch up, listening for the droid's distinctive clacking, striving to keep it in earshot. The machine's tarnished casing reflected little light, even as Orfei's eyes adjusted to the coming of darkness. He would now know night—see firsthand the stars and the Milky Way that had fascinated mankind through the ages; the thought thrilled him, though he wished his guide would slow down. He considered stopping until a shrill cry sounded in the distance and all the tales of the surface he'd heard in his youth came back to haunt him. Nine-eyed, fanged mutants became very real, and though the stars emerged in heavenly brilliance above, he dared not chance a glance skyward and risk losing his way.

The darkness of night consumed all, and Orfei began to run, the sound of his own breathing obscuring all other sounds. When a dim light cut through the shadows ahead he abandoned caution and raced for its sanctuary; rounding a large outcrop of boulders, he found the droid stopped, the light emanating from a lantern in its head that momentarily blinded him. It was then that he paid for his recklessness— from beneath his feet came the crunch of dried roots giving way to his weight; a step later he tripped and fell headlong among the carnivorous weeds.

Time seemed to freeze. The leaves of the plants felt cool against his cheek, and, rather than the smell of death, a more pleasant odor teased his nostrils—an intoxicating scent that sent cold spears of pleasure down his spine. When the vines coiled around him they were the arms of a lover that he embraced, his skin on fire and unable to feel the tiny needles piercing his flesh, the tiny mouths commencing to feast. A music blossomed nearby, a brilliant flute chased by falsetto voice, and everything within and without felt like magic. He opened his eyes and found an empty skull the size of a small child's staring back—even this was beautiful. Overhead the stars danced to the music, a harmony to the melody of his death.

His death, he thought. They were killing him! He struggled to move, but the vines lashed him firmly in place; he tried to scream, but when he opened his mouth a thick stalk squeezed between his teeth and shot for the back of his throat, making him gag and gasp for air. Without warning, the music turned dark and dissonant—he realized it indeed came from beyond, outside his mind. The vines around him began to thrash, even the one that had lodged in his throat. He bit down hard and an acrid taste filled his mouth; he spit out and retched, heaving—when he pushed up with his arms now the vines gave way, falling off, withering—the entire patch was a writhing mass—he pushed forward with his legs and found he could move. After a few hard thrusts he was clear, stretched flat, his heart pounding, his weight bearing down heavily on solid earth.

The music without continued, evolving from dissonance back into melody before giving way to silence, the thrashing of the plants gone still as well. Now Orfei heard voices in a strange tongue—voices of men and women. Hands grabbed and lifted him, and he looked about, the world still

lit by the droid's lantern. Even so, his eyes played tricks—
the faces around him came in and out of focus as the poi-
sons in his blood continued exacting their toll. They were
dark faces—golden skinned with small brown eyes. One
smiled at him, twirling a flute with long, sinuous fingers.
They all smiled. The arms holding him up felt firm, and he
realized he'd been saved from certain death, the flutist's
strange song disrupting whatever instinct controlled the
plants' concerted attack—an appropriate irony that an alien
music had saved his life—he the great, exalted composer
of the world beneath their feet. . . .

"You almost died," said a voice—now he could understand their words. Unable to stand on his own, he felt safe
among these people, whether they were mutants or another
sinister manifestation of man—they were certainly not his
own kind; their eyes were too small, their skin too darkened
by the sun; even those of negroid descent in Novyraj had
long past lost the dark pigmentations of their surface-
dwelling ancestors. No—Orfei had found a new society;
the droid may indeed have led him to where he wished to
go.

At the command of one of his saviors, the air beyond
the droid split like a curtain, as if opening into a new world.
In single file, his companions stepped through; when they'd
helped him reach the portal he stood on the lip of a low
valley lit by lanterns planted like stakes in the ground. The
curtain closed behind him. "We can see out," said one of
his escorts, "but they can't see in." Running along the
ground where the air had split was a series of metal
boxes—reflective cloaking technology from the wars of the
twenty-first century; Orfei knew this immediately without
knowing how—only Soul might have seen such devices
before. Here again he possessed knowledge not his own.

The small band took him downward; first came a pen
filled with large domesticated reptiles that leered wild-eyed
at his passing, then an overhang propped up by pillars—a
deep, man-made cave of some sort. The rows of lanterns
continued on into the structure, and all about were sturdy
little buildings resembling the surface houses of old. They
passed between the pillars—the cave was immense, with

recesses to all sides; Orfei couldn't shake the feeling that he'd been there before.

In the light, his hands glistened a bright red—his own blood. He wondered how quickly he would have died among the vines had he not been saved. Even free of them he felt pieces of himself missing, his eyes for instance—only now did he notice the face of one of those who carried him, the face of an older man, but pale like his own. "Yes," said the man. "I know where you're from. My home once as well."

They came to a room with benches cut into the ground; Orfei was laid on one, and the pale man clapped his hands. From the shadows came others with young faces that swam in Orfei's inconstant vision. Beautiful eyes all around him. . . . They washed his wounds with cool rags while the pale man looked on with concern. "I am Heng," he said, pressing a finger to Orfei's lips. "Don't try to talk—at best you'll only confuse yourself, at worst you'll bite off your tongue. You fell among strechellis, but you should be fine by morning. Best to lie back and let the time pass until then; the plants' secretions attack the brain, so expect anything. We'll stay with you; just remember you've got nothing to fear."

Orfei nodded. *Strechellis*, he thought—with the "r" rolling up from the back of the throat. . . .

Heng grinned and patted his shoulder. "Don't worry," he added, "it's easy to enjoy. These people chop it up and make a brew from time to time—better than anything down under. Be happy you're all in one piece. I had a similar experience once, though they only got my arm." He held up his left hand; half of it was missing. "That's how I got my name—short for Hengdala 'en grell which translates something like 'he who chops his hand to walk away laughing.' That's what I did, or so I'm told. They called me Ka-len below." The man's lips fluttered, but he sounded sincere; Orfei was surprised he could follow the words. The name Ka-len, however, aroused no memories.

"Didn't think you'd know it," Heng continued from a distance. "I was a scholar of engineering, the old kind, and there never were too many of us. What could Novyraj need

of men dreaming of towers and bridges, or even micro-
chips? Goliath provides all—I could do nothing but read
texts and contemplate theories and dream of frontiers man
had already crossed. No sect would have me—not *me* at
any rate—so I left.''

Heng shifted, dividing momentarily into three figures as
if refracting in the diffuse light before settling again like a
pool going quiet after the disrupting fall of a leaf. He took
Orfei's hand as his tale evolved, drawing the young rememberer halfway into his world where he imagined he
could see what Heng had seen and hear the sounds of the
past, a simple feat for Orfei, who already knew a far more
immediate communion. Heng became a waking dream
while Soul slept, and Orfei found within him echoes of his
father as strong as any he'd felt since Agamon's death.

They sheltered, Orfei learned, in a wing of an ancient
building dug out by some unknown people lost to history.
Their hosts called themselves Nuzi; Heng said that meant
''God's tribe''—they'd come up from the south about
when he'd left Novyraj, twenty years before. He'd ascended, not unburdened like Orfei, but with sacks full of
gadgets and electronic toys and diagrams and all the tools
he could carry. He'd found the excavated ruin, then the
Nuzi had found him just in time to save him from starving
to death. They'd taught him to live on what the land offered, how to draw water from the earth and how to stalk
and catch the native rodents in their nests, where a good
hunter could find enough meat to feed ten or more. The
Nuzi had brought the beasts in the pen from the south. They
weren't exactly reptiles, Orfei learned, as they gave milk
and produced a thick, curly coat in the cold seasons that
Nuzi women could weave into useful fabric, but their meat
was the quality Heng most admired; he detailed his first
meal and its heady aromas and flamed steaks; these were
the rewards of the surface—none in Novyraj could know
the taste of real food when all came from Goliath.

Heng in turn had given the Nuzi lost knowledge; together
they'd explored a new home, salvaging treasures mysteriously abandoned by its previous masters, who Heng supposed might themselves have come from the depths to rule

the surface for a time. The building still kept its mysteries; it dated from the old world, but they'd opened chambers remarkably preserved, as if some great cataclysm of the wars had buried it under tons of earth and sealed it in an instant. On discovering this he'd built the cloaking mechanisms to hide the haven from the outside; there were sects below who might brave the surface and plunder all should they know what existed, and Heng didn't feel they deserved it.

Of the world beyond, Heng knew little and yet far more than any in Novyraj could imagine. The Nuzi had migrated freely, but not from any great distance and for no concrete reason. Their legends placed their homelands in the distant southeast, the old nation of India to which they'd never tried to return. The old technologies, however, still lived; over the years Heng had five times seen airborne craft, always in the distance, and always a signal for the Nuzi to hide. He supposed new civilizations thrived, if only in pockets—perhaps not a good thing. If the old technology lived, so might the old ways of destruction, and so might history repeat with conflicts over what scarce resources the still-wounded planet had to give. For this reason he thought those below right after all—they remained safe in a world opulent in contrast. The surface could never sustain them.

On the other hand, the nine-eyed mutants were myth, as were other tales Novyraj told its young. Of the land's real dangers, Orfei had already met the most insidious—the deadly strechellis—and survived.

The grip of the plants eased slowly; by the time Heng ran short of words, Orfei could sit. The disjointed and cracked visual world coalesced into one with a softened sheen, its harder edges smeared by the slightest motion but retaining their shapes—to these eyes Heng indeed looked older and weathered, but never twenty years; he'd have been far younger than Orfei when he'd left or else the surface had treated him kindly.

The Nuzi themselves were a beautiful people, small in frame and all with dark brown eyes and richly golden skin. His attendants were mostly young, but now he noticed elders looking on from the farthest benches, each wearing the same passive smile.

"You are welcome here," Heng said now. "That is, as long as you understand you cannot go back."

A young woman frowned and bent close, dabbing Orfei's forehead with a cloth that came away red with fresh blood. The sudden renewed contact struck him in ways he didn't expect; her hair brushed his cheek like cool fire, and the smell of her skin came warm and strong, without a trace of perfume. Her bare breasts almost touched him, innocently, a movement only of grace with no sexual content. When she'd finished she backed away to examine her work, smiling shyly when their eyes met.

"Ah," Heng commented, "you've noticed Aresh. I've grown tired; perhaps I should leave you in her care?"

Orfei swallowed, unable to find his tongue or even avert his gaze while the young woman returned it. The dreams of Soul bubbled up, their mix with the intoxicants of the plants spreading like mystic wildfire over the plain of his awareness—all focused on Aresh. She offered her hand, and he took it. They walked together back through the avenue of lanterns and under the open sky.

It became a night of no sleep, as if the strechellis drew on reserves of energy inaccessible to an untainted mind. Aresh led him to a small spring away from the lights; the water was warm and luxurious, and it washed from his skin the last traces of the plants' attack. When she spoke to him he shook his head; he couldn't understand a word. Instead of speaking they lay side by side in the pool and gazed at the universe of stars above.

At dawn they took a walk, Orfei gladly following the woman, whose dark beauty grew still more apparent in the light of the sun. The clothes she wore covered little—only her hips and waist, and even the swath of cloth there seemed unnecessary. She wore an ornamented belt that kept a small knife next to her hip, more a piece of jewelry in Orfei's eyes than a tool or a weapon.

As they walked, Aresh pointed out details of the terrain; at every turn there were small insects to be found on the ground, miniature monsters scavenging for what little food the land offered and battling among themselves. And in a place where the land dipped into a gully they found a stream, its banks dotted with flowering plants grazed by small mammals and a few flying insects. Creatures thrived in the water itself, food for an odd species of bird that couldn't fly but only flap small stubby wings in a sad parody of its airborne ancestors. Orfei had long been fascinated by the avian images in Goliath's archives, and he'd studied them carefully in designing the dragon for his light-opera: These strange creatures reminded him not to let the rebirth of surface life lull him into believing all was well. From the old writings he'd learned flightless birds evolved only in environments free of predators, usually islands far from men. But here was ancient Moscow—not an island but a great city in the heart of a continent. Had all the predators of the world gone extinct, deprived of prey, victims of hunger or irradiated carrion? They'd not survived here—hadn't been here for thousands of years if birds had lost the need for wings. And why no flying species in the air? Flight in a world ruled by moving clouds of death and huge, lifeless stretches of land might perhaps be a dangerous thing. During migration, whole species would perish for lack of food—only the strays reaching small patches of livable land would stand a chance of survival.

He sat on the bank and watched; if he stayed still, the birds would approach him. Up close he examined their mats of feathers, in many places grown dense like fur; they'd adapted like the reptiles to withstand the demands of winter. Still, he wondered how they could survive without migration; he watched one disappear into an underground burrow and decided they might hibernate. Life, according to the old writings, was capable of many miraculous things. . . . His attention moved to a feather that fluttered on a stone next to the stream. A ground insect—an ant—took its shaft in its pincers and proceeded to haul it up to a higher stone. Scarcely breathing, Orfei watched. The feather dwarfed the ant by a factor of hundreds; a slight breeze blew and lifted it a few inches in the air, and still the ant held on, anchoring the feather until the wind let it down. The insect moved

again and lost its footing; the feather fell to where it had
started, and the ant again set to hauling it up. What could
a creature that size want with such an object? Only it could
know.

When Orfei's eyes finally strayed he discovered Aresh
gone. Panic gripped him; he wanted to jump up and chase
after her but had no idea of the direction she'd gone. He
stood; the flightless birds began gathering around his feet
and emitting strangled chirps, as if empathetically sensing
his concern, but he could think of little beyond finding
Aresh—they'd come far from her settlement and he had no
confidence he could make his way back by himself.

Long moments passed before her head finally popped
above the crest of a nearby hill. Orfei sighed, but his sense
of relief didn't last long. In her hands were flowers, and
tied around her waist was a swath of bright red cloth; as
Orfei ran to meet her he grew increasingly certain of the
cloth's origin—beyond doubt a cape of the sort worn by
the girl who'd followed him up the lift shaft. Aresh offered
him the flowers while he grabbed at the cape, trying to
communicate his alarm. She didn't seem to understand, and
he struggled to think out the best course of action. The
strechellis *still* muddled his thoughts—should he press
Aresh to show him where she'd found the cape, or lead
them in exactly the opposite direction? If the cycles of the
sun had any bearing on the counting of days below, this
was the day of the festival and the culmination of Lysis's
plans.

Lysis must have persuaded the girl's cult to bring him
back—and the cape abandoned? Perhaps its owner had
found it too stifling in the warmth of the surface.

He decided the best course was return to the safety of
Aresh's people. After several frustrating attempts, he made
his desire known, but not before she made him take the
flowers she'd brought him as gifts.

Heng found the cape as troubling as Orfei. He questioned
Aresh and told Orfei she'd indeed found it abandoned, its
owner nowhere in sight. Neither of them could say they'd

not been seen, though Orfei didn't think they'd been followed.

"She should not have led you so far from the enclave," Heng said. "My mistake; I assumed you'd ride out the drug in her bed."

Orfei shook his head. "That didn't happen."

"So I see." Heng ran his fingers over the fabric. "Only these ones ever surface and return," he said. "It's been years, though. The last time, three of them died."

"How?"

Heng's expression went cold. "Those below cannot learn of this place—these people. We are comfortable here, they are comfortable there, and that's how it must remain. The surface *can't* sustain them; they must continue to fear it, even if such fears are exaggerated or wrong—Novyraj is a cocoon that must not open."

Orfei thought in silence; his host spoke of death—*intentional* and premeditated—the ancient ways come to life all over again. And yet, more horribly, it made sense; in Novyraj conflict bred not blood but new halls, new sects, and soon—perhaps this very moment—new worlds. Novyraj kept men safe from one another, kept their lusts in check—he'd arrived again at the dilemma posed before he'd elected the lift shaft: Wasn't what Lysis and Clystra proposed a *good* thing? Did he dislike it simply because of *Dragon Dance*, because the thought of his creation made real offended him or made him afraid? Because it would make him like a god? Yet divinity of a sort was central to all art—a man in the process of creation was like a god, limited only by his talent and imagination. An artist constructed worlds; Clystra merely offered a way of attaining them in physical terms. Could such technology provide man a final liberation?

Some philosophers thought art man's reflection of nature, his attempt to make sense of it, to recreate it in his own image. Perhaps that offended Orfei, especially now, after knowing the real surface world, seeing it with his own eyes. The stream—the intricate interlocked ecosystem in perfect balance—here was life's creation *in spite of man*. Man could only observe it as he had, savor its delicacy—but if

he touched it, it would break. And even science had never
fully understood nature, so how could an artist attempt to
match it? Orfei, with his supposed greatness, could only
marvel, only sit before it and be amazed; his art, and that
of other men, would forever remain imperfect, flawed reflections of the true genius of life itself.

Heng was right, and so were Lysis and Clystra. Were
the hordes below to surface, even slowly, tragedy would
surely follow. At first they might come in small numbers,
cultivate the land, perhaps improve it. Over time they could
only destroy it—again. Heng spoke of necessary death—
ironic proof of the teleological tragedy at the end of all
roads. In man, nature had birthed its own downfall, its most
horrible agent of change. What amazed him was that mankind had evolved at all; only by his existence could nature's
judgment be questioned. And what the Fourth Council intended below—the creation of new worlds within Novyraj—imperfect, but a way to contain man nevertheless.
Heng called the world beneath them a cocoon, a hopeful
term implying mankind might grow within it. Lysis's plans
might strengthen the shell, harden it, extend the period of
incubation.

"They must have come up while the droid led you
here," Heng said. "Otherwise, we'd have known—the
droid is our eyes on the shafts."

Orfei still thought of death and conflict and war—the
paradoxes of civilization; now they'd entered him like
crafty snakes, crawled out of the dead past to dig into fresh,
still-fertile soil. In accepting Heng's defense of violence,
he'd become part of the problem. He could never rejoin
Lysis and Clystra now—whatever virtues their plans might
have. He'd defiled himself, become even less worthy. Far
too much was at stake. "Why didn't you kill me?" he
finally asked Heng. "You don't even know who I am."

Heng smiled. "You are the son of Agamon. By your
presence we are honored."

He stared back blankly, and Heng laughed. "Novyraj is
not entirely contained, holomage. To the east of here are
deep caverns where droids construct devices on the direction of Goliath. I've been there a few times; it's a strange,

dark world, but from it comes the luxuries used below—
all designed without the need for men, for engineers like
myself. On my first trip I brought back a vidscreen; I've
seen much of what's happened below, including your ascent to the Fourth Council.''

"But—" Orfei protested, confused. "Nothing stopped
you?"

"Goliath lets me take what I want. And he gives what I
ask—he gave me the design for the cloaking devices.''

Orfei tried to meaningfully digest the new information
but it was too much. The strechellis had released him and
fatigue was creeping in to take its place. Heng, meanwhile,
sent Aresh away; she returned shortly, accompanied by a
group of young men armed with long metal rods that could
only be weapons. Heng showed them the red cape, spoke
with them briefly, then dispatched them on a mission Orfei
understood without asking.

"They're after me," he said when the men had left.

"Shouldn't be," Heng countered. "It's coincidence—
nobody's important enough to be followed up.''

"No," he insisted. "They're after *me*. I'm surprised Lysis let as much time pass as she did.''

"Why?"

Orfei looked cautiously at the other man and related his
story—he left out Soul, but not Lysis's plan for *Dragon
Dance*. Before he could finish, Heng led him deeper into
the cavern to another depression where all benches faced a
flat wall—the vidscreen from the depths; he activated the
panel, and when it cleared, Orfei found his own face looking back at him.

Soul stirred, but Orfei pushed him back. In Novyraj, the
festival of Beltene went on, and Lysis had stolen his face.
On the vid, Orfei Agamon spoke to the people. "This is a
new dawn," said the stolen face. "We, the children of Soul,
stand on a new frontier, the greatest since the Great Descent. Witness *Dragon Dance*—" The vid wiped to show
the Hall of Meeting, the largest room in all of Novyraj.
Orfei's light-opera played in its center while other works
danced colorfully in other corners of the hall. People of all
sects filled the empty spaces, a cheering cacophony of voice

and music rising up from the floor. Lysis and Clystra stood on a raised platform at the near end of the hall, smiling down—she'd wanted him beside them but had satisfied herself by stealing his image, no doubt reconstructed by Goliath.

The chair of the Fourth Council raised her hands above her head and clapped them together; Clystra turned his attention to a device set on a pedestal before him—he touched it, and the mountainous terrain of *Dragon Dance* unfolded like a carpet, its ghostly landscape quickly filling the hall, quenching the other light-operas like a wind blowing out candles. Villages sprang up in the distance; the landscape defied the walls of the hall and stretched out to infinity, and the crowd bathed in its light gasped and fell silent. "*Dragon Dance*"—his voice repeated over the scene—"by the power of the great Clystra no longer a dream but reality!"

Light in the hall shifted suddenly, revealing ranks of men, women, and children arrayed behind Lysis, all in the garb of sects fond of humanity's more fantastic legends and tales—worlds of chivalry and magic and legend they pretended to live in their isolated halls. The vid panned their faces, uniformly ecstatic and awed by the scene before them. Next to Clystra a shimmering archway took shape, and Lysis took the hand of the first man behind her and led him to the portal—he stepped through, his body attaining the ghostly transparency of Orfei's work. Amazement rippled through the onlooking crowd as, one by one, the members of the chosen sects passed under the archway into *Dragon Dance*'s ethereal universe. When all were through, Lysis again clapped her hands, Clystra manipulated his device, and the immense hologram faded slowly like a dissipating fog.

Orfei's face reappeared on the screen. He began to speak, but deafening cheers from the floor overwhelmed his voice. Before the cheers died down, Heng jumped suddenly to his feet and killed the vid.

So it was done, Orfei thought. Even without him.

Heng whirled away, running back for the entrance of the cavern. The crowds below still chanted in Orfei's mind; it took him long moments to realize some shouts were more real—nearby. Aresh grabbed his hand, her nails digging into his flesh; something terrible was happening—he tried to follow Heng but Aresh desperately pulled him back. From the distance came screams now. Metal flashed under bursts of light, droids blasting the cavern with destructive beams of power. He stood his ground as figures began to take shape in the distant shadows, some outlined in red. . . . Heng's cavern—and the Nuzi—had been discovered.

Without Aresh, Orfei could not have moved. Fatigue came in waves, smearing reality, images flashing and blending in his mind—first the evolution of *Dragon Dance*, now the swift, brutal assault of the League of New Order against the Nuzi—somehow they must have defeated the cloaking devices—tracked him here. To capture or kill? He couldn't even feel fear; it didn't feel real. Perhaps the strechellis still held him—perhaps he'd never been freed. . . . Perhaps—perhaps he'd never even braved the lift shaft—he might still be in his room below, all experience since only imagined, tricks of the mind-bytes, or tricks of his own mind. How much could one man take? The link to Soul alone could push a mind past its limits—insanity made more sense than the life he'd led since. If he could withstand Soul, he could withstand more vivid hallucinations. Aresh, however, tugged frantically on his arm; without conscious effort or consent, his feet began to follow her.

They went deeper into darkness; Aresh eventually produced a light-stick, a torch that cut little more than twenty feet into the shadows. She stopped at a blank wall, handed him the torch, and ran her fingers over the rock. He looked back nervously; after all that had happened, anything could lurk in the darkness beyond the torch's reach. She mumbled in soft tones; as he turned to her, the wall gave way, a panel easing inward, then popping. The chamber beyond sucked in air in a raging gulp.

Something hit him in the chest—Aresh, diving at him, pressing and holding him against the wall as the moving air quickened, a brief but furious gale feeding a vacuous hunger beyond. He felt alone in his fear until Aresh lifted

her eyes; though they couldn't speak, he knew her thoughts:
This was an escape never taken, a desperate measure to be
used but once. Her people, behind them, were dying, and
they stood on the brink of the unknown.

The wind died as quickly as it had risen, but dust filled
the new chamber in a choking cloud. Aresh tore at Orfei's
robe with her knife, cutting two swaths of cloth, placing
one over her nose and mouth. Before he could do the same,
a beam of light shot out of the shadows and struck Aresh's
side, setting it on blue fire; she howled painfully and fell
limply to the floor.

Obeying some instinct, Orfei dived away and then
wished he hadn't. The light-stick rolled in the opposite direction, away from Aresh, each revolution illuminating
nothing but blank wall and empty air. Aresh's form and the
opening in the wall quickly disappeared as the darkness
consumed all. Then a voice cut through the silence—"I
know you're there, holomage," it said. "Your adventure is
finished." He recognized it—the girl from the lift shaft,
from the League of New Order.

Through the light went a flash of red motion, then the
light-stick rose in the air and he saw her feral eyes. She
waved some ancient weapon in the other hand. "Up," she
commanded, pointing the weapon his way. He rose unsteadily. As he stepped forward there was another flash, and
the woman stumbled, then dropped her weapon to the floor.

When Orfei reached her she fell into his arms, already
lifeless and unforgiving. He laid her down gently. The hilt
of Aresh's small knife grew unnaturally from the side of
her neck. He pried the torch from her fingers and shone it
on her face, a frozen mask of astonishment—the same un-
believing eyes she'd offered him in the lift shaft, when he'd
told her where he was going. Blood was everywhere, on
his hands and arms, his robe—especially the Nuzi knife.
Death had truly come again to the surface, and he at the
heart of it. As he eased the knife's blade free he fought
back tears—for the girl and for mankind; after so many
thousands of years, they'd still not learned.

He found Aresh by crawling. Her eyes were closed now;
the act of killing the other girl had taken the last of her

strength. He put his ear to her breast and found she still breathed. The torch revealed a horrible, oozing wound at her waist—he couldn't just leave her here. With great effort he stood, lifting her in his arms. Once up, she felt amazingly light. Jamming the light-stick between his teeth, he shifted her weight. The dust in the new chamber had mostly settled now; he stepped in, struggled to close the portal behind him, and moved off into this new, unknown darkness.

Soul again was his guide. Through twists and turns, he felt the ancient with him—he remembered. These had been shops where merchants had plied their trades, the architecture borrowed from the great malls of Los Angeles or Boston—any great American city where too many people shared too little space, only now dust ruled. Where fine dresses had once lined walls and aisles in neat racks, tattered cobwebs rained down in silvery curtains, fluttering like ghostly, waving hands at his passage; their predecessors had become mere mounds of thread among the debris beneath them. Anything organic had long since decayed, but where the churning air from without had cleared the dusty carpet, colorful floor tiles retained some small fraction of their former bright glory, and glass, metal, and plastics stood resolutely preserved like serene gods of the surreal, time-weathered halls: In one shop the stacked metal cases of electronic appliances rose up like totemic idols from the wavy drifts of decay; in another naked mannequins struck poses, engaged in a private, static dance of a duration their designers could never have dreamed. And Orfei found less reassuring artifacts as well—brittle human skeletons looked on in small groups that neatly lined the old walls, as if they'd sat down together to rest, perhaps while some force stole the very air from their lungs. The sight returned Orfei's eyes to his burden, Aresh's limp weight. Her wet blood seeped through his robe to collect on his chest, at once both viscous and oily as the flow coagulated slowly. She needed his attention; he had to stop her bleeding, but this was no place to rest. Then, beyond the soft glow of the light-stick, another light emerged. As

he neared it the omnipresent dust thinned and the soft sound
of moving water broke the dark silence. Rounding a bend,
Orfei carried Aresh into a world of light, a small corner of
the mall kept miraculously alive and into which Orfei entered as if in dream—in fact, he could assimilate it in no
other way; the floor, though scarred and broken in places,
was clean, its center boasting a small fountain that bubbled
with fresh water. Light came from strips in the ceiling
above, and several shops along one wall seemed similarly
alive. While he looked on, a maintenance droid glided silently into the open on hoverjets, crossing over the floor in
a deliberate pattern before disappearing into a housing in
the opposite wall. Cautiously, Orfei approached the fountain.

Though the water must have flowed freely for thousands
of years, it looked clean except for a few oxidized coins
sprouting like strange plants from the bottom of the pool.
Orfei laid Aresh on the cool floor and examined her wound
gently; the blast had seared her right side from her hip to
just beneath her armpit, leaving a raw mass of blisters
around a red, bleeding center at the point of impact. With
cupped hands he dipped water from the pool and released
it over the blisters; he thought a pained moan passed from
the girl's lips, but she didn't waken. It struck him to treat
the wound with cobwebs, though the source of the idea was
a mystery; still, he obeyed it, leaving her momentarily to
return with a mass of the ghostly fibers draped over his
arm. Aresh's wound absorbed the substance greedily, and
the delicate bandage all but stemmed the flow of blood.
When he was done he tore a long strip of cloth from the
bottom of his robe and washed it clean of dirt and dust in
the pool. He cleaned Aresh's face and body—carefully so
as not to disturb his earlier work—then stripped and
cleaned himself. He washed out the cloth again before
wrapping it around Aresh's waist—that was the last thing
he could think of doing for her. She rested easily now, her
expression peaceful. He hoped desperately that she
wouldn't die. The furious turn of events had intertwined
their lives, and she seemed his only connection to anything
even remotely real or meaningful.

On this Orfei thought as he sat next to her. Though the presence of Soul within him had calmed upon gaining the surface, its capacity to well up into his consciousness had not disappeared, only grown more subtle. And still it answered no questions; it simply descended like a mist into his mind to give him knowledge of things he couldn't himself know, show him worlds real only in another's memory and fully fantastic in his own. Especially this place—it couldn't be real, could it? Certainly nothing could survive so long, so well. Yet here he was, half in dream, at a crossroads in time somewhere between then and now. Were Aresh not with him he'd think his mind completely lost.

With events finally at rest, Orfei felt hunger. He devoured two of the food-cakes he'd brought from below, washing them down with water from the pool. He knelt next to Aresh and dripped the water on her lips as well; they parted, and the water dribbled inside. She sputtered and swallowed, and her eyelids moved, if only slightly. Encouraged, he lifted her head and gave her more to drink from his cupped hand. When her thirst seemed sated, he laid down her head and looked at her; even weak and wounded, she was beautiful, perhaps even more than he'd acknowledged before. Her eyes opened unexpectedly, and relief washed through him. It occurred to him he might be falling in love. "You're alive," he said. It seemed a silly thing to say, once it was out, especially as she couldn't understand him.

She smiled and whispered something. That was all they said; her eyes closed again, and he was on his own.

As time passed, he thought to the future, wondering what would come. Aresh had found the door they'd used to enter this place; moreover she'd actually led him directly to it. Certainly she wouldn't have been alone among her people in such knowledge, so others would eventually follow. If they hadn't all been killed. . . . The unsettling idea came like a terrible weight, and the thought of Heng's death especially disturbed him. If it had happened, it was Orfei's fault—all the death was his burden to bear. And he began to wonder if his safety now was an illusion—if those sent after him *had* defeated Heng, they would eventually discover the dead girl's body and signs of the struggle, including Aresh's blood perilously near the door. And if they found the door, they'd have no problem following the trail of his footsteps through the dust—that was a very chilling thought, and he had to do something. After a moment of hesitation he stood and took up the light-stick, then struck out once again into the darkness from which he'd come, doing his best to obscure the signs of his passage, only to decide in the end these efforts were of little use.

Returning to Aresh, Orfei looked around. He needed to explore the area further; perhaps he could find another way out. In the wall where the maintenance droid came and went was a large metal flap; he tried to open it manually but failed. If that was a possible means of escape, he would have to wait.

At the very least he needed to get Aresh out of sight. Lifting her gingerly, he carried her into one of the cleaned shops, one filled with small, brittle silver disks and metallic cubes—a vendor, he knew through Soul, of ancient recorded music and vid.

It was here, in the ghostly bosom of the distant past, with the life of Soul settled deep within him and the life of the wounded Nuzi girl held close to his breast, that Orfei's adventure took its ultimate, pivotal twist.

What happened has no plausible explanation in a world confined by the laws of chance, for not only was the probability alone infinitesimally small, but Orfei's experience of Soul, independent of this event, would have had little meaning. The entity he knew as Goliath must therefore have engineered it, and when all that is now known is ultimately understood, the only lingering mystery is how *it was done. In retrospect it is plain that Orfei's abandoning Novyraj was meant solely to lead him here, to this precise moment with Aresh in his arms and love in his heart. Here, the most impossible, yet crucial moment of this history:*

As Orfei moved to the back of the shop, a sudden flash filled the room, and something clattered behind him. He turned to lock eyes with a tall, thin woman bathed in a misty glow. The surprise on her face was as deep as his, but while Orfei froze, disoriented, she was moving, frantically manipulating a device worn on her wrist. As she did so, the reality of the room unraveled, peeling away into a featureless void that suddenly collapsed inward, knocking all breath from his lungs and plunging his mind into darkness. His last thought was for Aresh, whom he still held tightly in his arms.

XXIII

ACROSS MEMORY, DREAMS CONVERGED. THE UNIVERSE shrunk to a cage of gray metal and transparent walls and large, bearded men looking on with dull eyes. The body flowed like liquid in the confining space, the mind left to contemplate the inconstancy of time and the hearts of stars. A journey was in the making; this could be seen through a gap in the gray where the stars drifted slowly by. Around the body, the brothers and sisters coalesced, all with questions. In the heart of them, the answer always was Wait, and so they did. Together, they divided time on parallel tracks, leaving their shells to amuse the large men. From the second track they watched and waited, obeying the heart.

"Hello," Holly said gently as Derek opened his eyes. Her face was a welcome comfort, all the more as a host of strange dreams drifted back from the moment—not only the dreams but the memory of the viaduct and Berlin. Without thinking he reached up to touch her cheek, her skin like fine silk against his fingers. She tilted her head, pinning his hand against her shoulder. Only then did he wonder what he was doing. "How long?" he managed to ask.

"Almost a full day," Holly said. "I got a good deal of sleep myself. Feel better?"

He withdrew his hand slowly. "A bit. I think I could use something to eat." In fact, his stomach was churning.

Her smile broadened. "I've taken care of that." She reached behind him and pulled his bed up to an angle. For a moment their bodies came together; it seemed to him she pulled away reluctantly. "I'll be just a moment," she said, getting up to leave.

For the first time now Derek could see his room, a surprisingly pleasant place, especially in contrast to the memory of his previous visit. The furnishings were simple but quaint, wooden in appearance—high-quality imitations at any rate. His bed was wide and soft, and where before he and Linda had settled for standard issue bedding, what covered him now was a thick quilt, brightly patterned in yellows and greens. He had a large wardrobe, a dressing table with a high, arched mirror, another table with a couple of chairs, and a desk, all bathed in a soft golden glow from two large, torch-style lamps. But what impressed him most was an active holo beside the bed, a very convincing rustic scene with trees and colorful birds and rolling hills in the distance. Everything moved; the birds flew, cotton white clouds rolled majestically along the horizon, and even the limbs of the trees swayed as if caressed by a gentle breeze. The holo was framed like a window with a wooden crossbar across the center and all the hardware normally involved in the real thing. He reached out with the thought to open it, then paused as he grew fearful of spoiling the illusion.

"Go ahead," Holly said as she returned, carrying a tray. "It works."

He glanced at her uncertainly before taking hold of the handle at the bottom of the frame and lifting up. The window came open easily, and the soft sounds of rustling leaves and chirping birds entered the room. A blower on the other side circulated cool air through the opening to complete the effect.

"It's not exactly symmetrical," Holly said, taking a seat

on the edge of his bed. "We've got quite a spectacular waterfall on my side. You'll have to come visit sometime, and we can always switch if we get bored. May even be able to dial up new scenes," she added after a moment of reflection. "I haven't thought to check on the programming."

"This is quite nice," Derek said a bit distantly. Too nice, he thought—the sort of thing that might have saved his marriage to Linda if they'd had it then. Apparently, somebody in Philadelphia had taken the trouble to address the human needs of those involved in the project since his previous visit. The rich aromas of coffee and food reached him now; Holly placed the tray so that it straddled his waist. There were eggs and hotcakes smothered in strawberries and syrup as well as portions of bacon and sausage and glasses of milk and fruit juices. Not to mention the coffee—the sort of spread only the very rich could normally afford stateside.

Holly laughed; he realized his chin had dropped in awe. "Go ahead," she said. "It's all real, believe it or not. They've put in hydroponic gardens and even a small farm. All underground—must've cost a mint."

Gingerly, he took up a fork and sliced into the hotcakes. He refused to believe his eyes until he'd tasted the first bite; after that he had no choice—eyes could be deceived, but taste buds could not. As he ate, Holly touched him lightly on the arm. "Is it really okay?" she asked.

The vulnerability in her voice caught him off guard. "Of course!" he said. "Probably the best breakfast I've ever had."

An unfettered smile spread across her face then. "I was afraid I might have botched something," she said happily. "I mean, everything came out looking okay, but you never know—"

"You're telling me you cooked this yourself?"

"Yes," she beamed. "Well, I mean I definitely had help from the kitchen systems," she added quickly.

Derek smiled, but he couldn't put down the sadness welling up within him. He felt cheated; this should have been his past with Linda—it would have been perfect then, but

with Holly now it felt strange and unreal, like an uncon-
summated honeymoon. She seemed to sense his mood because she asked again if everything was okay. "It's
nothing," he answered. "I'm just thinking." Thankfully,
she didn't press him, and after a moment, on the pretense
of bringing fresh coffee, she left him alone to finish eating.

After he'd cleaned his plate he got up to explore, finding
a large room behind the door Holly used and a small toilet
and bath behind another. He showered and shaved and had
time to dress before she knocked and brought in the coffee,
one for him, and one for herself. They sat at the small table
and drank in silence for several minutes before she reached
out and touched his hand. "I'm sorry if I made you un-
comfortable, Derek," she said. "It's just that I'm afraid,
and I don't want things the way we left them in Berlin.
We've got to *communicate*, help each other. We're a team,
whether you like it or not."

"I never said I didn't like it."

She frowned. "You're a stubborn man, Derek. Please
don't play games with me. I've got things to tell you, but
I'm not even going to start unless you promise you'll drop
your conspiracy theories, at least any that treat me as part
of the plot. First off, I did *not* invent that CIS memo. I
know it's weird, impossibly so, but I've a bad feeling things
are going to get weirder. You've got to trust me, because
I've got to trust you. Right now you're the only person I'm
sure I want to trust."

"Why?"

"That's cheating," she said. "I asked for a promise."

Derek ran his finger thoughtfully around the rim of his
cup. "How can I make that kind of promise, Holly?" he
asked at last. "I hardly know you, and I sure as hell don't
have a clue yet what's going on around here. I've got disappearing people, evidence—if I'm to believe it—that
someone or something wants or wanted me dead, a bizarre
vidholo that makes absolutely no sense, and I never asked
for any of it. I'm supposed to be solving a mystery, but
every time I turn around I find a new one, all spoon-fed
me by you, I might add."

"Look," she said, moving her chair around the table so

their knees touched. "I'm in this as much as you are, and if I've handed you mysteries, it's because I've tried to help. Maybe they're connected, maybe they're not, but we're in this together, and not once since we've met have I tried to deceive you about anything."

"Shit!" he spit distastefully; it was getting difficult to disbelieve her. "Why me, Holly? I'm not a goddamn detective, and I never have been."

"Another mystery. Add to it why I got orders to come with you."

"Okay," he said, looking at her wearily. "I'll trust you, at least until that breakfast wears off." He tried to smile. "Tell me what you've got."

"Not yet," she said, taking his hand between hers. "I want you to understand how much you can trust me." She pressed his hand to her breast and slid it under her blouse. Her flesh was warm and soft, and the action caught him by surprise; he found his fingers responding, moving over her skin without conscious effort, his little finger brushing against her nipple, which hardened suddenly at the contact.

He started to tell her no, but then she didn't do any more, just held his hand there where he could feel her heartbeat and her warmth. They sat that way for a long time before she finally stood and led him into the next room.

The lounge had a local terminal Holly had been using; she had Derek connect Juliet piggyback and set up a four-by-four projection display in the air so they could work comfortably. To begin, she brought up a detailed three-dimensional rendering of the entire complex, an intricate maze of tunnels in seven uneven layers with crisscrossing ramps, a visual image that evoked something between a multitiered cake and an ant farm—though he'd been dispatched on a highly urgent mission, this was Derek's first complete view of Moscow's anatomy; bureaucratic paranoia tended to keep all but the grossest details of the place under tight guard from anyone who didn't have a need to know. Holly used a joystick to move a circle of light near one end of the second level. "We're just about here," she said. "As you know, the Sovs went to great effort to shut these corridors down. Most of the current excavation work is on the two levels below; apparently we've already picked the upper levels clean. The systems report a population of about sixteen thousand, and the department's still bringing in new personnel through the viaduct at the rate of fifteen to twenty a day.''

"But fifty are missing."

"Fifty-three."

"Still no witnesses?"

"None." She manipulated the display, and the white dot multiplied into a clustered pattern. "This is the 'last seen' distribution. The earlier locations tend to be concentrated on the exploratory frontiers on the fourth level, but lately it doesn't seem to matter. A good number of people seem to have disappeared from their quarters."

Derek studied the display; Holly hadn't needed to mention that a couple of the dots were disturbingly close to their present location. From that perspective the mystery grew even more baffling—no witnesses, no signs of violence, and now no definable spatial limits. And he was supposed to get to the bottom of it?

"Dr. Soul?" Juliet asked unexpectedly.

"Yes."

"I have a code one transmission coming in from Philadelphia HQ. You do not have authority to deny vidconnect."

Before he could ask why he'd want to, Juliet's static display shimmered a moment, then metamorphosed into a life-size hologram of Secretary Collier behind his desk. "Derek!" Collier said jovially. "I see you made it in one piece after all! You were beginning to worry me."

To his surprise, Derek found the hologram of the secretary a welcome sight, almost substantial enough to transport him, mentally, at any rate, back to the safety of home. He couldn't help but smile broadly. "And well you should have," he said. "I see you haven't moved."

"At my age," Collier came back, "that can be dangerous. After your antics in Berlin, the systems here didn't trust your handling this alone, so I decided to send Holly along with you. Everything working out okay?"

"We're only just getting started, sir."

"Well I'm sure you'll manage. Listen," he said, growing serious, "I'm going to level with you, and I want to be sure you understand. My sources in Berlin informed me of some friction between you two, and I want you to quit pansy-assing around and get to work. The departmental psych systems just recommended I call you back, Derek; they figure your behavior suggests some undue bias in this assignment, that you're still carrying a torch for Linda. If that's true, son, you'd better forget it; your ex-wife's a suspect in this case as much as anyone else, so keep your distance. That's one of the main reasons I gave you Holly."

"What do you mean?"

Collier smiled. "You figure it out."

Derek looked askance at his partner; if the old man was playing matchmaker, he had to admit he'd done a reasonable job of it. "Think of it this way, Soul," Collier continued. "The faster you sort this mess out, the fewer people we lose. Keep it close; don't trust anyone who's been there a while. You've got Dr. Linn, plus two dozen fresh, topnotch marines at your disposal—"

"Excuse me? Marines?"

"Dammit, boy! You *must* be nearsighted!"

"They're right outside," Holly interrupted. "We haven't gotten that far, sir," she said to the secretary. "Derek's only just woke up."

"Well, okay," Collier conceded, though his irritation was evident. "You have full access to anything you need, including full authority to shut that place down if you have to. Don't blow it! And if you need help, you'd better damn well call me—Juliet can reach me anytime, here, home, wherever. This channel's as secure as any on this planet."

"Thank you, sir," Derek said. "That's a comfort to know."

Collier laughed. "I'm sure it is, boy! I'm sure it is. That's it, kids—now get to work." The hologram abruptly dissolved.

"Well that answers one question," Holly said while Juliet reconstructed the cross section of tunnels.

"What's that?"

"Why I got orders to follow you—see, Derek? These mysteries can be solved!" She was smiling, and before Derek could say more she second-guessed him. "No conspiracy theories," she said. "You promised, remember? Anyway, the boss is right—you can't let past feelings for her get in the way of this. Since that one conversation, she's refused all my calls, and I must have tried twenty times by now. However you want to look at it, that is *not right*!"

"But I told you! She met me at the viaduct."

"Well," she said, sounding burdened. "We'll get back to that in a minute, okay?" She got up and went to a nearby table—obviously where she'd been working as it was cluttered with documents and other items in disarray. When she sat back down next to Derek she had a holographic clipboard. "I compiled this earlier," she said, punching a button to page through the board's chapters; each began with a set of official RD mug shots—faces of all types: male, female, young, old, black, white, yellow . . . no hint of any obvious, unifying thread. "Everything we know about the disappeared," she said. "I made two copies—this one's yours, so you can study it whenever you like." She handed it to him; the display showed a brunette woman in her early thirties named Sheila Lorenz, a hygiene specialist who'd been missing only a few days, last seen coming off duty from the fourth level command post. "Juliet?"

"Yes, Dr. Linn."

"Would you have Lieutenant Morris come in here for a moment?"

"Contact successful, Doctor," the computer replied. The main doors to the lounge opened promptly, and a young officer stepped smartly into the room and snapped to attention. "At ease," Holly said, but the marine didn't seem to relax much. "I mean really at ease, Lieutenant. Come over here and take a look at the display on Dr. Soul's clipboard."

Morris obeyed, moving behind Derek and looking over his shoulder.

"You've seen this woman before?" Holly asked.

"Yes, ma'am. Like I told you earlier."

"When and where?"

"Just outside, ma'am—when Dr. Soul arrived. She's the one who brought him here."

Holly put her hand firmly over Derek's. "That's all for now," she told the other man; the marine quickly left the room. "They're good boys," she said to Derek, trying to sound reassuring. "I'm not usually much on the heavy artillery, but I'm kinda glad we have them around for this."

He nodded, unable to react yet to the new mystery staring him in the face. "Is she the one you saw?" he eventually managed to ask. "That time I woke up—didn't you tell me you saw someone?"

"Yes—I mean, I thought she looked familiar, but I didn't even think to ask them about it until about an hour before you woke up. Several of his men gave the same answer, all quite confidently."

"Then she and these others may be alive?"

"Unfortunately I don't think we can jump to that conclusion," Holly said. "The best we can safely do is adjust the time of her disappearance ahead a few hours. The strangest thing is why she'd meet you—nothing to do with her job as I understand it, and something else to ask Linda about whenever she grants us the courtesy of an audience. What did she talk to you about, Derek?"

"I told you," he answered wearily. "I talked to Linda—nothing ambiguous about it—she looked, talked, and acted like Linda. If it wasn't her, then we can't trust anything about my memory; it must have been the viaduct drug still working."

Holly stood up. "You're right," she said. "I guess we'd better get out and start asking some questions."

The marines sent them by Philadelphia were housed in a spacious complex of rooms between the lounge and the arterial tunnel beyond. They seemed an efficient and eager group, and Derek was glad for their support in the face of unknown peril. Still, as he thought ahead he feared they'd become an irritant—a gauntlet he and Holly would have to run whenever they wished to go out or come in. Then again they'd be able to keep out just about anything trying to enter uninvited; he promised himself he'd try to keep a positive outlook, at least for the time being. He wasn't used to this sort of treatment, or authority for that matter.

Lieutenant Morris wanted to go with them, but Derek rejected the suggestion and felt a bit better about things when the officer graciously took it in stride. He had little doubt Secretary Collier had given the marines tailored instructions with respect to how far he could go—for instance, he didn't think he could order them away—but that could well be the extent of it. If things weren't so serious, he'd be tempted to try; he'd never felt very comfortable in the presence of uniforms, even though he now wore one himself. He wouldn't have bothered with that, but Holly had convinced him it was best until they had more of a handle on what they were doing. As they prepared to leave, he found himself happy to have her in spite of his earlier ambivalence; she'd done good work while he'd been incapacitated, and he had to concede she was doing her best to approach rationally what might lie ahead. She had, in fact, propelled the investigation forward entirely on her own. Without her—especially after Berlin and the viaduct—he might very well have done absolutely nothing beyond brood in his quarters until Collier ordered the jarheads in to carry him out in a straitjacket. Now that was an odd term—*jarhead*; he remembered hearing it from his father. It struck him as strange that a man with such undiluted patriotism would use what was certainly a derogatory term in reference to the military's most elite branch—it could only be an odd sort of bigotry from the days his father spent in the regular army as a young man. Even the righteous, he reflected, showed their flaws.

The marines equipped them with secure comm devices and tried to give them blasters; Derek refused the latter on the same grounds as the presence of the marines themselves—until he had evidence otherwise, the mysteries they faced seemed subtle ones, certainly not the type he could solve by brute firepower. For now he only had questions to ask; if he needed intimidation to accomplish the task, his uniform and rank ought to manage.

They took a t-bug, Holly at the wheel and Derek in the

passenger's seat. At first he tried to study the clipboard, but the data was too much to handle on a relatively short journey; he satisfied himself by paging through the chapters, attempting, if nothing else, to memorize each face.

XXIV

WITHIN ORFEI, SOUL DRIFTED BACK INTO DARKNESS. IN
the background, the images played on, the winding tunnels
beneath Moscow rushing past, Holly Linn's hair whipping
about in the artificial breeze, the faces of lost men and
women passing by in endless succession. As Orfei pulled
away the images slowed, as if they had no life without his
attention; again, the mind-bytes had altered their grip; fascinated by the effect, he pushed his self-awareness down
and rejoined Soul, then he again pulled away and again the
images held. For now, at least, they would wait for him.

Awaking slowly and distracted by the past, he at first
failed to connect with his own present, imagining that the
ground on which he rested was the barren earth of Moscow
over Novyraj from which he'd just emerged. What memory
he had of events past that—the droid, the strechellis, Heng,
Aresh, and the ancient mall—all seemed less real than Soul
in the tunnels. Besides, he could feel the warmth of the sun
on his face; with Aresh in the dusty, mysterious caverns,
he'd been far from the sun. But he had to concede there
was a certain weight on his chest—not enough, however,
to be the girl. As he came nearer to full awareness with

these thoughts he felt a deep sadness in his heart: If Aresh
had been a dream, then his unanticipated feelings for her
were equally unreal. All his life, as he'd never fallen in
love, he'd only been able to imagine it; was he now cursed
to dream it as well?

Unexpectedly, the weight on him shifted, and something
slid across his stomach. From above came a chiming sound
accompanied by the thumping of slowly beating wings.
When he opened his eyes, the sunlight streamed down in
blinding waves, then shattered above his midsection in
spectacular cascades of color. He shaded his eyes with a
hand; a great prism seemed perched on his chest, but it had
shape, and it moved. All the colors of the rainbow danced
along its edges, too dazzling for him to assimilate into a
meaningful form. For the moment, he concentrated on two
circular purple orbs in the center of the mass of color—
eyes, he guessed; at least they so appeared.

"You're not Manilow," said a voice from the heart of
the rainbow.

"Of course he isn't, you idiot eagle," came a woman's
voice from farther away. "Now I'm stuck with this useless
primitive and a fritzed-out temporal transporter and I don't
know what I'm going to do!"

Orfei's eyes began to adjust; the thing on his chest coalesced and took on definite form, but it wasn't an eagle.
In fact, it looked identical to the holographic star of *Dragon
Dance*, shrunk to the size of a small child. "You'll get
another transporter," the dragon protested. "The proxy of
Lord He-who-knows just promised you, only moments
ago."

"So what am I supposed to do?" returned the woman.
"Just wait?" Orfei craned his neck in search of the source
of the voice—she sat behind him, cross-legged in the grass.
Only then did he remember his last moments with Aresh,
the sudden flash and the tall woman appearing without
warning in the dusty world—this was she.

"That would appear to be the most rational course," the
dragon said.

"Well I don't wait well!" the woman snapped back. The
movements of her lips didn't at all match the words Orfei

heard. . . . "*Especially* if it means I have to wait for my transporter while he dissects that other primitive!"

"He won't do that," the dragon countered calmly. "He's a scientist. He'll repair her first."

"Wait a minute!" Orfei protested, pushing the dragon away, his hands first disappearing into the rainbow before contacting physical form. He gained his feet, almost lost his balance, and turned on the woman. "What other primitive?"

She backed fearfully away across the grass. "He speaks!" The consistent desynchronization of her lips and her words remained unsettling. Orfei rubbed at his eyes to correct the problem; the part of him that was Soul felt as though he watched a poorly dubbed vid.

"Did you think he wouldn't?" asked the dragon, flapping his wings to gain a hovering height of about four feet. "All but the very earliest primitives had advanced language capable of abstract thought and future projection—how else could they build societies, sciences, philosophies?"

"But I can understand him! He speaks the high tongue!"

"No he doesn't," the dragon corrected her. "I'm translating for both of you. That's why I am here; aural panlinguistic conversion is but one of my many talents."

"Oh," she said, then she looked at Orfei. "Are you going to kill me?"

"He has no weapon," the dragon chided her.

"How do I know he's not a ninja?"

"A what?" Orfei injected into the confusion. Was he to understand that the animated dragon was translating their words in midair, as they spoke them?

"He's not," the dragon said. "Besides, he's *your* prisoner."

"Wait!" Orfei shouted; he took a deep breath and stepped back from both of them. "I want to know what you're talking about! What did you say about another primitive?" He was sure they spoke of Aresh—dissection?

"A female primitive," the dragon offered helpfully. "Lady Cassandra just traded her to Lord He-who-knows for a new temporal transporter."

"That I won't get in time anyway," the woman added.

"How am I going to host a festival-by-the-gate with no new music!" She waved her arms frantically—all around them on the grass were fragments of the ancient store's decayed stock. "This junk is useless. I missed by *thousands* of years!"

Orfei took another step back and closed his eyes, determined to will the crazy situation away. If, as he'd reflected while waking, Aresh was a dream, then so was this. He tried to suppress his self-awareness, but the attempt succeeded only marginally. Deep within him, Soul cruised along through the Moscow corridors; Orfei nearly reached him, but the outward distractions pulled him back. The dragon hovered close to him; he could feel the beating of the crystal wings. "What's he doing?" the woman asked in the distance. "Maybe he's meditating," came the dragon's puzzled answer. "Be careful," said the woman, "he might explode—matter from the past can be peculiarly unstable—"

"That's it!" Orfei pronounced sternly. "Get out of my mind!"

"I'm afraid you're ontologically confused," said the dragon. "Your eyes reveal external entities, not mental processes which you might attempt to disrupt. This is one of the fundamental existential problems confronting all sentient life, and arguably the root cause of most human endeavors."

The woman—Lady Cassandra—clapped hysterically. "Our eagle has marvelous moments of insight!" she exclaimed to Orfei. "Don't you agree?"

With shaded eyes, he studied her; she remained on the ground, her limbs splayed out like an ungainly spider's. Her hair was a deep red and her torso nearly shapeless—if she had breasts, they were no larger than a young girl's. He noted a blackened band of metal around her wrist—the "fritzed-out temporal transporter"? She smiled at him now, awaiting his response to the latest twist in the convoluted conversation. What the *hell*—as Soul might have put it—had happened?

"Well?" Cassandra insisted.

"That's not an eagle," he said, indicating the dragon.

"What?" the creature shrieked. "I am an eagle by the very definition of the word—my name is Keriktik—translated for you that means Eagle-of-the-clearest-ideal!"

"You've upset him now," Cassandra said. "That wasn't very kind, even for a primitive."

"An eagle is a bird," he tried to point out. "It must have feathers and a—"

"But I have feathers!" the dragon said, positioning himself directly before Orfei's eyes. "See?"

The creature indeed had feathered wings—Orfei wanted to answer that he had feathers because *he'd* put them there; he had to be dreaming this—he was arguing with an externalization of his own creation, his own art. "I see them," he said, "but you're not an eagle. You're a dragon."

"That's preposterous," the dragon harrumphed. "Dragons are evil creatures from the legends, fictions invented by primitive men to allay fears of reptilian domination—manifestations of mammalian racial memory!"

"You're sure?"

"Of course I am! It's *known*!"

"Well I've seen renditions of dragons—re-creations—and you look exactly like one in particular."

"I've got you there," the dragon said with satisfaction. "Being an uneducated primitive, you wouldn't know that I *am* a rendition of an eagle. Lord He-who-knows gave me my freedom. Before that I was only a hologram."

"It's true," the woman chimed in. "This is a very famous eagle and you should be ashamed not to recognize him. *Everybody* in all the gateworlds knows the famous allegorical work *The Eagle Unleashed!* You've really never seen it?"

"No," Orfei answered impatiently; the frantic gymnastics of her lips was beginning to hurt his eyes.

"Well I'll show it to you then." The dragon harrumphed, lighting on the ground and extending one wing to its full length. A beam shot out from the wing tip, projecting a holofield over the grass. Orfei watched in alarm as the piece began; it *was*, beyond question, *Dragon Dance*.

"Go forward to the battle over the village," Lady Cassandra said, "that's the crucial part." The dragon obeyed her, jumping the light-opera ahead to its climax, where an army of men engage the dragon in a terrible battle and finally manage to kill it. "The eagle," Lady Cassandra said loudly over the music, "represents all that is free; it's a perfect creation, far better than any man. In its rightful role, men respect and worship it—that is, men worship freedom, but here we see the past, when men were ignorant. Here we see men denying the symbol of freedom, fearing it because it is better than themselves, and destroying what they do not understand. See how noble the great eagle seems as he dies? In its eyes we see reflected the folly of human ignorance." She smiled at Orfei. "It's a beautiful allegory, yes?"

Somewhat stunned, he attempted to follow her logic. He couldn't imagine a more misinformed interpretation of his work. It was true he'd injected ambiguity into the piece's central conflict, and it was true his dragon possessed noble qualities, but this woman had transposed philosophical significance onto the tale where none was intended. Maybe he had meant to present the dragon's demise as a tragic event—that, in fact, had been one of his points, but all this nonsense over symbolism had never crossed his mind. When he'd begun the work, he'd intended nothing more than a retelling of an old popular legend in which the dragon *had* been fully evil; he'd modified the plot after the tradition of all artists in Novyraj—nobody *ever* represented a conflict artistically without presenting both sides of the story; it just wasn't done—*that*, according to his artistic heritage, was the folly of human ignorance. In reality, every conflict had at least two sides worthy of unbiased presentation. "That's nonsense," Orfei finally told her. "If that dragon was so special, why did he start attacking the human villages?"

"Eagle!" she insisted obstinately. "The *eagle* attacked only after men attacked him first!"

"The men didn't attack until *after* he'd eaten half their goats and sheep and the people were starving," he pointed out.

"What presumption!" Lady Cassandra squealed. "Do you suppose a creature as free as an eagle would stop to consider such human concepts as ownership of property? To an eagle, all life is free!''

"To be eaten?" Orfei asked incredulously.

"Stop!" the dragon demanded, leveling a critical, violet eye on Orfei. "*You* said you didn't know *The Eagle Unleashed;* that's why I played it for you. But now you're talking about parts I didn't show you—that means you lied!''

"I didn't lie," Orfei said. "And that," he added, pointing at the still-active light-opera, "was never called *The Eagle Unleashed.* It's called *Dragon Dance*; that thing stuck with human arrows and lances is called a dragon, and you, therefore, are not an eagle. Now, if you don't mind, I'd like to wake up!"

"Blasphemy!" Lady Cassandra gasped.

"You're not asleep!" the dragon stated only slightly more calmly.

"Then where the hell am I?"

"We should ask who the hell are you to say such unspeakable things!" the woman came back.

"I am called Orfei," he said flatly. "Son of Agamon."

"More blasphemy!" the woman squealed, but then the dragon pointed his snout to the sky and roared, a terrible fountain of flame erupting from his maw to tower above them. When the flames died down, Cassandra, wide-eyed and fearful, remained silent.

Orfei shared the woman's fear, the dragon's unexpected display of ferocity having placed the confrontation on a new, unanticipated level. The violet eyes locked now on his own, two pools of murky fire. "You," the dragon said with a growl, "have now staked your life on the truth of your words! In this hologram from which I have been justly freed—what was my most prized possession?"

"Your gemstones," he answered hesitantly, "that you scratched from the rock of the earth. Specifically a large blue gem in which you imagined you could see the future."

"Imagined?"

"I suppose—some of what you saw did come to pass."

"In what key is the music when I am first attacked in my lair?"

"C major—shifting to D minor as soon as you're hit."

"And when the humans are planning my death."

"F minor."

"And when I'm reading the future in the blue crystal?"

"D-flat minor—it's a pentatonic scale."

The dragon sat back on his haunches, looking at Orfei now with amazement. "Then I'm not an eagle," he said, his voice tinged with sorrow.

"What?" the woman protested.

"He *is* Orfei," the dragon told her. "I have met my creator, and if my creator says I'm a dragon, then it must be true."

"You are what you feel you are," she told the creature. She turned on Orfei, her petulance clearly evident. "That wasn't fair," she seethed. "You should have told us!"

"You didn't ask."

"That's all you can say? You've just destroyed his world, and that's all you can say!"

"I haven't destroyed anything! It isn't my fault you misinterpreted my work!"

"Then who's fault is it? You're the one who committed the crime—whoever heard of a noble dragon? That's not logical!"

"I never meant to be logical." He sighed. "Look—why didn't you just ask Goliath? He could have explained—"

"You're insane!" She laughed. "Ask Goliath? Now I've heard everything! I suppose you talk to Goliath all the time?" she asked sarcastically.

"Not lately," he said. Not since he'd left Novyraj anyway.

"But you've done so?"

"Certainly."

Lady Cassandra fell into fits of hysteric laughter; only the dragon was finally able to calm her down. "You mustn't forget that he's from the past," the creature told her. "He's from before the first gateworlds, Cassandra— this is important. Some legends suggest they knew Goliath then, that anybody could speak with him."

"You believe those fairy tales?" she asked when her laughter subsided.

"It's true," Orfei injected.

"We'd better take him to Lord He-who-knows," the dragon told the woman. "I think you may have to relinquish claim of ownership over this primitive; Orfei Agamon is too important a being to be possessed."

"I'm not sure I want him," she said with scorn. "He is too full of silly ideas."

"Please!" Orfei interrupted them. "Tell me where I am?"

"This is the Style Concillate, creator," the dragon offered. "Spatially, your present location is approximate to wherever you were when Lady Cassandra found you, only much time has passed since then."

"How much time?"

"That's difficult to say; time in the gateworlds is only perceived linearly, but in fact it's subject to occasional burps—that's probably what happened to Lady Cassandra's temporal transporter; she picked an unfortunate moment to activate it. My guess is you've come nine hundred thousand, twenty years into your future, give or take a few thousand years either way."

"I think I'd like to wake up now," Orfei said in response.

"You are not asleep, creator," the dragon said, "so waking up is not a viable option. We must take you to see Lord He-who-knows; in our present circumstances, we have great need for his wisdom."

"Is that who has Aresh?" he asked.

"Is that the name of the other primitive—I mean, is that the name of the companion of Orfei Agamon?"

"That's what her people call her."

"Then that is where she is." The creature paused, his purple gaze resting softly on Orfei. "If I hear her speak, I shall be able to tell you the meaning of her name. Would that please you, creator?"

He nodded; actually, it would please him very much, and he couldn't fault the dragon's choice of destinations. If he was cursed to dream this dream, then it would certainly improve upon the reappearance of the Nuzi girl who had stolen his heart. And if—by some impossible stretching of

circumstances—this wasn't a dream, finding Aresh was all
the more important. The sooner they got going the better;
somewhere back through the convolutions of conversation
he recalled hearing something about dissection, and the imagery that statement had evoked sent new chills up his
spine.

They traveled in a flying machine fashioned of transparent material and shaped like the boats used by the ancients
to traverse waterways. During the journey the dragon al-
ternately flew ahead of the boat and rested on the gunwale
next to Orfei when he wished to comment on the scenery
below.

From the air, the land the dragon called the Style Concillate revealed itself as a fractured patchwork of inconsis-
tent landscapes, as if some great being had taken a knife,
carved the surface of the Earth into chunks, and rearranged
them in random fashion. There were rivers and streams that
came from nowhere and ended nowhere, starting and stopping in grassy fields. Mountains would begin, then end in
abrupt, vertical cliffs of dizzying height. Rolling, white-
crested waves crashed down on ocean beaches that dotted
parts of the land like crescent moons, only there was no
sea. If the land had a theme, it was expanses of grassland,
like the place to which Cassandra had brought Orfei. This
could never be the surface, Orfei realized; it struck him as
much more likely that he dreamed a potential result of the
thing Lysis and Clystra had planned—had already done?—
with *Dragon Dance*. In no other way could nature be so
bizarrely defiled.

From time to time they saw movement, people far below.
The area was vast, but its population disproportionately
small. From what he gleaned from the dragon, everybody
they saw was Lord or Lady this-or-that; he had little interest
in remembering the names. In general, the places where
people lived appeared greatly excessive in size, but the architectural imagination involved in their design never
strayed from two basic designs, the first a sleek castlelike
structure of polished marble, the second an open-roofed
maze of rooms in the rough shape of a crab with walls and

corridors veering off at the most unlikely angles. This latter design suggested that, though the clouds in the sky appeared real, they never actually rained. Orfei verified this by asking the dragon, getting in response a request he define the concept of rain; as he did so he realized with discomfort that the words were not his, but Derek Soul's. In Novyraj, rain was as much an impossibility as it appeared to be here, and that made him think again that this was the future as Lysis and Clystra had conceived it. The dragon told him this was a gateworld; the creature knew little of other gateworlds, but he insisted they did exist, and he guessed that they numbered in the tens or hundreds of thousands. Lord He-who-knows, the dragon suggested, could tell him much more.

For the latter part of the journey, Orfei let these ideas sink in. As much as it alarmed him to admit it, he could suppose no reason why this world could *not* be a logical extension of the plans Lysis and Clystra had laid out before him. And if this wasn't a dream, and if what had transpired with Heng and Aresh had been equally real, then he had watched those very plans reach fruition without and in spite of him.

Still, nine hundred thousand years was an incomprehensible stretch of time, many times longer than the period separating his Novyraj from the days of Derek Soul—it was too great a space for human imagination to comprehend adequately, yet in support of it was this woman; now that he stood next to her in the airboat he could easily see she towered over him by at least a foot—that and her lack of visible breasts suggested some sort of evolution; he couldn't call it an improvement, for she was in no way an attractive sight. He suspected that humanity—oi this strain at any rate—had lost the need for sexual procreation.

When they finally arrived at the home of Lord He-who-knows, he was surprised to find it the most modest dwelling in appearance of any he'd seen; from without it seemed little more than a small mansion, European-style, with a thatched roof and an immaculate garden. Directly behind the house, a sheer cliff stretched a good half kilometer into the sky, but beyond that the grounds were the model of twentieth-century British sensibilities (now how could he know that, were it not for Soul?). They were greeted by an animated construction in the shape of a female human, very similar in substance to the dragon, only her crystal flesh was infused with swirls of lavender and rose. He wondered if Lord He-who-knows made a habit of ''freeing'' characters from the holograms of the past. This one he'd never seen, but he'd never pretended to know the work of every artist who'd flirted with the medium.

Orfei and the dragon were left in a waiting hall while the crystal woman took Lady Cassandra deeper into the mansion. The dragon hopped around in front of him and gazed up at him with wide, unrevealing eyes. Orfei let several tense moments pass before he finally broke the silence. ''So what should I expect of this man—Lord He-who-knows? He is a person, isn't he?''

''Oh, yes,'' the dragon said. ''Quite human.''

''Would he really dissect Aresh? That's not a very human thing to do.''

''He's a *scientist*, creator,'' the dragon replied. ''He wouldn't dissect her unless she was dead. Lady Cassandra thought she was dead; that's why she traded her away. But I'm sure Lord He-who-knows will have repaired her by now; he's very good—after all, it was he who gave me my freedom.''

''Let's hope so.''

''Your every hope,'' the dragon said, ''is mine, creator.''

''Don't keep calling me that.''

The dragon paused, bewildered. ''But why? That is who you are! I am the most fortunate sentient creature ever to live, for I have met in my lifetime my creator. Men throughout time have sought their God, but now I, Keriktik the eagle—I mean, the dragon—have succeeded where the saints of the past have failed. If not creator, then what shall I call you?''

''Orfei will do fine.''

''Then I will try, but do not chastise me, creator, if I fail from time to time. I am not perfect.''

''Listen, Keriktik,'' Orfei said. ''I am not your creator in the way that you think. If I created you, I gave you only an image, a shape. What makes you unique is your mind, and that I had nothing to do with.''

''And that is the noble act of a god—you've granted me free will, the choice to please or displease you by my acts. But I am no Cain, my lord, and I shall never betray your trust. From this moment I pledge to you my life—here in the house of Lord He-who-knows I take this solemn vow.''

''This conversation is getting silly,'' Orfei said in exasperation.

''Silly?'' the dragon said, his sadness almost palpable; for a moment he let the word echo in the room, then, just as suddenly, he regained his enthusiasm. ''You've just tested me, haven't you, creator? You make light of my pledge in order to test my loyalty—my first trial, and I have passed it! This moment will be carved in stone in the first book of Orfei, God of the Dragons!''

''You mean there are more of you?''

''Perhaps,'' the dragon said. ''In other gateworlds I may have similarly been granted freedom. And then if you create me a female—''

''I can't do that,'' he said abruptly.

''I understand,'' Keriktik said. ''First I must please you, then you will create me a mate.''

He was spared the need to reply by the reappearance of the crystal woman. ''Lord He-who-knows wishes to greet you, Orfei Agamon,'' she said in a lilting voice. He gave the dragon a worried glance, then they followed her into the house.

Lord He-who-knows was a large man, as tall as Lady Cassandra but with bulk enough to betray the fact that he enjoyed his food; Orfei guessed he weighed at least three hundred pounds. He wore a white, tailored suit as anachronistic as his home, and most of his features were hidden beneath a dark, bushy beard that, though not unkempt, seemed to have been pruned rather than trimmed. His eyes, however, were bright and cheerful; were they not, Orfei would have thought himself in the presence of an ogre. He greeted Orfei and seated him at a large, round table. Lady Cassandra was already there; the dragon took a perch on

Orfei's chairback. "So you are the great artist," Lord He-who-knows said.

"Great is a matter of opinion," Orfei said. He was anxious; he'd hoped to see Aresh by now.

"Well," Lord He-who-knows said, leaving the word suspended for a moment as if it expressed a complete thought, then he smiled broadly. "You do realize your presence here violates the second and third principles of temporal flow?"

"I've never heard of them," he answered.

"The second principle is no travel into the future," the dragon offered, "very basic, but the third is more subtle. Before the advent of temporal transference technology, many thought it impossible if only because the potential paradoxes were so vast that if time travel were possible, those in the future who'd discovered it would have made a complete mess out of history. The *facts* however, maintain that temporal transference is a restrictive possibility— you might wonder what would happen if you prevented the mating of your biological parents, but the third principle states that you can't—not that you might approach success but fail, but that you can't get anywhere near such an event because time itself won't let you. Time is a living thing, and the events that shape its course cannot be changed. The corridors between past and present are not linear, but if you think of them in a linear fashion, most are completely blocked; time itself resists event modification—if a particular coordinate in space/time represents an event of *any* conceivable significance, even the premature death of an insect that would otherwise have had offspring, the future can never be stretched back to reach it. It's very elementary."

"You've failed to understand my point, Keriktik," He-who-knows said. "His is not a human mind," he told Orfei. "Immense in terms of logical power, but very irregular regarding insight." He turned back to the dragon. "During normal temporal transference, we are restricted to the most sanitized moments, are we not? Lifeless moments in abandoned rooms, deserted cities—who has ever even seen a primitive human at close range?"

"Nobody," the dragon said, sounding agitated, then,

"Oh! I know—Lady Cassandra should not have met my creator at all—but not necessarily," he added quickly. "There are no violations if you suppose this *is* the natural future of Orfei Agamon and company; the second principle is not violated because temporal transference cannot apply to one's own natural future, and the third is not violated because Lady Cassandra, the only true transferee, could not possibly have affected the event in any case. Assuming it was natural, of course."

"You may have a point," the large man said, furrows creasing his brow. "Thank you for your analysis, though your logic isn't binding."

Pleased with the compliment, Keriktik grinned, translucent lips pulling back to reveal transparent fangs. "I see no inconsistencies," he said with a flourish of finality.

"Well," the big man said simply, again letting the single word strive to express his position. He turned to Orfei. "Perhaps you have a theory of your own?"

Orfei shifted uncomfortably; Lord He-who-knows's lips, like Lady Cassandra's, moved independently of his words. In a sense he was growing accustomed to the effect, but it remained unnerving when he thought about it. "I have no theories," he answered, "except that this is a dream."

"Well that won't do," his host said with a frown. "When do you expect to wake up?"

"I've been trying."

"Perhaps I can help you."

"How?"

Lord He-who-knows didn't answer; he only smiled. Orfei couldn't seem to remove his eyes from the other man's grin. The face around it, along with the physical reality of the room, went elastic and began to fade. The chair beneath him disappeared, and he fell to the ground—a vast flatness stretching out in all directions, the mouth before him the only feature now in sight. He thought for a moment he'd been proved correct—that he did dream—then the mouth dropped to the ground and opened into a dark, gaping hole, and an army of slithering reptiles emerged—snakes with wings that flew at him, wrapping about his body and face. He lost all opportunity for idle thought; he tried to run, but the snakes had bound his legs. Before his eyes, fangs dripped acidic venom that burned his flesh. The weight of the reptiles grew unbearable, and he began to scream, the sound of his tortured voice growing deafening in the featureless void that now closed in on him, crushing him. He screamed and screamed until his heart felt ready to burst, and then, without warning, the reptiles disappeared. The next instant, he was back where he'd begun, at the table, seated across from his host, Lord He-who-knows's smile now gone. "I apologize for inducing that illusion," the man said in very solemn tones. "I hope in doing so I proved the incorrectness of your thinking. Such a nightmare would certainly have awakened any man, as waking is the human body's natural defense against such extreme terror. Do you follow my reasoning?"

"Please," Orfei said, shaking his head, trying to purge the images; the sound of his screams still echoed in his mind. "Don't do that!"

"I already apologized."

"You should believe him, creator," Keriktik said. "You are not dreaming."

"What about *my* problem?" Lady Cassandra suddenly blurted out. Orfei had forgotten she was there, but after that horrible vision of snakes, he was grateful for the distraction.

"But you haven't stated it—" Keriktik began.

"The hell I haven't! I'm out a temporal transporter, and now I'm out two prizes! You won't get away with this He-who-knows!"

"I haven't attempted to get away with anything. We have problems before us—haven't you been listening?"

"Principle this," she spit, mocking the dragon, "principle that. All I want's another temporal transporter; you give me that, I'll get the hell out of here, and you can principle yourself into the next century!"

"That isn't wise," Lord He-who-knows said very calmly. "In the present circumstances, with the anomalies we have before us, any manipulation of temporal currents could have unpredictable and possibly disastrous results. Not one, but two principles of temporal flow have been violated for the first time in history; if you'd practiced responsible living, you would have recognized these facts and their ramifications when the violations occurred. Instead, you negotiated a trade with my proxies for what you thought a useless dead body, fretted over what you'd do with a live one, and never stopped to realize nothing live had ever, ever been brought forward from the past.''

''What about Lord Cameron's Chinese harlot?''

''That's an automaton, and you're a fool for believing him.''

She'd grown quite red in the face. ''I have a right to believe what I wish!''

''That is true.''

''Then I demand a replacement for this!'' she shouted, holding up her arm with the blackened metallic band.

''Very well,'' Lord He-who-knows said, opening his palm before her. The air there shimmered, and a shiny twin of her device materialized. Lady Cassandra quickly snatched it up. ''Thank you,'' she said.

''I'm happy it pleases you,'' he said; before she could stand up, he added, ''but it won't work. I have disabled the controller software for all devices in the Style Concillate with the potential for temporal manipulation until these mysteries are solved. Until then, there *will* be no disturbances in local temporal flow of any kind.''

''How dare you!''

''I don't dare, my child. I am Keeper of this gateworld; it's my responsibility.''

''I am hosting the festival-by-the-gate! I *must* have new music!''

''Then make some up.''

''That's preposterous!''

''No, Cassandra, that's creativity—if you'd tune your mind more than once every few decades, you might rediscover it.''

Lady Cassandra's face turned a livid shade of red; now, she let out an explosive breath and stood up in a frantic flurry of ungainly limbs. She glared at Lord He-who-knows, then turned her angry eyes on Orfei before storming out of the room.

''She's really quite pleasant in less exciting times,'' Lord

He-who-knows said after she'd gone. "Must have given you a very confusing first view of our world."

Orfei nodded, unsure of anything to say. He felt out of balance, his mind in a state of flux, plagued by a vertigo of consciousness. If this was reality, there was too much of it to assimilate. His host, at once benevolent and tyrannically domineering, stood as an anomaly within any conception of human potential and limits; if here was the future, there was too much power. "Aresh," he said in the end. "I came here to get the woman you have."

"And then you will leave?" Lord He-who-knows asked. "Where are you going?"

"I don't know," he answered. He didn't; beyond a reunion with Aresh, his future loomed like a dark, unrevealing abyss. There would be Soul, but beyond that?

"Well," the other man said; this time he continued on: "You really shouldn't leave. I have much thinking to do, and you appear to need rest. Please stay here for the present; I have already prepared accommodations for you and your mate."

"Then she is okay? I will see her?"

"Of course!" Lord He-who-knows replied with a chuckle. He waved his hand in the direction of Cassandra's departure, and a stairwell materialized in the air. "I never said otherwise."

Orfei stood and approached the stairwell, hesitantly testing the first step. "Go on," his host encouraged him. "You will find her at the top. We will speak again when you've slept." Orfei ascended then, only half-aware of the dragon following closely behind.

The room above was of breathtaking design, its decor rose and gray, its main wall a seductive hologram of a Bacchanalian feast. In a four-poster bed he found Aresh, the girl fast asleep beneath layers of silken sheets; he pulled them back to inspect her wounds, but the horrible red marks were gone. She was naked; he looked at her for a long while before stripping off his clothes and sliding next to her beneath the sheets. As he pulled her close to his body, she stirred and rolled to face him.

"Orfei," she said, her eyes fluttering open.

"I'm here."

"This is a dream," she said. "I understand your words."

"That's what I thought. Keriktik must be nearby."

"Who?"

"You will see," he answered.

"What of Heng?"

"I don't know," he said wearily. "I really don't know."

She leaned back and stretched, reveling in the softness of the bed. "This is a wonderful dream," she sighed. "There's this kind, grandfatherly man who made my pain go away, but he didn't talk much. Where are we?"

"I'm not sure of that either." He again pulled her close to him and closed his eyes. Sleep came quickly; he thought, *I love you*, and wondered whether he'd said it aloud, then shadows enveloped him and he felt himself falling into Aresh's warmth.

XXV

THE UNCUT, STONY GRAIN OF THE TUNNEL WALLS MADE streaklike patterns as Holly pumped the t-bug's hoverjets, accelerating down a long, straight corridor. For Derek, the streaks were a brief meditation; they converged and crossed like a network of parallel roads seen from the air; for some reason he imagined them the legacy of a giant, gouging claw.

They went first to whence he'd come, the viaduct terminal where Linda—or Sheila Lorenz—had greeted him on his arrival. Prior to reaching their destination, they had to clear two security checkpoints, each manned by a stern contingent of heavily armed marines, weapons prominently on display. Each demanded both fingerprint and voice identification; at the second checkpoint Derek noticed a large vidmonitor where several men unblinkingly observed their counterparts at the first—a very strict security arrangement designed to be inviolable; were the first checkpoint overcome, the second would either shoot to kill the perpetrators or cave in the tunnel itself if faced with significant opposition. Derek found the situation quite disturbing; it was obviously designed more to keep the workers of the complex from reaching the terminal than for keeping unwelcome arrivals out. Moreover, he remembered none of it from before, but both checkpoints confirmed he had passed through on arrival, and at least one man at each location recognized the holographic image of Sheila Lorenz—more reason for him to discount everything he remembered as hallucination. Beyond that the marines knew nothing about the woman except that their authorization systems had allowed her to pass both ways.

To his clear mind, the Moscow terminal seemed every bit as cold and clinical as its counterpart on the Berlin side. There were few human workers; it was an environment for machines, where human intervention could only complicate and hinder operations. As such, they had little difficulty locating Tech Specialist Willis, the man who'd established voice-comm with Derek during the viaduct journey. Willis's office was a terminal-lined control booth looking out over the platform; he came out to greet them while Holly powered down the t-bug.

"Hello, Doctor," he said to Derek, sounding slightly nervous. "It's good to see you looking well. I hope there's not a problem."

"Why should there be?"

"Well," Willis said, "some men might want to blame the kind of experience you had on a human factor. In this case that would mean me."

Derek would have laughed in less serious circumstances. "You've got nothing to worry about, Mr. Willis."

"Thank you, sir," the man said, smiling now. "Why don't you come up to the booth? I have real coffee and think I might be able to scrounge up a couple of clean cups."

"That sounds good," Holly said, preempting Derek's reply.

Willis led them up a short flight of stairs and gave them seats; the control room was surprisingly spacious. "Security in the access tunnels is rather tight," Derek commented as the other man dug through a drawer in search of the promised cups.

"Yeah," Willis said, looking up and sighing. "And a

pain in my ass, too. Makes it really lonely around here; I work four day shifts on and off with another guy—used to be they'd let my friends through for visits, but not anymore. Now I'm not sure I even have any friends.''

''Why's that?''

Willis found the cups and set to filling them from a small metal percolator. ''Everybody's scared shitless, sir. They want out of here, and everybody who knows me and where I work thinks I'm their ticket. Doesn't matter that I couldn't do a damned thing to help them even if I wanted to—they just don't see it that way.''

''I'm sorry,'' Derek said. ''I think I understand your problem.''

''Well,'' the man said with a smile as he passed out the cups, ''life's a bitch. So it's good to see you two—I don't suppose this is a social visit?''

''Not really,'' Holly said. ''Your coffee's very good though—we may have to come back!''

''It's the best,'' he said in agreement. ''Commander Kramer gets it shipped in special from somewhere in South America. A little spills out here, a little there—you know how it goes?''

Derek nodded and raised an eyebrow. ''Don't you think it a bit risky advertising that fact?''

''Well, Mr. Inspector General,'' he said, ''feel free to slap my wrist and ship me back to Berlin.''

''That sounds like a request.''

''It is.''

Derek sipped on his coffee and didn't answer. It occurred to him that he could well do what the man asked—his authority certainly extended that far.

''So why *did* you come here?'' Willis asked before the silence grew strained. ''I don't know anything about what's happening past the rumors.''

''Such as?'' Holly asked before Derek could show the man his clipboard.

''Such as giant snakes that swallow people whole, or squads of killer droids left behind by the Sovs. Disintegration beams. Invisible mutants—you name it. The latest and scariest is that it's one of us—some maniac murderer who got past the psych exams or went crazy being down under too long.''

''What do you think?'' Holly pressed him.

''I don't. I mean, I do my damnedest not to think about it. Just like everybody else. What do you think?''

Holly thought a moment before answering. ''The snakes and invisible mutants are a bit farfetched.'' Derek watched her; on the surface she appeared calm, but her voice had a funny edge. Inside, he guessed the man's speculations terrified her.

''I suppose it was too much to hope that you'd already cracked this,'' Willis said distantly. ''I sure as hell hope you do, though—and soon.''

''We're trying,'' Derek said, taking over. He pushed the clipboard in front of the man now. ''Do you recognize this woman?''

''Sure,'' Willis said. ''She's the one came to meet you— Sheila, right?''

''You know her?''

''Not personally. One of the guys who inspects the loader droids does.''

''Is he around?''

''I think so.'' Willis mashed a button on his console. ''You there, Jamie?''

''Sure, Jeff,'' came a voice from a speaker. ''What's up?''

''The IG's in here asking about that Sheila friend of yours—can you come up?''

''Sure.''

''He won't be a minute,'' Willis said, letting up on the button. ''Want more coffee?'' The new man arrived as he refilled their cups. ''This is Jamie Parsons, sir.''

Derek greeted the man and motioned him to sit.

''Is something wrong with Sheila?'' Jamie asked. He was a tall, blond boy in his early twenties. His eyes went from Derek to Holly. ''Shit!'' he said before they could answer. ''Her too? She was just here a couple days ago!''

''The administrative systems already had her listed as missing then.''

The new information seemed to stun the man. ''That's

too weird," he said distantly. "Jeff and I were just talking about her yesterday, weren't we Jeff? I was telling him how strange it was they'd send her to greet an IG—she's no big shot."

"You didn't know she was missing?"

Jamie shook his head. "We don't get told much, especially about all this. Has to get around word of mouth, and we haven't been off shift since then."

"Did you speak to her while she was here?"

"No," he answered. "I was busy double-checking all systems for trouble after what happened to you, sir. She saw me, though. I think she waved."

"How well did you know her?" Holly asked.

"Pretty well, ma'am. We didn't have anything between us or anything like that if that's what you think. Sheila was a wild one—too much for a country boy like me. Know what I mean?"

"I think so, but maybe you should explain anyway."

"Wild, you know?" he said, struggling and looking rather embarrassed. "She slept around with a lot of guys. Had a lot of energy—whenever there was any kind of party, you could be sure she'd be there. I don't know when she ever slept."

Derek took back his clipboard. "Thanks," he said. He didn't think the two men had much more to tell them.

"Is that all?" Jamie asked. "I know where you might learn more."

"Where's that?"

"Place that calls itself The Last Rattle—it's a rec joint on the fourth level where Sheila usually hung out."

"Thank you," Holly said.

As they left, Jamie called out after them. "Sir!" he shouted. "If you go there, don't go in uniform!"

Derek stopped and turned. "Why's that?"

"You want to see what it's really like, don't you?"

Derek nodded and smiled at the man, then joined Holly at the t-bug.

They stayed silent until they'd crossed back through the security checkpoints, then Holly throttled down the hoverjets to a crawl, put the t-bug on auto-nav, and suggested they compare notes.

"Whatever it is," Derek said, "it's operating with very high access."

"I agree—because of the security authorization. She was listed as missing in the central administrative system, yet specifically authorized to pass security to meet you at the terminal. Want to know something else?"

"What's that?"

"Linda issued an executive order a couple weeks ago—to the effect that all security levels for the disappeared be reduced to zero immediately on confirmation of their missing status."

"Which in Sheila Lorenz's case occurred," Derek said, reviewing the clipboard, "twenty-six hours before I arrived here in Moscow. Is there any chance these date and time stamps could be faulty?"

"No," Holly answered. "I thought of that while you were still asleep. Did a brief remote interview with the confirming officer—some shift foreman on level four—and he was positive the system had it right. I suppose we could cut Juliet loose on it; she'd be able to sift through the system archives and make sure we haven't missed anything."

"That's a good idea," Derek said. He was staring at Sheila Lorenz's holo on the clipboard; no matter how hard he tried, he couldn't remember her face—it was no different than the rest of the board's faces, faces of strangers, though all evidence now suggested he'd spent at least fifteen minutes in her presence only a couple days before. In his memory, those fifteen minutes belonged to Linda. "I don't get it, Holly," he said after a long pause. "Let's say this Sheila Lorenz did meet me at the terminal, that she was missing, and her meeting me was important enough to whomever or whatever it is we're up against that it necessitated high-level manipulation of system data to bring about—what was the *point*? What was accomplished? I didn't speak with this woman; hell, I can't even remember her face!"

Holly didn't immediately respond; she held up a finger to request his patience—her other hand was busy punching codes into the comm device given her by Lieutenant Morris. "Juliet," she said into the device. "We want you to double-check the date/time data associated with the Sheila Lorenz reports—I want a thorough archival verification. And find out where the authorization for Lorenz to pass the viaduct checkpoints came from—who and where."

"Requests understood," the computer replied. Holly looked up at Derek. "Sorry about that," she said. "The sooner we ask, the sooner we have an answer."

He nodded. "Were you listening to what I said?"

"Yeah," she said. "I'm not sure what to think. I want to find hope in it—after all, everything we learn hints that you were in the enemy's power, so to speak. Yet you didn't disappear, and seem perfectly normal as best as I can tell. There is one thing, though—once when you woke up, you mumbled something about what you thought Linda told you about everybody being safe, remember? The exact words?"

Derek closed his eyes to dredge up the memory. "She said, 'I'm sure they're okay—he promised me.' Before that she said something about moving the headquarters closer to the work to improve morale, and that's about it really."

Holly mulled it over, frowning. "He?"

"I remember thinking the same question. But haven't we decided none of this matters—that it was all hallucination?"

"Maybe," Holly said distantly. "Maybe we need to re-think it. Please think back—is there *anything* that happened you haven't told me?"

"My mind was a mess, Holly. The bullet car drugged me, then the control computers went out, leaving me to fend for myself. For the most part I relived my past with Linda—came to near the end and talked to Willis a while, then spent the rest of the trip phasing in and out and trying to hang on. There is one more thing, but I can't imagine how it matters."

"Tell me anyway."

"Well," he said, "remember when I first got to Berlin and went out on the streets? That little girl that cop of yours hit with a truncheon?"

"He wasn't *my* cop."

"But you know what I'm talking about?"

"I think so."

"Well, that's who I thought met me at the bullet car—for the first few seconds, before I saw it really was Linda."

Holly glanced at him, but didn't immediately answer. Juliet came back during the pause: The dates and times on the reports on Sheila Lorenz were definitely correct, but her authorization to pass the checkpoints was untraceable; the records in question had simply appeared on file with no hint of origin at least ten minutes but no more than an hour prior to Derek's arrival.

"That's about what I would have predicted," Derek said.

Holly was still lost in thought. "At the risk of you thinking me crazy again," she said eventually, "that may be important—that little girl, your seeing Linda, everything. . . . I don't really know how yet, but think about it: We've been concentrating on Sheila, just this one little corner of the mystery, and we've come up with our first solid fact—whatever's behind this is in the system, you said so yourself. Well if we stretch that we can tie it back to Berlin, to that CIS memo—that was something in the system too, wasn't it? We've got computers involved at every turn—a mysterious authorization here, an unexplainable stray memo there, a system malfunction in the viaduct. And didn't the stateside AI systems choose you for this mission over any objection you could put into words?"

"Yes, but—"

"Systems again, Derek," she said, cutting him off. "Everywhere. And almost all of it's got something to do with you; I keep wanting to think that you're the point, the reason for all of it. You're a bureaucrat sent out to do detective work—not that you're doing such a bad job, but it isn't difficult to imagine there must be somebody more qualified; your past experience here with Linda can't give you *that* much of an edge. And then that memo—it suggests that one system in the past recommended your death, but another system hijacked it. Beyond that your TravelDoc malfunctioned, but who's to say systems leave the picture at that point? Those drugs induce a very suggestible state, then the systems plant seeds and act as guides for the subsequent induced hallucinations—the technical term is virtual reality, it's sort of like stepping into an active hologram, except it's *all* internal in this case, in the head. Can I ask you a very personal question?''

''You can try.''

''Why did you leave Linda? She was very much in love with you.''

''I'm surprised she never told you; I found her on the floor one afternoon with Paul—the guy she's married to now.''

''That's what I heard you thought. You never confronted her, did you? She didn't even know why you'd left until a month later when that story came back to her as a rumor.''

''That's bullshit,'' he said with distaste. ''She sure as hell saw me when I walked into her office.''

''She swears that never happened. Told me she wrote you about it but you never replied.'' Holly paused for a moment, searching his eyes. ''You know, for the past several decades, the biggest debate in psych circles has been over the philosophical applications of virtual reality—what are the implications when it's perceived as ordinary experiences, and are there really any meaningful differences? Where does ordinary human reality end, and the reality fashioned by a computerized world begin?''

''Are you trying to tell me I never saw what I think I saw?''

''No,'' she said quickly. ''Well, maybe—I don't really know, but if you think about it, it's not necessarily any stranger than anything going on here now. Maybe I'm just trying to get you to think, to question things. When Linda heard that rumor she went back to the activity logs for that day to find proof you were wrong, but it turned out she and Paul *were* meeting together at the time to discuss some shift-scheduling problems; there were no human witnesses to corroborate that story—rather inconvenient for disproving your side of things.''

''Along with the fact they're married now.''

''That's not necessarily relevant,'' Holly said. ''Psychologically speaking, it could even be that your accusation planted the suggestion. I'm not trying to hurt you, Derek,'' she said, taking his hand. "It's just that all this other stuff about systems makes me think about it—here we might have an instance where someone or something wanted you *out* of Moscow."

"That's really stretching it, Holly."

"Maybe," she said. She had both of her hands on his now, and her eyes searched his in a way that increased his discomfort, as if he could do nothing to keep her from seeing straight through to his heart. "It could be me," she said in a very soft voice. "I *could* be crazy because I want to think all this might be true—everything I've been suggesting to you. You see, if it is, then what's going on here may not be so horrible. I keep thinking about that man Willis talking about giant snakes and murderers—*horrible* possibilities, Derek! But if I shift into this big theory, there's hope—like Sheila Lorenz-slash-Linda assuring you they're all okay—alive, not eaten or murdered. If this revolves around you, Derek, then it may all be benign!"

He wanted to push her away, but, inexplicably, he reached out and pulled her to him, placing her head on his shoulder; it was as if the turmoil in his mind had disconnected him from the moment, relieving him of the task of controlling his physical actions. In a few brief minutes of conversation, Holly had called his entire existence into question and asked him to do the same—it *was* crazy, and she'd pushed just about every emotional button he imagined he had, and yet . . . She had him thinking—she'd done her job well. Bubbling up through the rekindled dark passions of his marriage came two disparate memories, disconnected moments that crystallized, lined up, and fell neatly into Holly's puzzle: The first was the way he'd been invited to discover Linda's infidelity—via an anonymous message in the system; the second was Linda describing over Indian food her recurring dream with the deformed people and the man who either cured or destroyed them— a man with his face, she'd said. This second memory gained greater significance in light of his hallucinations in the viaduct—this was the moment they'd focused on, the one played over and over again, as if to stress the moment, to underline it. . . . Why? In retrospect, Linda's recurrent dream, unless it was a fabrication, might be viewed as the basis of their entire relationship, the very foundation of their marriage. Without it, she might never have given him a second glance at that embassy party, and that would have been the end of it. So what was he thinking? In the context of Holly's theory, Linda's dream might fall into the category of virtual reality, something imposed upon her in Moscow for the purpose of attracting him there. In the context of Holly's theory, he could make it all fit; the final problem was he himself—what made him so special?

While Derek thought, Holly pulled away and took over the t-bug's controls. "I think it's time we called on Linda," she said. Derek, only half-aware of her, nodded in agreement and fell back into thought.

XXVI

ORFEI STIRRED; SOMETHING WAS ROCKING HIM GENTLY—
Aresh's hand on his shoulder. He could feel her breath, a
soft rhythmic warmth on his ear and the back of his neck.
"Are you okay?" came her whisper. He rolled over to face
her; her blue eyes took on hues of silver in the chamber's
rosy ambience, and her dark skin seemed to absorb the light
and glow like polished stone. "You were moaning," she
said. "You've had troubling dreams?"

"Not dreams," he answered. Now that they could speak,
he saw no sense in hiding anything from her; he told her
about the mind-bytes and Derek Soul—everything that had
happened since the Room of the Fourth, everything he
could tell her about Novyraj to help her understand. In
whispers he spoke of Lysis's attempt to violate his mind,
of what she and Clystra had planned and done with *Dragon
Dance*—Aresh herself had been at his side to witness this
last event. When he was finished he looked away from her
and asked if she believed him.

"Of course I do, Orfei," she said. "It is no small thing
to have visions; you are a very special man."

"I have visions of my people's past, and now I'm thrust into their future. Is this a dream?"

"I do not know," she said, kissing his forehead. "I hope not."

"I think I only want one thing now," he whispered. Her skin was like warm satin against his cheek; he kissed it and slid lower in the bed to find her breasts. As he kissed her nipples, he reached between her legs and stroked her slowly, each caress making her tremble and press against him ever more firmly. In the end it was she who pulled him back up and forced him inside her; they made love like that, lying on their sides until the final moments of passion when she pushed him onto his back and rose up above him. As they came together he thought how he'd never seen such a beautiful sight as this girl moving on top of him, her skin speckled with perspiration, her every breath an exhalation of the aroma of life itself. When she rolled away and curled up next him, they lay motionless, holding each other in silence until sleep came again.

XXVII

"LINDA WON'T ACCEPT ANYBODY'S CALLS ON THE GEN-
eral comm channels," Paul Kramer told Holly. They were
in a large lobby outside the administrative offices; he'd
greeted them with a smile, but Holly had pushed the conversation straight into business. "She's got a blanket rejec-
tion order in effect—doesn't even keep track of who's
trying to get through. People who need to reach her get
through on designated frequencies only."

"Then she should have had the courtesy to mention that
fact when I talked with her," Holly said bluntly.

"Why?" he asked. "You're here at the department's direction, not ours. This is our problem, and we're working
on it; we didn't ask for your help, nor do we want it."

"But we're here," she said.

"That's true, and if you want to do us a favor, you'll
leave. Do you want to destroy our careers?"

Holly laughed; by the sound of it she was getting very
tense. "What on Earth gave you that idea?"

He nodded at her clipboard. "That," he said. "It's *our*
problem to solve, not yours."

Derek looked on, glad to let Holly take the brunt of it.

He'd met Paul Kramer socially on several occasions in the past; Moscow's operational manager had never struck him as much more than the average stuffed shirt—he'd often wondered what hurt him more, that Linda had betrayed him, or that she'd done so with this unexceptional man. He got the impression Holly knew him as well, but that the two were not on friendly terms. "Well I think I'll discuss that with Linda," said Derek's partner. "Where is she?"

"She's in her office," Paul said, walking away.

"We'll get back to you," Holly called after him. "In the meantime you might want to give some consideration to the fact that this is the department's problem, not your own personal goddamned test of manhood!" The barb didn't faze him; he just shrugged and kept walking. "I *don't like* that man!" Holly seethed under her breath; Derek didn't argue with her.

They found Linda seated behind her desk, nervously tapping her fingers together as they entered. "It's about time you two decided to drop by!" she said. Her eyes went from Holly to Derek; he thought they softened then, if only slightly. "Hello, Derek," she said.

He had to clear his throat. "Hi, Linda," he managed. *Long time no see. . . .*

Holly pushed Derek toward a chair, then seated herself. "I can't count the number of times I called you, Linda. What am I supposed to do if you don't answer?"

Linda raised an eyebrow, then shrugged. "I'm getting tired of Collier's games," she finally said. She was tapping her fingertips together like a fast-paced metronome. As Derek watched her he was shocked at her appearance; time had treated her cruelly—she looked ten years older than he remembered, her hair a uniform gray now, her body withering, cheeks caving in. . . . He was again glad to have Holly; the simple sight of his ex-wife made him want to cry out of pity, and that was no perspective from which to conduct an investigation.

"What games?" Holly was asking.

"These games!" Linda answered, the declaration almost a shout. "You—him, all of this!"

"It isn't a game, Linda. People are disappearing!"

"Very astute, Holmes," she spit. "They're deserting, to be more precise. And as soon as I catch the ringleader, you can pack up your fingerprint kits and go home."

Holly sat back, brushing her index finger against her lower lip. "Deserting? That's the first we've heard of that .... How's it possible, Linda? These tunnels are all mapped out—where are they going to go that you can't find them?"

Linda emitted a sound somewhere between a grunt and a hiss. "I'm just supposed to lay it out in front of you and give you the glory? I asked Collier for more security forces, and instead he sends an IG!"

"We're on the same side," Holly insisted wearily.

"Are we?" Her eyes fell coldly on Derek.

"Of course!" Holly said.

"I was asking *him*!"

"The same side," Derek confirmed softly. He'd never thought she could grow so bitter. . . .

"Well now *that's* good news!" she returned sarcastically.

"Linda, I—" Derek began, then paused to clear his throat. In a twisted sense, he imagined she might be enjoying this—him squirming in a chair before her. "I never asked for this assignment. I tried to refuse it, but they wouldn't let me."

"We're on the *same* side," Holly repeated quickly, reasserting her presence. "If you're withholding information relevant to this investigation, we've got a right to it! Where's your support for this desertion theory?"

"That's not your concern!"

"The hell it isn't!" She flipped open her comm device and angrily mashed its buttons, never taking her eyes off the other woman. "Juliet!" she said. "I want a full frontal assault on the personal files of Linda and Paul Kramer—shut 'em off, track down any aliases, and melt anything that—"

"Wait!" Linda protested, jumping up.

"Pause command, Juliet," Holly said. "I'm sorry, Linda. It isn't easy for me either—the last I knew, you were my friend."

Like a puppet with cut strings, Linda collapsed into her

chair. "Everything you don't know," she said wearily, "is under an alias called Toastem. The password is—" She paused to look up at Derek, tears welling in her eyes. "The password is Drak. Leave the rest of our data alone—you have my word they're irrelevant."

"Thank you," Holly said. "Modify command, Juliet. Dump Linda Kramer alias Toastem—password is Drak."

"Dump successful," the computer said after a moment.

"That's it, Juliet." She shut off the comm device and snapped it back on her belt.

"If you're still my friend, Holly, don't tell Paul. He's done most of the work, and it means a lot to him."

"I'll keep that in mind. I've got one more question."

"Go ahead."

"Who did you assign to greet us at the terminal?"

"One of my aides."

"Can we talk to him?"

"You can try."

"Where?"

"Try your clipboard," Linda said, waving her arm in a lazy gesture. "We confirmed him missing about an hour after you arrived. If that's it, I'll ask you to leave now. I feel very tired."

Derek found it difficult to keep his eyes on her; she looked far worse now than when they'd come in— wounded, mentally raped. "That was brutal," he told Holly when they were back in the t-bug.

"I didn't enjoy it any more than you did. Christ, Derek— she's aged five years in the last six months!"

"You should be in charge here," he said distantly. "I couldn't have done that, no matter how necessary it was." He would have broken down in tears first. . . .

"Well I'm not so pleased with myself," she said. "After seeing those two like that, my better judgment tells me to dump all their goddamned files anyway. That's what Collier's going to tell us to do."

"I know," he said, "but only if we tell him everything. Do me a favor and don't, not yet at least. I don't think she was lying."

"I'm not sure she'd realize it if she was, but it's not her I'm worried about."

His heart sinking, he realized she was right. If they had a real problem, it was Paul Kramer, not Linda. The ordeal had worn her down, but he was very much alive and kicking, obstinately so. It wasn't very hard to imagine him with an agenda of his own, concealed even from his wife—hell, with the state she was in, he doubted they were even sleeping together. . . . He thought back on Holly's suggestion that he'd more or less imagined the circumstances that ended his marriage—a horrible possibility if true. He couldn't help thinking she'd still be whole if he'd never left.

No, he decided adamantly. It was life here that had destroyed her, just as it had been destroying him before he left. It was the place, not the people; without this place, there'd have been no problem.

Holly took them back to their quarters and wasted no time, going straight to Juliet and the dump of Linda's files. Derek left her to it, excusing himself to take a shower; the humidity in the corridors had left his skin clammy and itching under his uniform, but along with that he felt an intense need to be alone; between Linda and Holly and the analytical demands of his job, he'd grown emotionally numb, at the same time realizing the day had blown large holes in his understanding of himself and his own past. Everything was so twisted and confused that he didn't know what to believe, but worse than that, he doubted believing would make any difference—with everything in flux, a mere attempt to believe might be the last act of a fool. Nothing was black-and-white anymore; Linda, whom he'd loved, was crushed and beyond him, so far away that what love he had left could only be cast from a distance in the form of pity. Holly, whom part of him wanted, had blasted her way into his life and become both destroyer and redeemer—so far, he might as well have been her pet dog; she'd all but dragged him through it by the nose. And what was he to her but the puzzle's wild card, some sort of human magnet for the mysteries to cling to like iron filings in an otherwise unpolarized, senseless void?

He showered, trying to wash it all away with the water, to dispel the impurities of the day into the mushrooming billows of steam condensing on the bathroom's ceiling. When he shaved it was a stranger's face that watched him in the mirror—there was too much within him for a reflection to understand. He felt broken apart, on the threshold of something new and undefined, and he didn't know whether to fear or welcome it; the one thing he felt he did know was that life's previous threshold was behind him: Since leaving Linda, she'd lurked like a ghost in the corner of every room, an ominous threat beyond every door—all that was behind him, the anxieties, questions, morose reveries over what might have been. . . . When he'd left, he'd left it incomplete, an unresolved melody whose discord life hadn't let him forget, but now, after seeing her, that final note had at last sounded. Collier's psych systems were right; he *had* harbored a twisted sort of love, though not for a woman, just a memory. The woman was—beyond him. . . . His life now and his past with her were distinct things that no force on the planet could hope to put back together. In more certain times, the revelation might have been cathartic—after all, it freed him of years of unsettling inner turmoil—but jubilation didn't now fill his heart, only sadness.

After the shower air-blasted him dry, he stretched out naked on his bed and gazed at the serene, rustic vidholo. The fake window remained open; the trees still swayed, the clouds tumbled, and the birds chirped, but what had struck him that morning as pleasant now simply felt wrong, just another example of mankind's tendency to destroy and reconstruct, to couch himself in illusions in order to forget the horrors he'd imposed on his world, that such simple pleasures were no longer to be found in nature while in the past they'd been real and alive and legion. The artist's eye, no matter how refined, could never capture such perfection; holographic art, like the rest of human endeavor, could not bestow life. He slipped into these morose thoughts until Holly rapped on his door and broke the spell.

"We've got something new," she said once Derek had pulled on a pair of pants and joined her in the lounge. She had the map of the Moscow underground up in Juliet's projection display. "Watch," she said, manipulating her joystick; in the space between the third and fourth levels at the exploratory frontiers, a limited web of red lines took slow shape, a few terminating on the corridors of one level or the other. "That's a superimposition of one of Linda's files. Supposedly, they're tunnels."

"Okay," Derek said uncertainly, squinting into the hologram. "Isn't that rather improbable? This master map is based on geological soundings, isn't it?"

"That's the problem—why I said 'supposedly.' There's also a report concerning a couple of nonspecialized technicians, both listed among the missing—Thomas Liebowicz and Shane Crawley. Paul Kramer interrogated Liebowicz after Crawley's disappearance; the man testified to an interesting sequence of events." Holly paused to create a pointer in the hologram and move it to one of the places where a red line touched on a fourth level corridor. "Liebowicz swore he and Crawley discovered an opening here, a sort of jagged crack in a recess in the unfinished wall about two feet wide. Crawley insisted on entering; Liebowicz followed. It was a dark tunnel, and all they had were a couple of emergency flash-wands. Crawley went exploring, moving out of sight of his partner who stayed by the opening when the tunnel twisted about twenty feet in. Liebowicz waited about five minutes, called after his friend, got no answer, and went in deeper. He swore the tunnel deadended another twenty feet past the twist, and there was no sign of Crawley."

"Hmm," Derek reflected. "That's about the nearest thing we've got to a firsthand account, isn't it?"

"Yeah," Holly said, "but it's a bit fishy. Both men went missing within hours of each other, both last seen on duty, Liebowicz's disappearance only about an hour after the time stamp of the report."

"Well we need to check it out."

"Very carefully," Holly said. "I don't like thinking about Liebowicz disappearing so soon after talking with Paul; the timing's too close to be coincidence."

Derek studied the hologram. "What about the rest of these red lines?"

"I don't know," Holly answered. "There was nothing else in the Toastem alias we didn't already know, so we don't know what evidence they have to support the map. My guess is they've got their reasons but kept most of them in their heads."

Derek frowned, finding Holly's supposition troubling. "They're not making it easy for us, are they?" *Surely* Linda knew she couldn't just give them sketchily documented data and expect all the questions to stop. . . .

"That's probably an understatement."

"Well," he said with a sigh, "what's our next move?"

"It's really up to you," she said. "I can't make up my mind. We need to grill Linda again on this map, take a look at this corridor Crawley supposedly disappeared in, and I don't want to forget Sheila Lorenz. I'd like to inspect her quarters and check out that place the man at the viaduct terminal mentioned."

"The Last Rattle—"

"That sounds like it."

That meant casual dress if they were to follow Jamie Parsons's advice. "I'll go put on a shirt then. Let's do the corridor first and put Linda on hold. Paul may not make it so easy for us the next time, and we may be better off finding out as much as we can on our own first. I'd like to respect Linda's wish that we don't let on to him what we know; at least until we've exhausted what we've got."

"You're right," Holly said. "But I'm afraid that might not take long at all."

They took the t-bug down long, ramping tunnels to the fourth level; Derek took the opportunity to review Sheila Lorenz's chapter in his clipboard. The red spot on their map was well into the area currently being excavated and explored, and they passed several teams of workers coming off shift and riding hover-platforms back to the residential sections. At the exact point in question, they came unexpectedly to a security post; the marines there weren't stopping anybody, they just stood behind a low partition of chains and watched, smiling and displaying their weapons for everyone who went by. The recess in the wall was behind them; the light wasn't very good, but Derek could make out the outline of what looked like a wide crack in the tunnel that had been sealed loosely with small boulders.

Holly slowed as they passed the security post, but she didn't stop or even look at Derek until they were a hundred feet clear of it. "Looks like we'll have to put that one off a while, too. If we show any interest in that crack, I'm sure Paul will hear of it."

"So it's back to Sheila Lorenz's?"

"No," Holly said after a moment. "Let's do a quick tour of the operations here—that's the sort of thing Paul will expect, so it shouldn't push any alarm buttons. We've got a couple more of these intersections on this level, and I think I can work them into a casual cruising pattern. I suspect we'll just find more security posts at each spot, but it's worth a try."

Derek nodded in agreement and soon found the decision rewarding insofar as it diverted his attention away from his somber thoughts. There was much to see, all of it interesting from one angle or another; the immediate area boasted no less than three extensive Sov laboratory complexes, one devoted to genetic studies, another to biochem, and the third full of an array of optical computing experiments—probably part of some long-term AI research project. Many of the RD workers wore lab coats and carried clipboards, meticulously cataloging every notable feature imaginable with the patient diligence of archaeologists; if Derek hadn't known what they were doing, he might have believed some of the Sov science still extant and manned by the RD whitecoats. In other places, excavation teams blasted neat holes into some of still sealed-off areas, using precision sonic devices for both preparation and execution. Worker and server droids buzzed through the corridors, carrying supplies and necessities, and in one section of the biochem complex, technicians directed a miniature robotics system in exploring the more dangerous rooms.

Derek particularly watched the workers. Tired, nervously active eyes and drooping shoulders betrayed the stress they were under, spoiling what otherwise appeared a model operation. Whenever they passed men and women in isolated locations they were greeted with looks first of alarm, then with relieved smiles—he sensed a pervasive atmosphere of paranoia everywhere they went; nobody seemed very much at ease, even around the security posts sprinkled here and there along the more prominent corridors—and in the places Holly had marked on her navigation display. They saw nothing at the other posts as prominent as the sealed crack in the first to hint at the existence of the unmapped tunnels, but the confirmation of Holly's suspicion they'd find more marines implied Paul Kramer was definitely trying to restrict access to the mysterious areas on his map. His reasons why, however, remained potentially broad, at least the way Derek saw it. The most admirable possibility was that Paul was protecting his people, keeping them away from areas he suspected or knew were related to at least some of the disappearances—that made Derek realize there still had to be more; these efforts had really done nothing to halt the events, which in fact were occurring ever more frequently. The placements of marines could also serve another purpose within the context of Linda's desertion theory—if people were somehow going renegade and deserting via the tunnels, the marines effectively shut them off and some of the officers probably had orders to expect deserters trying to get back in.

When they finally left the area, Derek voiced aloud the thought that the desertion theory had some strong grounding if the mysterious tunnels actually existed.

"I don't like it," Holly said. "It doesn't even begin to explain everything."

"You're not being critical," he told her. "You don't like it because it's a simple, mundane explanation of what's been happening. It makes all your fantastic theories absurd."

"What about Sheila Lorenz, Derek? She greeted you *after* she was missing, and she appeared to you as Linda!"

"So adjust the time of her disappearance ahead a few hours, and blame what I saw on the viaduct drug."

"And the CIS memo recommending your death?"

"A practical joke—maybe planted by Paul or Linda to scare me away, keep me off their turf."

"Lorenz's security authorization to pick you up?"

"Another false lead planted by Paul to keep us guessing. Hell, it's even possible they faked her disappearance—she may be alive and well and chuckling at us right alongside them. And you can chalk up the computer malfunction in the viaduct to their meddling as well; between them, they've got enough authority *in the system* to do just about anything we can."

Holly gave him a troubled glance and sighed. "At least I know now you're thinking. . . . Do you actually believe all that?"

"I'm not sure," he answered. "It's as likely as anything else we've supposed and has the added benefit of plausibility to its credit—I find that particularly refreshing at the moment."

"Except the disappearances haven't stopped, Derek. Except that these tunnels, if they exist, *aren't right*, not if the geoscan missed them."

"Maybe they're shielded."

Holly frowned again and detached her comm device from her belt. "Juliet!" she commanded. "Get a new geoscan of the Moscow tunnel system and have it thoroughly analyzed and accuracy-graded by the best specialist available."

"That may take some time, Dr. Linn," the computer answered.

"Why's that?"

"The geosynchronous satellite that did the original scan is a nondedicated asset; there is a three-day wait in its queue for work submitted at your authorization level."

"Then get my authority boosted—contact the systems at HQ, and if that doesn't work, have Secretary Collier handle it personally. I want the work completed and ready for my review within four hours."

"I will try."

"Thank you, Juliet," Holly said. When she'd killed the link, she let out a short laugh. "I just thanked a computer, didn't I? She's so advanced I keep forgetting she's not hu-

man. Actually, I think I want to forget—did you know the
psychs have a term for that? Techno-empathy—it used to
be an isolated problem among the less educated, but it's
spread almost exponentially since the war.''

Derek nodded; more than a few people talked to and
about their home systems, or systems in their vehicles or
elsewhere as if they were pets or members of the family,
as if their software was alive instead of some abstract, complex organization of ones and zeros. A memory surfaced
from a few years back—there'd been a landmark court case
between an eccentric vidstar and the state of Pennsylvania.
The man had commissioned an advanced android, tried to
marry it, and eventually sued the state over its refusal to
allow the match. Derek remembered his face clearly from
the vidnews, proclaiming love for the android to all who'd
watch and listen, insisting she was the only one who understood him. What disturbed many who witnessed the
spectacle was not so much that the man obviously believed
what he said, but that his proclamation had a certain reso-
nance—they'd known what he was talking about; he'd just
slipped a bit more deeply into things than most.

''Anyway,'' Holly said, ''we'll give the desertion theory
equal treatment for the time being. Have to wait for that
report though—unless you've got a better idea, I think it's
still time to follow the Sheila Lorenz thing.''

Derek mumbled his acquiescence; he was still thinking
about computers and men—at his apartment in Philadelphia
he had a vintage pet-brain he'd named Alfred—a good,
butlerlike name. He found himself admitting he actually
missed Alfred, a completely irrational emotion in light of
the fact he currently had more AI support at his fingertips
than he could ever imagine using. He wanted to attribute
the feeling to the idea that what he really missed was home,
and Alfred only by extension, the computer no more than
a symbol of home—in other words, he missed Alfred the
way he missed his own bed. . . . The only problem there
was that he'd never talked to his bed when he was
lonely. . . .

In Sheila Lorenz's quarters they found all the debris one
might expect to find in the wake of a suddenly departed,

unattached young woman: more than a practical number and variety of clothes, a state-of-the-art collection of cosmetics, thickly decorated walls, and a cupboard with a wide range of nonnutritional, recreational foods. Sheila had had a roommate, a girl named Jean, who arrived midway through their inspection and asked if anything was wrong. Holly told her they were conducting a follow-up to the normal investigation.

"Well I hope you find her," Jean said; before she could leave, Holly asked about Sheila's day-to-day habits. "I didn't really know her that well," the girl said. "She didn't hang around here much, but when she did she mostly slept. But I never saw anything strange, if that's what you're asking—she ate, watched the occasional vid, shot the breeze with me from time to time, but never anything deep."

"Is that all?" Holly asked. "Did she have any boyfriends?"

"I'm sure she did, but I got the impression she liked music more than men; she was always talking about going dancing—how she used to win contests back home. I don't think she was in love; she wasn't secretive, so I'm sure she would have told me. Never had a man in here to my knowledge."

Derek was hardly listening; Jean had already been interviewed by installation security, and he'd read all about it on their journey down to the fourth level. Holly wasn't getting anything new. He let her ask her questions and wandered off through the girls' rooms on his own. The one Sheila had slept in was small but comfortably arranged, with her bed against one wall, a vidprojection system opposite, and her clothes overflowing a corner closet. He sat on her bed; on a small stand next to it was a bracelet—a sort of charm bracelet, but designed to hold vidchips; he'd seen the type before; they'd recently become fashionable stateside, made for men as well as women. They had little metal brackets for a handful of standard vidchips, and people usually filled them up with home-shot footage of their families during holidays and on vacations. He'd learned to avoid most people who wore them; the contents of the chips inevitably became a topic of conversation, and since vid equipment was almost always at hand, the result was usually a few hours of Dad making faces at the camera or one little kid pulling another's hair.

While he toyed with Sheila's bracelet, he casually flipped on her vidprojector, and the unexpected result came as shock enough for him to drop the bracelet clattering back on her nightstand. The holofield filled quickly with black, roiling clouds, and Derek fumbled frantically with the equipment to shut it off—the last thing he wanted now was *The Shining Wall*'s weird intoxication muddying his mind. After banishing the clouds, he popped the chip out of the projector and eyed it. It had scared the hell out of him, but now that the room was visually still, he didn't think it much of a surprise. Hadn't Holly told him the vid originated here in Moscow? If so, it would be perfectly ordinary to find any number of people there watching it. He dropped it in his pocket and glanced out the door, wondering if Holly had noticed what had happened; his partner was still talking to Jean—Derek really hoped she hadn't seen it; if he knew anything about her, the mere possibility of the weird piece tying into everything else she had in her head would be too tempting for her to resist.

When Holly finally finished with Sheila's roommate, she suggested they go straight on to The Last Rattle. Derek asked her if she'd learned anything new, and she shook her head in obvious frustration. "And you?" she asked.

"Nothing," he said. "That's another round in favor of the deserters."

"Maybe," she said. She checked in with Juliet on the geoscan; the computer had needed Collier's help, but it had gotten their authority bumped up. The scan was under way now; it would only be another couple of hours before Holly would have everything she'd asked for. "Let's get the pictures first."

"So it's still The Last Rattle?"

"I don't see why not."

"Well," he said thoughtfully, "I hope they have food and something to drink. Your breakfast was wonderful, but it's wearing off."

She looked at him with a momentarily absent expression

before breaking into a broad smile. "Thank you, Derek,"
she said, as if his compliment had brushed all the burdens
of the investigation off her shoulders. He felt it too, though
it was her smile and not his words that improved his spirits;
he'd almost forgotten he'd spent the day in the presence of
a beautiful woman.

The Last Rattle was in a large, dark room with tables
placed on tiers that rose up from a dance floor next to a
small stage; they took a table just above the dance floor
and waited a minute for a server droid to appear; Holly
asked for a chef's salad, and Derek ordered a soybean
steak—apparently the kitchen stocks Holly had tapped that
morning weren't available to everybody as these were the
most ambitious items on the menu. They sipped Scotch
before the food arrived, and Derek asked Holly what she
expected to do now.

"I don't know," she said, looking around. They shared
the place with about thirty other people, most sitting at the
tables, a few on the dance floor moving slowly to a low-
volume electronic pulse. There was nobody on stage, and
nothing particularly unusual happening. "This place must
be driven by shifts—I don't suppose normal day-night patterns mean much down here."

"They don't," he agreed. "Looks like it may be picking
up, though." He indicated the entrance; a group of three
men and four women had just entered and were looking for
a table.

"Let's just relax," she said. "It's been a long day, and
half the point of coming here is to wind it down a little.
As for the rest of it, I guess we just watch. We don't have
a clue as to who to talk to or what to ask regarding Sheila
Lorenz yet."

"Depends on what you're looking for—you might learn
a lot from some of these men if you're wanting to compile
the sexual exploits of a dance-crazed debutante," he said,
a little distracted. Someone had activated a light show on
the stage; he wondered if the entertainment was about to
come on.

"That was a mean thing to say, Derek!" Holly protested.

"I'm sorry," he said, looking back at her. She *was* right, of course. "I was just being sarcastic. Seems a little silly we bothered to come here in retrospect; I think I expected secret societies, orgies, or maybe even blood sacrifice the way Jamie Parsons talked about this place."

Holly giggled, almost choking on her drink. "You know," she said, wiping at her lips with her napkin, "so did I! It's hard not to think you're going to discover the worst every time you turn around. It's really quite pleasant here."

"I'm not arguing," he said. Even the whiskey was passable; he took a couple of sips, letting the liquid slip slowly over his tongue while he watched the stage. The lights there began to grow more coherent, then they suddenly coalesced into a holographic image of a head—a sort of animated caricature, in fact, of Paul Kramer's head. Derek laughed, directing Holly's attention to the stage. "I think that's why Jamie wanted us to come out of uniform."

She nodded, watching the disembodied hologram; its lips were twitching, and it began to speak. "No danger," it said. "My f-f-fel-fel-fellow workers, you are under no d-d-danger-danger." Someone had taken one of Paul's announcements, inserted some fast, cut-style editing, and put it to this computer-generated caricature. The head repeated the same lines over and over again, its voice growing a little faster and a little higher in pitch for each repetition, and snatches of frantic drumming came in from the background, further accelerating the rhythm and beat. Derek looked around; everybody in the bar was watching the stage, some of them laughing at the caricature of their boss, but most of them chanting along with the words and pounding their fists in the air in time, as if they intimately knew the twisted rhythms, and their interaction with the vid had taken on aspects of ritual. When the piece neared its dizzying conclusion, the head exploded in a shower of sickly green ooze, and the drums went through a clattering finale that eventually gave way to the constant, kick drum beat of an aggressive, fast-paced tune Derek remembered being popular a few years before. People laughed and cheered as the vid ended, then flooded onto the dance floor for the new song; on the stage the green ooze settled into holographic cracks, and the random light show it had replaced returned.

Derek was laughing along with everybody else. "If I know Paul, seeing that might actually *make* him explode!" When he looked back to Holly, though, her expression was pensive. The server droid came with their food then, and they began to eat in silence.

"I do have one thought," Holly finally said as she neared the end of her meal. "I'd like to know who put that together. Remember *The Shining Wall?*"

"Yeah," he said hesitantly. He knew where she was going before she spelled it out, and he was briefly struck by a feeling of guilt for concealing the vidchip from Sheila's bedroom. "I've been waiting for you to bring that back up," he added without enthusiasm.

"It could be important," she said. "The systems traced its origins here, but the department isn't aware of exactly where or by whom it was made. Maybe the people who did that to Paul made it, or know who did. I know it doesn't sound very relevant, but it would be useful to get the mystery out of the way."

"Holly," Derek sighed. "It *isn't* relevant. It's somebody's idea of art and entertainment, and if it has meditative or unsettling qualities, then all that means is the artist was good at getting what he wanted. It's a goddamned *vid*—an illusion, not real!"

"I know," she said, but her concession made her look so defeated Derek almost told her about Sheila's vidchip copy—he would have if he hadn't already known how she'd react. He was tired of scouting for flimsy, irrelevant leads—not while they had substantial problems such as Paul's mysterious tunnels to explore. Instead of disclosing what he'd found, he gently took Holly's hand and suggested they have a couple more whiskeys. After that they could get back to Juliet and see what had come out of the geoscan, which, he reminded her, had been her idea. She agreed, and little else happened until they finished their after dinner drinks and left The Last Rattle.

Back in the t-bug, Derek began to feel the effects of the

four whiskeys he'd consumed; his head was light, and all the tension had fallen out of his arms and legs—his movements felt slightly liquid. He wasn't drunk, but he knew it wouldn't take much more to get there if that was what he wanted. Holly hadn't drunk as much, but she did show signs of an enhanced sensitivity to humor; when she sat next to him, he made a funny face at her, and she burst out in laughter.

"Admit it," she said once they were under way.

"Admit what?"

"That I'm not such a bad partner. That I'm not conspiring with Linda to destroy you, and that, in fact, you enjoy my company very much."

"Right on all points," he said, laughing. "Actually, you're a great partner. With a few exceptions, I could almost hand the whole thing over to you and consider this a vacation, maybe go up to the surface and try to get a tan under the Russian sun."

"I don't think you'd be very successful," she came back.

Derek didn't answer; he was happy just to watch her—she seemed to take particular pleasure in operating the t-bug, giggling as they rounded each curve like a child operating a bumper-hover at an amusement park. He was watching her face, the way her lips moved when she smiled, when the unexpected happened: As they banked onto the upward ramp leading from the third level to the second, a powerful, subsonic shudder rippled up from below, the walls and floor of the tunnel shaking violently. Holly lost control of the hovercraft, and it skidded up one wall and bounced off the ceiling, then the floor, finally executing a stabilizing horizontal flip before leveling back into its course. Derek was thrown jerkily from side to side, and though the t-bug's shielding over the passenger area kept them both in their seats, during the horizontal flip his head cracked hard against Holly's knee, and he knew a brief moment of intense pain before losing consciousness.

XXVIII

O<small>RFEI BOLTED UPRIGHT; THE SHOCK OF</small> D<small>EREK'S INJURY</small>
left a numbing, pulsing pain lingering at his temples. He
reached for Aresh, but she'd left the bed; after a moment
of listening he separated the nearby sound of her voice from
the chaotic noise within him and moved toward it. He
pushed back the bed's curtains and discovered her talking
to Keriktik.

"—but I swear I never saw him until two days ago,"
she was saying, her back to him.

"My creator has awakened," Keriktik pointed out, looking up at Orfei.

Aresh turned; she hadn't bothered to dress, and the sight
of her wiped away the last of the pain in his head. "Orfei!"
she said excitedly, moving toward him. "You didn't tell
me you created Keriktik!"

"Only technically."

"Lord He-who-knows wants to speak with you about
Derek Soul," she told him more seriously.

"But—" Orfei said. "Did you tell him about it?"

"No," she said, lowering her eyes. "He is like a god,
Orfei, and this is his house. Remember when you woke up

171

and told me what you dreamed? I think he learned then. Since I've been awake, he asked me about it; he is very interested in what you told me—he says it might change everything.''

He reached out and caressed her hair. ''It's okay,'' he said. ''He scares me as well. He says this is the future.''

''Have you looked at the sky?'' she asked in a tense whisper.

''What do you mean?'' he replied softly, though if what she'd said about their host was true, he doubted the volume of their speech made any difference.

''I don't think the sun sets, Orfei! It marks the night by growing dim, and no stars come out—it's not natural!''

He looked at her, searching her eyes. In his entire life, he'd spent only the one night on the surface, under the true starry brilliance of the universe, but he knew exactly what she felt. How could he begin to make her truly understand what he suspected Lysis and Clystra had done? ''I know,'' he finally said. He kissed her forehead and fell back on their bed, closing his mind and searching for Soul—all he could find was the oblivion of Soul's unconsciousness. When the attempt failed, he got up to dress and told Aresh they might as well go along with things for the moment, unless she had a better idea, which she unfortunately did not.

They found Lord He-who-knows in the gardens behind his house—under a sunny gazebo. The rose-colored automaton brought them a liquid to drink out of crystal cups; Orfei had no idea what it was, but it tasted little different than lightly sugared, carbonated water. ''Well,'' He-who-knows greeted them happily, ''Keriktik has told me you spoke in your day with Goliath! That is a long-postulated hypothesis I would very much like to confirm.''

''He was an ordinary part of life,'' Orfei said. ''The computer at the heart of Novyraj—no different really than the small systems the ancient surface societies had in their lives.''

''I must disagree,'' Lord He-who-knows argued. ''You are right that Goliath was the heart of Novyraj, as he is now the heart of the gateworlds, but you are wrong to think him a computer—he is far more than that, I'm afraid. Goliath is alive.''

"That's not something I would know," Orfei said, though the words came out in stutters; the mind-bytes in his head were buzzing and coming to life, but they weren't showing him anything.

"Are you not stable?" Lord He-who-knows asked from a distance.

Orfei shook his head from side to side until the mind-bytes went still. "It's the mind-bytes," he told his host. "Aresh said you know of them—do I need to explain?"

"Well," Lord He-who-knows said with satisfaction, "you are proving my point. These mental disturbances of yours—your visions of the man who built Novyraj—they come from what you call mind-bytes, correct? And did Goliath not insert them into your mind?"

Orfei nodded. "As I understand it."

"You are the recipient of an unprecedented gift, Orfei of Novyraj. In the civilized gateworlds, you are already revered for *The Eagle Unleashed*, but I must tell you the learned have long debated your actual worth, and I've been at times among your detractors. Nevertheless you are a legend come to life; I have digested the events you related to your mate and must now believe the following: Foremost, you are who you say you are; furthermore, the holographic work of art you titled *Dragon Dance* has significance beyond any previously imagined and was, in fact, the source of the first gateworld; additionally, you have been projected into the future in spite of the principles of temporal flow from a precise and compellingly significant point in time, that being the temporal junction that witnessed the birth of the gateworlds which, in more colorful language, might be called the initial mutation on the road to modern reality. I am confirming, in other words, much of the conjecture you presented to Aresh. Does this please you?"

"I guess so," he answered uncertainly. Somehow, Lord He-who-knows had not only addressed concerns he'd posed to Aresh, but some he'd thought confined to his own head.

"I thought you'd approve," his host said happily. "Now, drawing on the premises just stated along with other knowledge I have come to have of reality, I feel I can safely assume that your presence here is meaningful—what is meant to be. Keriktik may well have been right when he suggested this was your natural future.''

The dragon squawked his pleasure. "May I inform the Lady Cassandra of your statement? She has formally requested immediate notification should you rescind your official ban on temporal manipulation.''

"Well,'' said Lord He-who-knows, "I don't think that is yet wise. We must first solve the problems of our visitor from the past before I'll feel ready to think that issue through.'' He turned to Orfei. "You, my friend, have been sent here by Goliath. Do you have any idea why?''

"No.''

"Then I think you must ask him. You must make a journey through the gateworlds, find the entity that cannot be found, and inquire as to your purpose. This is the only logical course available, but if you don't mind, I would first like to observe you in your visions. What do Goliath's proxies show you now?''

"Proxies?''

"The mind-bytes,'' Lord He-who-knows said. "What are they showing you?''

"Nothing. Before I woke up, Soul was injured—when I search for him I find only darkness.''

"Well,'' the other man said thoughtfully. "Perhaps I can help you resume your visions. Will you allow it?''

Orfei glanced at Aresh; the Nuzi girl's eyes darted nervously between the two men. "Will it hurt him?'' she asked.

"I expect not. It may not work—I must, however, lightly touch his mind.''

Orfei looked to Aresh again, then to his host. After a moment, he acquiesced and nodded—he couldn't think of anything else to do; and, were he truthful, the state of Derek Soul concerned him—nothing would make sense to him if the man had actually died.

"Very well,'' Lord He-who-knows said. He reached out for Orfei, and his hand grew large, in much the same way as had his mouth when he'd imposed on Orfei the image of the snakes. Orfei felt the fingers touch him, then his mind spiraled away into darkness, bouncing off the oblivion that was Soul before coming again to life, this time in a different form.

XXIX

"GET YOUR BOSS!" HOLLY COMMANDED THE MARINE who stood watch outside their quarters; Lieutenant Morris was at her side within seconds. "What the hell was that?"

"Earthquake, ma'am. Five-point-something—it wasn't too bad here, but I gather some of the lower areas got rocked pretty good." He turned to the one who'd summoned him. "Get Simpson and Turner and carry Dr. Soul to his room—*move!*"

"Be careful!" Holly told them. "The left side of his head especially—he cracked it against my knee." Now that she was standing with her weight on that leg, she grew even more concerned; if Derek's head felt anything like her knee. . . . She could imagine the headlines: *Human Passengers Collide in Tunnel Accident—Hovercraft Emerges Unscathed.* "Any casualty reports?" she asked Morris as his men gingerly lifted Derek free of the t-bug.

"About ten injured so far—it's all still coming in through the security channels. I think a couple guys died when some old Sov equipment collapsed on them on level three, but haven't heard confirmation of that, only the initial report."

Holly hated to feel relieved, but she did; she'd been afraid of serious cave-ins—casualties in the hundreds or thousands. "Let's get Derek inside," she said. As they passed through the lounge, she asked Juliet for a full seismic analysis of the event, then she helped the marines ease Derek onto his bed. Thankfully, nobody else had commandeered his biomonitoring system; it had retracted into a corner of the ceiling. She pulled it down and positioned it over the bed. "You can leave now," she told Morris. "Keep on top of the damage reports."

"Yes, ma'am," the marine said, taking his men and leaving quietly.

Holly tried to arrange Derek's head comfortably on his pillow, turning it to the left. He already had a huge bruise around his temple. She clicked on the biosystem, and it quickly confirmed her suspicion of concussion, though she was greatly relieved it reported nothing more. Still, tears pooled in her eyes; she sat at his side and ran her fingers over his forehead, brushing the hair off his sweating skin. "We just can't keep you on your feet, can we?" she said. Part of her sorrow was selfish, but realizing that only made matters worse; she'd been sure the night would have brought them together—God knows she needed him; there was a part of her that had wanted to take him since the moment they'd met. Maybe it had something to do with a maternal desire to heal the open wounds he still bore from his marriage, or maybe it was something else—she didn't know, but couldn't, at any rate, help the way she felt.

It was hard for her to get up, but in the end she managed, leaving the biosystem to do its work. According to the machine's analysis it could have Derek on his feet in sixteen to twenty hours, but until then she'd be on her own. She went back to the lounge and slumped in her chair next to Juliet. "I want a direct vidconnect to Linda Kramer," she said after a long moment of silence. "She's got some kind of code barrier up to keep out unwanted calls—break it."

"That won't be necessary, Dr. Linn," the computer said. "She's sent you an authorized code."

"Awful nice of her," Holly muttered.

"Excuse me?"

"Nothing, Juliet. Get me that vidconnect."

"Yes, Holly," came Linda's voice as her hologram coalesced.

"Sorry to bother you, Linda. Just wondering what the hell happened—my guy tells me it was an earthquake."

"As best as we know," the other woman said wearily, "that's correct."

"Any history of seismic activity around here?"

"None." Linda rubbed her eyes; Holly had to credit her for monitoring the situation from her office—she ought to be in bed; she looked ready to collapse. "There must be something wrong with the initial reports, though; they put the epicenter at the edge of the third level, nowhere near a known fault line."

"There's no chance it was explosives?"

Linda laughed. "Wishful thinking, dear? Have you any idea of the force required to generate what we just felt?"

"I'm not a geologist," Holly said, trying not to sound irritated—for all she knew, she'd deserved Linda's sarcasm. "I've got more to ask you when you've got a moment."

"I expected you would," Linda said. "Save it, okay? I'm not trying to put you off, but there's a lot happening right now. Paul's down on level four trying to contain the situation, and he'll be mad as hell if I don't get back to him soon."

"I understand," Holly said. She told Juliet to drop vidconnect, and the holofield immediately twisted and expanded, Linda replaced by Collier behind his desk, glaring at her from midair. The secretary's sudden appearance made her bolt upright in her seat. "Sir, I—"

"What the hell's going on there, Holly?"

"Earthquake, sir. Derek's been hurt."

"*Shit!*" Collier said, though the anger in his eyes quickly gave way to concern. "Is it serious?"

"Concussion—he'll be back at it in a day or so."

"I guess that's okay then." He sighed. "We got these damned satellite reports of a geological disturbance and I didn't know what to think!"

"I guess earthquakes happen, sir. Rather inconvenient, but I don't know what else to say."

"Any major damage?"

"Not that I've heard. A few injuries—some dead, but not many. Unless a geological analysis tells you differently, I don't think you've much to worry about from a policy side."

"That's good," he said, looking relieved. "Well, how's the investigation going? Why the hell did you ask Juliet to have me authorize a priority one geoscan?"

"Paul Kramer seems to think he has tunnels not on the master map."

"Does he?"

"I don't know—do we have that analysis yet, Juliet?"

"Not yet, Dr. Linn. I project completion twenty minutes from now."

"That's about all I can tell you, sir," Holly told Collier. "We're just getting into this. I'll try to do what I can on my own, but I can't promise much until Derek's back in action."

"Well you just be careful. If anything major comes to light—and I mean *anything*—you get back to me!"

"I will, sir."

"Is that all?"

"Yes, sir."

Collier smiled. "Keep your chin up, girl," he said. "I've got a lot of faith in you."

"Thank you," she said. The secretary faded into mist, and she was finally left to her thoughts in silence. She tried to picture Derek again, making that funny face at her in the t-bug, but it only made her more depressed. In the end, she decided to get back to work—if she could sink deeply enough into it, the next day might perhaps pass more quickly. Work a little, she thought, *then get some sleep.* . . . Now that events had slowed, the clouds planted in her mind by the whiskey began to come back—ghosts of inebriation, too weak to make her giggle, but strong enough to make themselves remembered. "So what have we got, Juliet?" she asked in a tired voice.

"I have the report you requested this morning," the computer said.

"What report?" she asked, though she remembered as she asked the question.

"About Derek. You wanted an analysis of the records of his tour here—all references anywhere in the system."

"Right," she said. "Let's have it then." Juliet's display flattened into two dimensions, giving Holly a menu. Lazily, she paged through the data, amazed at the sheer bulk of it all; Juliet had found everything imaginable, from every command Derek had issued in the course of his job, to an exacting inventory of everything he ate on any given day. She sifted through it all for a while before concentrating on what she'd really wanted—references to Derek in areas of the system other than his own. It had been a hunch, something she'd thought of doing while he'd showered; she'd hoped to find something to shed light on the mysterious CIS memo, maybe evidence that somebody important didn't like him—anything to help get him to take her theories seriously. Juliet hadn't uncovered exactly that, but she had come close—Derek had apparently made some waves; there were several official complaints logged by supervisors of various supply areas, criticizing his to-the-letter oversight practices. She realized he must have been bored if he'd taken his job that seriously. She found another memo, apparently triggered by an independent security subsystem, requesting a thorough background check of Derek's past, and the report returned from the States was full of other instances of maverick behavior and a lot of critical statements by old associates to the effect that he'd been a liberal nutcase as a young man. The stamp on the security report was only days before he'd supposedly found Linda with Paul Kramer and fled Moscow in a fit of heartbreak and despair.

Holly sat back and tried to put it all together. Considering the normal, paranoid security surrounding the installation, a report on Derek like that could well have triggered the garbled memo with which she'd been plagued in Berlin. Whether it might have really been acted upon was another matter, but if Linda had told the truth in insisting she'd never been with Paul before Derek left—implying, therefore, that Derek had been made to believe he'd witnessed his wife's adultery, but that it hadn't actually happened—then it was as if he'd had some benevolent guardian angel looking over his shoulder, hurrying him out of Moscow and out of harm's way after the report was received, then hijacking the subsequent memo resulting from it all. Why? And had the same guardian angel really manipulated the selection systems in Philadelphia to call him back now? Maybe she *was* crazy—she kept thinking that rhetorically, but she could almost believe it was true. . . . Everything she was thinking—it all had to revolve around Derek or the entire exercise was pointless, but now he again was bedridden, and it seemed ridiculous to imagine he'd been brought back to Moscow to get knocked out against her knee. . . .

"I have the geoscan, Dr. Linn," Juliet said, drawing Holly back to the present.

"Fine," she said.

Juliet brought up the display, and Holly peered into the area between the third and fourth levels where Paul's map had shown tunnels. In the new map, there were a few light spots in the area, most of them shaded pink. "What do the colorations signify?"

"Aberrations, according to the analysts."

"Why aberrations?"

"The report says, 'Light density, excessive to indicate open space—probable satellite error.' "

"Any mention of possible shielding in that area—something to cause the satellite problems?"

"No chance of it, according to the analyst. Shielding would show as impenetrable space, as dense or denser than the surrounding rock—the substratum here is all smooth material."

"Thank you," Holly said. "You can kill the display." She was getting tired—too tired to reliably speculate on what the analyst meant, what the mysterious tunnels meant. *Excessive density to indicate open space?*

"Your other report is ready, Dr. Linn," Juliet said.

"What report?" Was she repeating herself?

"The seismic analysis."

"All right," she said. "Give me a visual."

Juliet regenerated the subterranean map. "The equations are functions over time—the total event occurred within a fifteen-second bracket." Thin blue lines representing shock waves began rolling through the display, emanating from roughly the vicinity of Paul's tunnels, perhaps a couple of hundred yards farther out near the perimeter—it was just as Linda had told her. "Is this an independent study?" Holly asked. "No relation to data provided to local administration?"

"My processing and authority are independent; however, the data may be the same. The output of seismic recording equipment is both limited and available to all."

"So you've confirmed the apparent epicenter?"

"Confirmed and verified—the data is anomalous with respect to the old geoscans, but a postevent survey just conducted on Philadelphia's orders shows the formation of a new fault line running perpendicular to the vertical axis of the epicenter, a ground shift of several inches. The geoscan you requested this afternoon has also been reevaluated for subsurface stress by the Philadelphia systems."

"And?"

"Minute pre-event indicators. Earthquake forecasting remains an art; there are too many relevant factors ruled by forces far beneath the planetary crust, and our satellite imaging systems are limited to a quarter mile penetration depth."

"So this was just an inconvenient geological event?"

"That's a reasonable assumption in light of the data."

Holly shook her head; it sounded too simple—she really was getting tired. She imagined her brain hurt, but in spite of her exhaustion, the influx of new information struggled to find the light of her attention, as if she'd pushed herself to think for so long and so hard that the analytical mechanisms she'd triggered refused to shut down. What were the odds that a natural event such as an earthquake might occur in the wake of so many unnatural events as she'd been pondering? Or did she have it backward—what worry should an earthquake have for the troubles of men? To the

biblical minded, the shaking earth was the hand of God.
. . . She wished terribly for Derek to wake up and help her,
tell her he was okay, that it was only a little bump—wasn't
that ironic? In his presence that day she'd felt free to let
her mind fly, to reach into the impossible and pull out
something that made sense; it didn't matter if he thought
her a little crazy—for a while, she really hadn't been sure
if he did—it only mattered that he'd been an anchor, a
receptacle for her imagination. Maybe the problem was that
she'd told him, babbled on about him being the heart of it,
passionately spilling out every wild thought she could bring
to bear on the subject and then some. It was as if in the
process of externalization she'd given herself irrevocably
to him, and her own validity somehow depended on the
consequences. She found it hard to remember how he'd
been in Berlin—open at times, at others cold and unreach-
able; they'd had a new start here, and she'd let it carry her
away. They'd made a lot of progress, but now he was gone,
and the information kept coming. . . . How was she going
to manage it? "Juliet," she finally said, rising wearily to
her feet. "Can you get me any music?"

"I can override your standard entertainment programs, if
that's what you wish. What would you like to hear?"

"Relax me," she said. "If I hear a drum, you're fired."
She stumbled in the direction of her room, glad when a
slowly pulsating mix of spacey, repeating guitar and electronic textures quickly filled the air, glad that Juliet had
been programmed levels above most systems she'd dealt
with, ones that could rarely if ever locate a musical piece
without having it spelled out by artist and title. This was
something she'd never heard; there were little scratchy
sounds in it that seemed to synch up with the movement
of her feet.

She stopped in her bathroom to wash her face. When she
looked up in the mirror, she paused. She'd always been
pleased with her nose, but suddenly it looked too small. . . .
After looking at Derek all day, the shock of her own image
was like a jolt back to the past. Was this how he saw her?
Red cheeks and dirty green eyes? Her lips gone dry and
bare? Her black hair cut short, wind-whipped by the tunnels

into an unruly, tangled mass? She took a brush to it, but it caught just below her left ear, yanking violently at her scalp; she put down the brush and closed her eyes, suddenly seeing Derek's face again, the way he'd cautiously raised an eyebrow at each unexpected twist in her logic—he wouldn't have known it, but he'd somehow given her ideas real life. Before—when he'd still been recovering from the viaduct trip—she'd managed well enough on her own, but then she supposed it had been out of fear; she'd pushed herself to work and think if only to avoid the fact she'd suddenly been plunged into what could well turn out to be a gruesome example of man's inhumanity to man. Every time she turned around, something in the back of her mind expected to find a bloodless, mutilated body, then another, and on and on until all fifty-odd of them were piled in a mound before her. As the image surfaced, she shuddered; she desperately wanted that *not* to be the truth of it. Maybe that was why she clung so to Derek now. Maybe that was why the thoughts she had came to her at all, but *dammit*, she thought, *they all fit!* Could she trust her intuition? Derek had done a passable job of debunking everything in the t-bug on the way to Sheila Lorenz's quarters. If he meant so much, why couldn't she take that seriously? The desertion theory could conceivably have some merit, but what bothered her most about it was where they were—what person of sound mind would go absent in an underground complex beneath a radioactive wasteland? Where would he go? What would he eat, drink? Those questions didn't pass the test.

As she made her way to her bed, the new information tugged at her again, the earthquake and the *excessive density* of Paul Kramer's tunnels. She brushed the questions aside; she *would* get some sleep. Perhaps then she'd have a sharp enough mind to readdress everything. She crawled beneath the covers and let the mattress absorb her; Juliet's music tugged at the tangled morass in her mind, pulling it out and massaging it before putting it back. Holly drifted into the twilight realm between sleep and awareness, the darkness of her room growing misty and textured, like an old-fashioned, matte-finished photograph. After a time she thought she heard voices in the shadows, the lilting voices of children. Fuzzy lights danced at the edges of her vision; she could still hear Juliet's music, the guitar melted into a bass, then a breathy flute or a trumpet—maybe a conch shell—blossomed out from the amorphous sea of sound. She thought to close her eyes, but when she realized they were already closed, she opened them. Before her, awash in shadows, stood Derek's little girl, blue eyes glowing faintly with a light of their own.

"Oh, my—" She struggled to push herself up on one elbow. The girl's gaze was like an open wound, her eyes like spears that cut through the sleep in Holly's mind and set it on fire. She reached out and touched the girl's arm; her flesh was warm and real. "What do you want?" she asked.

The girl backed out of reach and said nothing, just looked at her. Holly sat up, taking her eyes off her visitor for only a moment, but when she looked back, the girl was gone. "Jesus Christ!" she whispered; a cold, tingling sensation still ran up and down her spine. "Juliet!" she called out. "Get Lieutenant Morris—quick!" She jumped out of bed, dressed quickly, and met the marine in the lounge. "Did you let somebody in here?" she asked.

"No, ma'am," he said, looking puzzled.

"Nothing strange—I mean, your men haven't logged anything unusual in the last half hour?"

"I can check," he said, "but I doubt it. They have very strict orders."

She looked down at her feet; they were bare, and somehow in the darkness she'd chosen her uniform—to the marine she must have been an appalling sight.

"Is there something wrong, ma'am?" Morris asked.

"I don't know," she said hesitantly. "Put your men on alert or whatever it's called. Keep their eyes open."

"I'll double the watch, ma'am," he said. When he left, Holly checked on Derek. The biosystem had lowered to mere inches over his face, one of its extensors extending down to his bruise. Other than that, all was normal. She sighed and closed his door, slumping again in her chair by Juliet. Things were getting too weird. . . . Had she dreamed that little girl? It had been like Derek reaching across the space between them and jolting her awake. Whatever it was it had worked—she sure as hell wasn't getting back to sleep anytime soon.

Work, she thought. Maybe she could exhaust herself fully; she desperately needed sleep. . . . Idly, she put Juliet in manual mode and shuffled absently through the day's data, flipping the various 3-D displays on and off, pulling up the file on Sheila Lorenz, and the file on Derek. It was then she suddenly remembered the one report in Linda Kramer's files, on Thomas Liebowicz and Shane Crawley. Liebowicz had been interviewed by Paul, then disappeared. That was—*fishy* was the only word. . . .

"Juliet," she said, clicking the computer out of manual. "This stuff you got on Derek—you know, the stuff on his eating habits, what vids he watched, et cetera?"

"Yes, Dr. Linn."

"Can you compile the same data on Thomas Liebowicz?"

"Is that a command?"

"Yes."

"I will have it for you shortly," the computer said.

"Thank you."

She wasn't really sure what she was after; parts of her mind were moving too fast—she just had a hunch.

"Compilation completed," Juliet said.

"Okay—" Now, what exactly was it she was trying to do. . . . "Uh—tabulate it," she said. "Let's assume Liebowicz was alive—not disappeared, I mean—for a period of time extending from his reported disappearance to possibly now or any moment in between. Scan all the logs of the supply and entertainment systems—try to pinpoint specific physical locales where normal requests for sustenance or anything else match the patterns established by Liebowicz you've just tabulated."

"You are not requesting an exacting analysis, Dr. Linn. Any number of other individuals may—"

"We'll sort that out later," Holly said, interrupting the machine. "Just try it. Let's see what we get, okay?"

"Understood," Juliet replied.

Holly sat back to wait. It was a terrible long shot—Maybe it had been the look in Paul Kramer's eyes when he'd smugly brushed her off; it hurt to ponder the psychology of the man, but if she assumed he took his desertion theory seriously, and Tom Liebowicz was his one main lead . . . She began to grow sure Liebowicz's disappearance had been engineered, that he'd probably not talked to anybody else after talking with Paul. The story about the tunnel had been withheld, absent from both his and Crawley's files. If it really was true, then the bastard had covered it up and removed Liebowicz to keep him from talking to anybody else. Holly could only hope for Linda's sake that Paul hadn't become a murderer in the process.

"Survey complete," Juliet said. "Five matches on your request."

"Put 'em up."

Once again, the hologram of the tunnels sprang up in Juliet's holofield, five red dots distributed through the occupied areas at random. Holly focused immediately on one on the second level, highlighting it with her joystick. "Where exactly is this?"

"The old guest quarters behind the command post."

"Old?"

"They've been inactive for months, downgraded after the quarters in this area were completed."

Goddamn! Holly thought. She'd been right—"What are the dates?" Juliet told her; the first was a couple of days after Liebowicz had reportedly disappeared, the most recent was today—he was alive! she thought excitedly. "Can I get in there—without going through Linda's work area?"

"The access is through the local headquarters, guarded by independently programmed identification systems—you would not be allowed to pass such security."

"There's got to be another way! What's this thin line?" She pointed at what looked like a ridge that wrapped around the side of the headquarters complex toward the red dot.

"A service tunnel, for droids."

Holly smiled—that would be large enough. "And the security there?"

"Primarily electronic handshake, but there are keypads for human overrides."

"That's all?"

"No other consumers of power as of your last scan."

Holly's smile turned into a chuckle. Trust Paul to think like an upper-class bureaucrat; he'd probably installed traps capable of killing any man who tried to get to Liebowicz via the obvious route, but he hadn't thought of droids, or if he had, he'd thought them appliances, and their tunnel perhaps some magic doorway through which no human could conceivably pass. . . . "I'll go that way," she told Juliet.

"Then you will require the keypad values?"

"Yes," she said. "Get that, and in the meantime run that same check on *everybody* else reported missing. Give me an active display; I want to see the distribution as you obtain it."

"I have initiated processing, Dr. Linn."

"Thank you, Juliet." She watched as new dots filled the hologram, one by one, each a different color—shaded to correspond to the individual files, Holly assumed. At first, she avidly watched the area where they'd pinpointed Liebowicz, but his red mark remained solitary and isolated from the others. So much for having cracked the puzzle entirely. . . . Now what was she going to do? With Paul busy managing the aftermath of the quake, this could be her best chance—maybe her only chance—to get to Tom Liebowicz covertly. *But how*? *Without Derek?* She thought of taking Morris, but that might only draw unwanted attention, and besides, if she could get to Liebowicz and get him out, she'd need a second t-bug, and the whole operation would likely end up a logistical mess. No, it was best to go alone, and quickly.

While Juliet continued to mark the hologram, Holly opened an audio message to Derek, just in case. Trying to keep her voice steady, she explained everything that had happened, starting with the earthquake and the geoscans, ending with the strategy she'd employed to find Paul's—prisoner? What other way might she describe it? She apologized to Derek for leaving him, then started to feel slightly silly—after all, she planned on getting out and back in a half hour. She suddenly felt as if she should go dressed in black like—who was that in the old vids? Modesty Blaise? "Well, Derek darling," she said, finishing up the message. May as well play up the drama. . . . "I'm leaving now. If you're hearing this, something must have gone horribly wrong."

Juliet announced the end of her processing; Liebowicz's dot remained alone, and the hologram otherwise resembled a double-banded, multicolored Milky Way across the second and third levels—easy to explain, Holly guessed; she'd probably been lucky Liebowicz's profile had produced only five dots, and not a hundred. "Unless I rescind the order," she told the computer, "give that message to Derek as soon as he is awake and alone."

"Understood, Dr. Linn."

She put on shoes and straightened out her uniform, stopping only briefly to talk to Morris on her way out. "Guard him with your life," she told the marine, then she left.

Near the command post, Holly struggled with second thoughts. Other than the occasional medical droid careening around the curves, the tunnels were unnaturally quiet, like an eerie calm over the bedlam one would certainly find on the levels below. She should have brought Morris—it wasn't as if it seemed likely they'd be seen. She almost turned back to get him, then laughed at herself. There was nobody in the tunnels—wasn't that what she wanted? What was she afraid of?

She guided the t-bug to the droid access tunnel and punched her way in with Juliet's codes. She had to tilt her hovercraft up on its side to fit it through the gate, then she powered it down and closed the entrance behind her. *Now* she needed to be careful—the rest of it had to be quiet, on foot. Liebowicz was only a hundred yards or so in. She crept along, through two more doors until her destination was visible at the end of a long, empty hall. Only then did she think how hastily she'd acted—how lucky, in fact, she'd been. She hadn't even given thought to the possibility of Paul using human guards—he hadn't, but she'd been an idiot not to consider it. She reached Liebowicz's room and pushed open the door, finding a two-room suite with an attached kitchen area and a bath. The man she'd come for was asleep on a couch. *Piece of cake!* she thought happily. ''Tom!'' she whispered. The man groaned and turned over. ''Tom!''

''What—'' He had a haggard look as he sat up—years older than the shot of him in Holly's clipboard. ''Where's Kramer?''

''Did you sleep through the earthquake? He's down below, handling it. I've come to get you out of here.''

''You're kidding.''

''No chance of that—hurry up!''

''Who the hell are you, lady? If you're one of his deserters, you can go the hell back to where you came from— get yourself killed if you want, but leave me out of it. I got a reputation and family back home to worry about!''

''Listen Tom Liebowicz,'' she said angrily. ''I haven't deserted anything! I'm with the goddamned IG, and the best thing you can do for your reputation right now is follow my orders!''

''Yes, ma'am,'' he said uncertainly, rising to his feet. ''Sorry for the misunderstanding, but this ain't been no picnic. Kramer's fucking crazy—you know how he smokes cigars from time to time? The bastard burned holes all over me. . . . Come to me and say, 'Where the hell are they? Who's their leader?' and shit like that. When I finally figured out what he was talking about, I told him what he wanted to hear—thought he was going to kill me otherwise.''

''Let's go, man!'' He'd walked toward her; now she grabbed his arm and pulled him from the room. They'd made it halfway back to the droid tunnel when the main access door opened, and Holly's worst fear became reality. Paul Kramer stepped through; surprised only momentarily, his expression growing quickly enraged. ''Oh, God!'' Holly said in a sinking voice. He was filthy with dirt and grime; for some reason, he still held a shovel tightly in his hands.

Holly felt Liebowicz slip away from her. ''She's crazy,

Mr. Kramer,'' came his voice from behind her. ''She must be one of them.''

Paul snarled and stepped forward. Holly dodged to the side and tried to dash past him, but he brought the shovel around against her arm with a sickening crack; the pain that exploded through her was enough to knock her to the floor. Before she could get up, he yanked her up by the wrist, sending more spears of pain up her battered arm. ''This wasn't smart!'' he seethed through clenched teeth.

''You—'' she could barely force out the word. ''You can't do this, Paul!'' Her head lolled against his chest; everything was spinning in and out of focus.

''Why not?'' he laughed. ''I don't see your goon squad anywhere, do I? Looks like you're all alone!'' He jerked her arm again, pushing her against the corridor wall. She felt his hand against her stomach, moving lower; for a moment she thought he might rape her, but he only grabbed at her belt and tore away her comm device, then he pushed her violently forward, and as she fell to the floor she heard a door slam shut behind her.

The pain came and went, like a physical thing in the silence, a great black hand come down from the air to thump against her arm and shoulder, pound her to the ground until nothing was left but the agony. She'd feel her mind going black, then the pain would ebb—it wouldn't let her pass out, but even when the promising darkness opened its arms to her, a part of her fought it—a part that feared she'd never again wake up.

In the dim light she found herself in an identical suite to Tom's. Looking around, she managed to sit up, wincing as her arm smacked limply on her ribs. She reached around with her good hand and grabbed her other elbow; the break was just above it, her flesh over the bone already growing discolored. Without letting herself think for too long, she pulled the elbow out, screaming as the shattered bone came back into line. With her eyes tightly shut, she rode out the new waves of pain and again defied the darkness. When it finally lessened, she slid across to the door and vainly tried to open it, the effort bringing tears to her eyes. She truly was trapped.

Somehow, Holly made it back across to the couch. She lay on her back, positioning her arm as best she could, trying to think of a way out, but she could barely think of anything. "Computer," she said feebly. "Do I have a computer here?" Her own voice in her ears was one of desperation, a voice she'd never heard in her life except in nightmares.

"Working and active," came an answering voice from the wall, cold, its personality programs either absent or deleted.

"Get me a medical droid—I have a serious injury."

"Request has been queued and awaiting clearance."

Shit! Somewhere, probably quite nearby, Paul Kramer was laughing at her. "I want comm then—vidconnect to Philadelphia."

"External comm is disabled in this location."

"I am Dr. Holly Linn, lieutenant inspector general!"

"Name identification meaningless," the computer replied. "All present here are titled occupant."

She let out a torturous sigh. There had to be *something.* . . . The more time passed, the closer she felt to death— Paul would have to kill her; once he'd thought it over, he'd see he had no other choice. Maybe she should just pass out, make it easy for him and end her pain. The thought grew tempting. . . . She thought of Derek—what a pair they made with him knocked out and her on her way. Maybe Collier would lose his job in the end; some independent authority was bound to question his idea of an investigative team, regardless of selection system recommendations. What were human decision makers for anyway? Paul Kramer was right, this was stupid.

Now she'd never know the answers, never see Derek again. . . . She wished that morning she'd kissed him— maybe that would have changed something. Maybe then they'd have been making love when the earthquake came, the ground shaking with, instead of against them. She thought briefly of Tom Liebowicz, cowering away when Paul attacked instead of fighting and saving them both—

she started to hate, but then pushed the emotion aside; if she was going to die, she'd rather her last thoughts be pleasant ones.

The pain condensed near her elbow, becoming a hot, hard thing. She needed morphine—she needed goddamned medical attention! What had she done to deserve such agony? "Goddamn you, Paul!" she cried. "Let me out of here!"

"Occupant?" the computer asked, its word caring, its tone devoid of color. "May I suggest a vidholo?"

Holly laughed until new tears came to her eyes. "Perfect!" she said, choking. "Just what I need." Through her tears, the room shivered. This was it, she thought—the darkness was opening up to take her. She brushed away her tears, and then Derek's little girl from Berlin—the blond urchin with blue eyes and no tongue—was again before her, standing and staring as she had in her room. Holly smiled at the hallucination. "You again," she whispered.

The little girl waved her hand, and the room's vidprojector came active; she stood in its light, casting a long shadow on the far wall. "Who are you?" Holly asked as the holofield overflowed with smoke and whalesong filled the air, inky black and plaintive, the opium dream of *The Shining Wall* come to tug on her heart. The girl faded into the fog, and after a moment, Holly rose and forgot her pain, the black clouds billowing around her, and the feeling of something in it, unknown and nearby, something watching, grew and swelled like a living thing within her. She thought of her fear, and it went away—the fog was like a cocoon, the watcher omnipotent yet benign—like a god, she thought, his arms the black fog, his bosom the cobblestones beneath her feet. The little girl was gone now, disappeared ahead of her into the darkness. She struggled with her feet, each step forward bringing her nearer the ecstasy of a god's embrace.

On the final step she fell back, the cobblestones sinking beneath her like lilies on the surface of a pool. She caught a brief glimpse of blue sky, then melted into the road.

XXX

ORFEI FELT A TINGLING SHOCK RUN THROUGH HIM, AND Holly was sucked away as Soul had never been. He dived back for her in his mind, but she wasn't there; for a moment, a world of white engulfed him, then the sensations of his own body came rushing back, filled him, and pulled him up. He was on his back, on the grass. Aresh caressed his face, and his head lay in her lap, his pillow the soft cushion of her thigh. "I think he's returned," she said.

"Well," said Lord He-who-knows in a grave voice.

Orfei opened his eyes; the big man sat a short distance away, and Aresh and the dragon, heads together and almost touching, peered down at his face from above. "She's gone."

"Who?" asked Aresh.

"The woman," Lord He-who-knows said. "Holly Linn—Derek Soul's companion. Now that I've seen what Orfei sees, I am certain these events are preconfigured. Do you know anything, holomage, of the mechanics of Goliath's proxies? The mind-bytes?"

Orfei sat up, shaking his head. He could still feel ghostly

remnants of Holly's pain, as if it had been his own arm Paul Kramer had shattered.

"Well," Lord He-who-knows continued, "your mind does not time travel as you might believe. What you see— all that you've seen and what may come—is recorded. Goliath has inserted his proxies into your mind to show you these things. I also believe he has propelled you here, though to what end I can only guess. You, therefore, must seek him out and ask him."

"That's quite improbable," the dragon said flatly.

"Perhaps," the man countered. "But so are the events to which we are presently witness. Some mystics among the Keepers claim Goliath may yet be directly accessed, that a gate-walker with a great deal of luck can find him."

Aresh eyed him skeptically. "I'm unsure how much of this I understand," she said, "but it seems to me that such an idea would have been tested before, if as many years have passed as you claim."

"Dear girl," he said, rather impatiently, "there is no record of a consistently successful gate-walker in the past half million years, and we Keepers have never ceased to consider the problem! I suppose I must explain the architecture of reality: As Keeper, I may establish communication with my counterparts in other gateworlds—they number precisely 7067. However, the precise number of gateworlds themselves is unknown; some estimates, in fact, exceed a million and are still growing as any Keeper has the knowledge to spawn a new world; but let's suppose the ratio is one in one hundred worlds protected by a Keeper— one out of one hundred describable as civilized. Now, the gates themselves are periodic, and the connections they provide nonsymmetrical, meaning once a gate-walker passes through, there is no direct route of return, and if the periods of the two gateworlds are not synchronized, the walker may have to wait from one hour to several weeks for the next opportunity to come. Meanwhile, there is but one chance in a hundred he's found a civilized world, with the possible dangers of the remaining ninety-nine chances too variable to predict. I'll trust you to calculate the probability of a traveler ever returning safely to the world from which he began.''

"One in 706,700,'' the dragon inserted. "Per attempt, and assuming all your figures exact.''

"It is a rare human who is willing to confront the risks,'' Lord He-who-knows said. "Especially when the new world option remains. One has only officially to petition his Keeper, and a new gateworld may be spawned to exacting specifications—this is the only certain way to abandon one world and be assured of a safe haven in the next.''

Just like Novyraj, Orfei thought, but instead of new corridors and rooms, new worlds.

"But you're suggesting Orfei take the risks of a gate-walker?'' Aresh pressed Lord He-who-knows. "You speak of dangers while saying that's what Orfei must do?''

"That's an accurate deduction,'' he told her. "However, we must have faith and trust in Goliath. Your presence here is incomprehensible lest it be his will; therefore, his will may well guide his chosen servant through the gates and beyond if necessary.''

"But what if you're *wrong!*'' she asked in exasperation.

"Impossible.''

"Wait,'' Orfei said, grabbing Aresh's arm. "I will go. If I understand what I've seen through Derek Soul, it is through Goliath that these gateworlds exist. I think Lord He-who-knows is right; if Goliath brought me here, there must be a reason, and if I don't yet know what it is, then I must attempt to learn it. Besides,'' he said, turning to Aresh, "what happens if we simply remain here? What would we do?''

"If you go,'' she said softly, "then so will I.''

"Me, too,'' the dragon chimed in. "I have to—without my dynamic translation capability, my creator will be unable to communicate, even with Aresh.''

"Very well,'' Lord He-who-knows said. "It is decided.''

In the Style Concillate, the gate had a period of nine days, its next appearance due that evening—the time, Orfei recalled, for which Cassandra had traveled back in time, to the ancient mall, in search of music. The people held a festival when the gate appeared—Keriktik called it tradition—so they might greet any gate-walker, or personally dispose of any hapless creature wandering in from an uncivilized world, tasks normally managed automatically by two armed droids that stood guard at all other times.

To reach the gate they again traversed the land in an airboat, flying until the landscape began to go flat, landing when the horizon showed nothing but a white, featureless void.

At the edge of the white, the people of the Style Concillate had begun to gather, hundreds of tall, regal men and women who eyed Orfei and Aresh with a mixture of curiosity and disgust. Were it not for Lord He-who-knows's patronage, Orfei would not have felt safe there. They landed, and others kept coming, arriving in the airboats until Orfei guessed they numbered over a thousand. Droids set up tables with food and drink, while Lady Cassandra directed the erection of a stage. As all this happened, the gate materialized.

Orfei missed seeing the actual event, but after Lord He-who-knows parted the sea of people in his way, he found himself in front of a tall glittering archway, a silvery, shimmering veil in place of a door. Like a curtain, he thought— a liquid curtain of water, or a mirror that absorbed reflections. The gate made a low hum, a warm sound like a purr. Orfei took Aresh's hand and immediately stepped toward it.

"Wait," Lord He-who-knows stopped him. "Eat first. Be prepared." He took them to the tables and let them be. Aresh eyed the food with disdain; it was mostly cakes and gelatinous globs of unknown content; she tasted nothing without letting Orfei go first.

Before they finished, Lady Cassandra came up in a huff and made a scene before the Keeper of the Style Concillate. "I hope you're happy," she told Lord He-who-knows. "If this night goes badly, you'll be to blame!"

"You'll be fine, Cassandra," he told her. "New music isn't everything."

"You owe me!" she said, stomping away.

Lord He-who-knows smiled amusedly at her passage,

then took Orfei, Aresh, and the dragon back to the gate. "She doesn't understand," he said on the way. "Neither do the others. That's why I am Keeper and they are not." Orfei looked around; Cassandra and her people scarcely watched them anymore—all were absorbed in food or whatever else interested them. This was probably the only time many of them met—once each nine days, conversations picking up where they left off nine days before. . . . Among many people in Novyraj, things had been much the same; people rarely cared for anything not perceived as directly concerning them.

Before them, the gate shimmered, silver and alive. Again, Orfei took Aresh's hand and stepped forward. The dragon flapped down, taking a place on Orfei's shoulder, and they all passed through the silvery veil together.

XXXI

DEREK SOUL CRAWLED UP THROUGH THE DARKNESS INTO the realm of dream. He was a child again, seven or eight maybe, in the family flyer with his mother—he could smell her, the warm, perfumed soapy smell that always told him she was nearby. He gazed down at the Kansas plains below. "I wish Daddy were here," he said.

"Your father's busy," his mother said. "You know that."

She was right—his father was in California, still trying to clean up San Francisco from when it got nuked; that was his father, back and forth to California the whole time he'd been in school. He hated it; they never even let him see pictures, and when San Francisco came on the vid, their computer, Chester, always turned it off. The pictures were not for children, his mother said; she didn't know it, but he had an interactive holo called Bay Commando where he became a supersoldier stalking terrorists through the San Francisco streets; he could shoot them with his automatic blaster or fight hand to hand—the hardest part was finding their headquarters and stopping the bomb before everything went red with fire. He'd won only once, and he'd gotten

199

so excited he'd almost told his mother. "Daddy could have stopped the terrorists," he said.

"Of course he could have, sweetheart," his mother said. "But he wasn't there. Now you must stop talking—I've got to keep an eye on the nav systems; there's some shielded toxic dumps outside St. Louis, and you don't want Mommy to get distracted and fly into one, do you?"

"No," he answered. Definitely not—one kid he knew on the edu-net said he lived near a secret toxic dump, said weird monsters came out at night and got into fights with the neighborhood dogs—any dog that got bit died.

"There's the arch!" his mother said. "See it way up ahead? Just keep watching it, we're almost there."

"Okay," he said. He watched the arch grow slowly, but he couldn't keep his eyes on it; on either side of the flyer, plexi domes rose up like ugly gray bubbles full of dark smoke with bright yellow fires deep inside. Around the domes—everywhere—the ground was black. If he squinted his eyes, he could see people in spacesuits going into and out of the domes, like ants crawling through cracks at the bottom of a door. He wondered if that was where they made the monsters the kid on the edu-net talked about.

They landed on a pad near the bank of a smelly river; he could still see the St. Louis arch from the side, rising up to the sky like a rocket ship. A server droid dressed in a funny black-and-white dress came up to the flyer as they got out, and Derek's mother told it she was going shopping for a few hours. The droid said, "Thank you," and took Derek to a huge playground, where there were hundreds of other kids playing in arcades and on slides and swings outside. The droid clamped a kid-finder bracelet on his wrist, told it his age (Derek wondered how it knew), and then gave him a light tap on his bottom, telling him to go on and enjoy himself. The arcade looked fun, with lots of new games he hadn't seen in Topeka, so he went there first; he charged in among the other kids but was quickly disappointed—all the good games kept telling him he was too young to play: The new version of Galactic Cowboy wanted him to be nine, Raid on Mecca said he had to be ten, and Bay Commando wouldn't let him play unless he was twelve! He made his stand in front of this last game, insisting obstinately that he could play if he wanted to until an irritated server droid grabbed him by the collar, told him his mother would punish him severely when she learned of his manners, and put him outside. After that, the arcade wouldn't let him back in.

Derek wandered miserably away; the droid had been mean to him, and he was crying—he certainly didn't want to be punished. He ran to the most distant set of swings, as far away from other kids as he could get, and tried to take out his anger by swinging dizzily high into the sky. Before he could succeed, though, the swing set demanded he slow down, and when he didn't it started screeching, "Alert, alert! Child in danger!" Tears streaming from his eyes, Derek jumped from the swing and ran off to a patch of grass, where he slumped to the ground, closed his eyes, and tried to imagine himself anywhere but where he was. The playgrounds in Topeka were much nicer than this!

"Why are you crying?" Now another kid was bothering him; he looked up—it was a little girl younger than him with bright blue eyes and blond hair. He wanted to say, "None of your business!" but something in the way she looked at him made him just say nothing. He noticed she didn't have a kid-finder on her wrist. After a moment, she smiled at him. "Want to see something?" she asked.

"Maybe," he said. "How'd you get the 'finder off?"

"Easy," she said, reaching forward, pinching the bracelet on his wrist between two small fingers; it came away, falling into her palm. "Now you have to come with me or you'll get in trouble."

He looked at his wrist, wide-eyed—he never seen *that* before! "How'd you do that?"

"I know the computer," she said. "Come on!" She began moving away, and Derek got up to follow her. She headed for the river, farther away from the other kids, the server droids, and the playground. They reached a high fence with signs that said DANGER! in big red letters, but the girl did something to the fence, and it opened up at the bottom so they could crawl through. They climbed down to the riverbank, where the smell was horrible, and Derek

grew scared, but when he thought of going back he decided
that was worse. The little girl was moving ahead, skipping
from rock to rock on the muddy bank to avoid the black,
oily muck in between; Derek scrambled after her.

They came to a cave in the bank, and the little girl disappeared inside a moment, tossing a torch back to Derek
before urging him to keep close behind her. The cave was
small and wet; an older child could never have crawled
through the entrance. A short way in it opened up, and there
was a small table with candles on it and old plastic crates
for chairs. "See?" the little girl said happily. She sat on
one of the crates, and Derek sat on the other.

"Wow!" Derek said as the girl lit the candles. It was
just like a vid about pirates or hobbits or something.
"What's your name?" he finally asked.

"I don't have one," she said with a smile. Her eyes
seemed to shine by themselves. "Yours is Derek Steven
Soul."

"How do you know?"

"I told you I know the computer," she said. "The computer likes you; it says you'll be a good man one day, and
you'll help my brother."

"What brother?" he asked, looking around suspiciously.
This had suddenly gotten spooky!

"Don't worry," she said with a laugh. "They've dam-
aged him gravely, but he is still asleep—he will sleep for
years. Then you'll help him."

"You're just trying to scare me," he said nervously.
"You're weird!"

"No," she said with a smile. "I won't scare you. . . .
Did you know the Earth is alive? It's alive, and it breathes,
and everything you see around you that's alive is what
comes out on the Earth's breath."

Now he didn't have a clue what she was talking about.
"I want to go back," he said. She still smiled at him with
her glowing eyes. "*Can* I go back?"

"Of course," she said. "Put this back on." She reached
forward and clamped the kid-finder back on his wrist. "I'll
tell the computer to let you do what you want—let you
play any game you want, so you'll stop crying."

He got up slowly, still eyeing her suspiciously, and crawled outside. Choking on the stench of the river, he hurried back to the playground and crawled through the fence, not slowing down until he'd reached the arcade. Outside it, he hesitated—if the little girl had lied he could get into more trouble, but he finally decided it wouldn't really matter. He walked confidently back through the arcade's gate, and nothing stopped him. At Bay Commando he pressed his thumb against the credit pad, his kid-finder bracelet came briefly to life, and his soldier icon materialized in the game's holofield. With practiced skill, he guided it across the entrance bridge into the heart of the terrorist-plagued city and played until the black-and-white-dressed server droid came to say his mother was back and escorted him to the flyer pad, never uttering a word about punishment.

XXXII

"WHERE ARE WE?" ARESH ASKED, FINALLY STANDING UP.
Orfei slept quietly on the dark ground, where he'd fallen
upon stepping through the gate.

"I don't know," the dragon said. They were in the mid-
dle of a vast, dark plain at twilight, thunderheads towering
up from low in the sky, their sides raked by lightning that
came and went in silence, never followed by thunder. Huge
shapes rolled and tumbled along the distant horizon, and a
warm, musty wind blew steadily from the direction of the
recently set sun. "We should be safe, though," he added
confidently. "The gate will return once my creator
awakes." They hadn't seen it since the moment they'd first
looked back, when it had dematerialized before their eyes.

"At least it's not getting any darker," she said. "I don't
think I'd like it here at night; this sun's just like the last
one—too stupid to move."

"What do you mean? The sun *doesn't* move—it's obvious."

Aresh sighed and tried to tell Keriktik what it was supposed to be like, how the sun rose in the morning, moved
slowly across the sky, and set, letting the moon shine and

bringing out the stars to follow in its path and fill the heavens with beauty until it rose again to light the land. Some among her people still believed the sun and moon were the gods of love, even though Heng, who'd come to lead them, explained it differently. But what the old ones meant was that the sun and moon spent so much time chasing each other, never going in opposite directions, that they must be lovers. Aresh had never been sure what she believed, but she did know enough about the sun to know it was supposed to move.

"Not the sun," Orfei said sleeping. "The Earth moves—around the sun in a circle." He leaned up on an elbow and tried to describe it visually, twirling one hand around the raised index finger of another. "That's the old science, what the ancients understood and taught. Did you know they sent ships to the stars? They are just like other suns, some with their own earths and moons."

"Orfei!" Aresh said happily. "I tried, but I couldn't wake you!"

"It was Soul," he said. "He was only dreaming, but it was powerful—I feel like something important will soon happen." He told her what he'd seen, then went back farther, Aresh and the dragon asking questions until he'd externalized it all and the three of them sat, pondering the meaning of the mind-bytes' tale. Where they were, there was little else to do except wait for the gate. *Trust Goliath*, he thought, trying not to notice the passage of time. These were Goliath's gates, and they had to be taking them somewhere.

"I don't understand the little girl," Aresh said. "Who is she?"

"She doesn't age," Orfei said. "From Derek's dream of when he was a little boy, until when he saw her in Berlin, she never grew older—she just lost her tongue. I think the dream was something that really happened; that's how I feel—how Goliath wants me to feel?"

"Look!" Keriktik said excitedly. "The gate!"

Orfei turned; once again the liquid silver portal had risen out of nowhere. Like a hologram, he thought. A hologram to invite them into another, then another, and on and on.

What had Clystra done to make this real? Quickly, the three of them stood to plunge into the unknown together.

This time they entered a world of crystal, like a reality carved of ice. "*Dragon Dance*," Orfei said in a whisper. Goliath was guiding them. They stood on the lip of a large amphitheater, the gate shriveling up behind them. Below, three figures knelt down on the tiered steps; when Orfei spoke, one looked up and gasped.

"Quick!" the figure said. It was a young woman in a dark brown robe. "Get the queen!" The woman next to her rose and began backing away.

"Look!" said the third. "A dragon image! They are demons!"

"No," the first said. "Remember the prophecy! *And then will come three—a warrior, his witch, and her familiar!*"

"A familiar's a cat!"

"Be still and wait for the queen!" the leader said, smiling nervously up at Orfei and pushing the other acolyte back to her knees. Orfei glanced at Aresh, and she shrugged.

"What do we do?" she asked softly.

"Wait for the gate," Keriktik said.

"Or the queen," she whispered. "Or whatever comes first?"

Orfei barely heard them; he sat down on the steps and looked around—here he was, within his own creation, the first of all the gateworlds. There was no chance he was mistaken; everything—every line of the amphitheater, every cloud in the sky—bore his mark; he could feel it as if it were still coming out of him, blossoming to life in his holofield, and all that was lacking was his music. Goliath had guided him here—was this where he was to find him and learn what purpose he served? Soul was stirring now, drifting in and out of cloudy dreams; he closed his eyes and sought the mind-bytes, urging them forward, demanding they show him more. Slowly, they obeyed his commands, and the ghostly realm of *Dragon Dance* faded away.

XXXIII

DEREK FELT A RUSH OF AWARENESS AS HIS BIOSYSTEM began countering his sedatives with bursts of amphetamines. What had happened? The last thing he remembered was the tunnel, everything shaking and turning upside down, Holly fighting to keep control of the t-bug. An earthquake? Behind these thoughts, the dream of his youth came back to him; he put it aside for the moment and rose stiffly from his bed. There was a dull ache in the back of his head; he checked the biosystem's display and learned he'd had a concussion—ninety-five percent repaired and recovered. He pulled on his pants and went out to find Holly. The lounge was empty, as was her room. "Juliet?" he said.

"Dr. Soul," the computer replied. "I have a message for you from Dr. Linn. Also, Mr. Paul Kramer has expressed a strong desire to see you."

"Okay," he said. "Let's hear the message." Juliet played it, and Derek sat down with a heavy sigh. "Damn!" he said. The message was fifteen hours old, and he didn't doubt her ending words—something had almost certainly gone terribly wrong. "Tell Kramer I'm on my way," he said, rising. He verified the time and nature of Holly's de-

parture with Lieutenant Morris and told the marine to com-
mandeer another t-bug. In the meantime he took a quick
shower and dressed in his uniform.

While he waited, he mulled things over critically. Too
much seemed to have happened for him to take in easily—
not only Holly's disappearance, but her other work, before
she'd left. Had she really found Tom Liebowicz—a prisoner of Paul Kramer? He began to feel guilty for whatever
had happened; pressing her seriously to consider Paul's
story of deserters was certainly his fault. Yet something felt
wrong about everything—the weird geoscan analysis, for
instance. Tunnels with *excessive* density? Paul knew how
to get into them—hell, he had the entrances blocked off!
So why hadn't he just taken a squad of marines down the
damned things and solved the mystery once and for all?

It amazed him that he hadn't thought about that same
question before. Maybe he'd assumed Paul was in no hurry,
that he didn't want to risk armed conflicts if the deserters
were armed. Maybe it was the excessive density entering
the equation—something to propel them back into Holly's
weird ideas and theories, only Holly wasn't with him anymore. If her message was to be believed, she might well
be dead at the hands of the man Derek was preparing to
visit. Well, he wouldn't make her mistake; Lieutenant Morris was going with him.

As the marine guided the t-bug through the tunnels, Derek realized how ominously high the stakes had grown.
Gone was the tension between Holly and himself, the competing ideas, the unspoken desires—all that which had
given the previous day the air of a game, as if they'd been
two fools playing detective. Now it was only he, his partner
whisked away, a trained killer in her place beside him.
There would be no room for him locking up now, for letting
his mind drift to memories of Linda where he could wallow
in depression. There'd be no room to ignore anything that
might happen; Holly's life could yet depend on his actions.
Reaching Moscow headquarters, he made his way straight
to Paul Kramer's office, pushing open the door without any
regard for decorum. "Where is she?" he demanded gruffly.

"Gone!" Kramer said, half-laughing. There was a hard, maniacal edge to his voice.

"I'm serious, Paul!"

"So am I, Derek!" he said, slapping his hands down on his desk. "She is *gone*. I put her in a room—locked her in a room, I should say—and the system reported her missing a half hour later."

Derek took a step back. Somehow, a small blaster had materialized in the other man's palm—slipped down from his sleeve? He was waving it at Morris. "Get out of here!" Paul screamed at the marine.

Derek glanced at Morris. "You'd better do what he says."

"But sir!"

"Go!" he commanded. Slowly, Morris backed out of the room, never taking his eyes off Paul. "You can't get away with this," Derek said. "It's gotten beyond you."

"Get away with what? Don't you get it? Your partner disappeared! Just like the rest—poof! I didn't *do* anything!"

"You locked her up!"

"That's right, but that's all—everything else just happened. She was spying on me, dammit!"

"She was looking for Tom Liebowicz."

"Ha!" Paul said. "I told you to stay out of my business—this is my investigation!"

"Is that why you're pointing that blaster at me?"

"I don't know—maybe I'll kill you."

"Paul—" He was cut short by a side door opening unexpectedly, Linda stepping unawares into the room. That was when Derek made his worst mistake; adrenaline had his muscles coiled tight, bursting for action, and when Paul's eyes went from him to Linda, he began to move—for Paul and the blaster. His opponent, however, was only momentarily distracted; before Derek could get halfway to the desk, the blaster swung back to point at his chest, and Paul's wild eyes pinned him in mid-stride, motionless and off-balance. Everything else was still moving. He heard Linda scream, "Paul! No!" then something struck him in the side.

As Derek fell to the floor, the blaster lit the room a cold white. A weight came down on top of him; he rolled away and discovered it was Linda—Paul's weapon had cut a clean hole through her neck, and her eyes stared at him, twisted into a mask of horror.

"Freeze!" came Morris's voice through the heavy silence of death. Derek heard the blaster clatter distantly to the floor, then he reached out to touch Linda's face, smoothing out her expression, trying to massage away her look of pain and terror. Blood was pouring from her wound; her lips moved uncertainly, but words were impossible. Tears filled her eyes; he knew there was no way to save her—she had only seconds left. After all that had happened, she'd saved his life and lost her own in the process. He eased her onto her back, kissed her gently on the lips, then held her tightly while her body convulsed once and went still.

XXXIV

IN THE CRYSTAL WORLD OF *DRAGON DANCE*, ORFEI CLUNG
to Soul, to Linda Kramer and the fragile light of her failing
life. In the past's agony lurked the present's salvation—this
he could only hope, else justice grew meaningless, like this
crystal world of dragons and knights and queens he'd so
carelessly given life, never imagining it might later gain
substance. Beyond his mind, it went on, an errant, dis-
obedient child:

"I don't think he hears us," Aresh said.

Keriktik ruffled his feathery wings. "My translation
function is not at fault," he said flatly.

"Orfei," Aresh said, "the queen has come to speak with
us!"

He *could* see her; the queen was tall and full-figured,
like a transplantation of Lysis across time. Her maroon
robes and ruby crown gave her added presence, setting her
apart from the icy architecture of his hologram, but her
voice was Orfei's music set to different words: "You are
the prophecies come true," she said. "You will both restore
and end the world."

He said nothing, his silence a solemn sentinel above

them. Soul's pain as he at last laid Linda's still body on the past's stony floor was far more real.

"I don't understand," Aresh said distantly. "Restore what?"

"The dragon," said the queen. "He was the heart of the world, but we killed him. Now, in his absence, the earth shakes and dissolves—can't you feel it?"

Goliath? Orfei thought. Somewhere, deep in his mind, the mind-bytes resonated with his thought of that name. . . . *Direct me, Goliath—make the path clear for me to see!* Soul's pain came on in waves, pulsing in and out of his mind, pulling him deeper and deeper, as if a great maw had opened to swallow him up.

"I feel nothing," Keriktik said from the other side of the world.

"He's gone again," were the words Aresh said to chase those of the dragon. Within the heart of the beast, Orfei cast a final glance outward: Aresh's dark beauty and her eyes—they sought him but couldn't see; the dragon's eyes had turned now to the crystal sky, its wings flinching, its animate heart battling the artificial instincts of an artificial world; between them, the queen stood like a nervous statue, a pillar of purpose and determination entrapped in the hologram—Orfei's world, from which he'd created no escape. . . . As he watched them, they shimmered. "You can't feel it?" came the queen's voice as song.

Orfei's vision fluctuated, began to break apart. Thick, vibrating pulses came up from beneath him to spread outward. . . . *I feel it*, he thought, then Goliath and the mind-bytes drew him deeper, Aresh, Keriktik, and the queen of Dragon Dance evaporating along the horizon of external reality while he sank, ever more rapidly, into infinity. There came worlds of misty blue-and-yellow haze, primordial seas wherein the universe began. The stuff of stars danced and flowed through him, wiping thought away, leaving nothing but wonder backed by a dark, terrible sense of power, as if on a whim he could shatter nascent stars with the slightest of breaths. This power filled him, then, like butterflies, the mind-bytes carried him gently through to a deeper void. Here there was solidity and warmth, and his power no longer made him afraid, for he was not alone—across the void were his brothers and sisters, their voices reaching him in celestial song, melodies that pierced through to the core of his existence, that called him to join in, but his voice was silent. He was not yet whole, and his wonder evolved into longing, and the longing into pain.

The void was gray substance that refused to embrace him, and his sad agony grew greater still. Somewhere beyond was a light, but when he reached out to touch it, he couldn't move. His heart had become a prism, and its refractions his chains.

XXXV

DEREK IDLY TAPPED HIS FINGERS AGAINST THE SIDE OF Juliet's manual keypad while Collier's image came to life in her holofield. "Soul!" the secretary bellowed. "What the hell's going on? I ordered you to report hours ago!"

"I'm sorry, sir. It's been a long day." It had—he'd no more wakened than Linda had been killed. Recovering from that had taken hours, and there'd still been Holly to worry about. Morris had arrested Paul Kramer on his authority, then they'd had to disable Kramer's security leading to the place Holly had been kept before indeed finding her absent. Tom Liebowicz had emerged unscathed, if somewhat cautiously; he'd told his story, then sworn he'd seen or heard nothing to disprove Paul's assertion that Holly had simply disappeared from her room. On top of all that, with Paul's downfall and Linda's death, Derek had suddenly found himself in charge of it all. He'd ordered an immediate halt to all work, but matters kept getting worse; since then he'd had no less than three fresh reports of disappearances. The very *last* thing he wanted on his mind was Collier. . . .

"C'mon, son," the secretary said. "Both our butts are on the line now!"

"They're still disappearing," Derek said wearily, finally opening up. "Three more today, since I canceled operations. Linda's dead, maybe Holly as well, and I'm doing everything I damn well can to keep myself together! We've got to shut this place down and get the people out of here— if you want to know the truth, that's the way I see it."

Collier grunted. "That'd be a helluva lot easier if we'd found the Sov archives on the star elves experiments."

"I'm aware of that, sir."

"You don't think Kramer's been sitting on that as well?"

"Honest answer? It never crossed my mind."

Collier eyed him steadily. "Dammit, Derek! The president's not going to—"

"That's my advice, sir," Derek said, cutting him off. "You've got to do something no matter what. I *can't* run this place; I'm not even remotely qualified. You're out two administrators, and the workers are scared to death— you've got to find new people to head this project anyway, so why not cut back to a minimal staff in the meantime?"

"I'll mull it over," Collier said. "What about you?"

Derek sighed. "I don't know. I don't think I can give this up—there're a few leads yet to follow. I've *got* to find out what happened to Holly; Paul swears she just disappeared from the room he locked her in."

"You believe it?"

"I don't know. I want to believe she's still alive."

"Ship that bastard back here, Derek. I can pull in a favor or two from Central Intelligence and still keep it in the family—pick his brain apart and make damn sure that's what really happened."

"Yeah," Derek said distantly; he didn't like the secretary's tone, but he needed to know. "Just keep him alive."

"Whatever you say, inspector general. In the meantime, you want another assistant?"

"No. I would, however, like to get back to work."

"For the moment," Collier said firmly, "I'll let you. But I want a *full* report filed on this whole thing with Holly and the Kramers."

"Will do, sir."

Collier's hologram dissolved. After a while, Derek told Lieutenant Morris to escort Paul Kramer to the viaduct for immediate transfer to Berlin, then file a detailed incident report on the events of the past twenty-four hours for the secretary's personal attention; after all, he knew as much as Derek did. "Write at the end that I'll—no, we'll—amend it if anything new comes to light," he said.

The last order actually made the marine smile. "Thank you, sir," he said. It took Derek a moment to realize he'd offhandedly given the officer a very choice opportunity to advance his career.

With Morris gone and Collier out of the way, he was finally left to think. The secretary had taken his mind off Linda—that was helpful, he supposed; he'd imagined a lot of things on his way to Moscow, but seeing his ex-wife gunned down by her husband before his eyes hadn't been one of them. He was amazed he could reflect on it at all with an objective mind; it was, perhaps, the result of shock, and if he gave it a chance, the grief would surely catch up with him. That wouldn't do Holly much good if she was still alive. It was time, he realized, to investigate Paul's tunnels. He took the t-bug himself, straight to the tunnel from the Liebowicz-Crawley report. Though he'd called off work, the marines had kept a three-man crew at each security post, apparently on orders from their own commanders. These three young men looked particularly glad to have his company; he supposed they'd had a hard enough time just maintaining their post in the empty excavation area.

"It's just a dead end, sir," one of them said as he rolled away the rocks sealing the crack in the tunnel wall. "They had us search it for hours for concealed passageways—ain't nothing there."

"Thanks," Derek said, "but I'll look anyway." The marine gave him a wide-angle lantern and escorted him through the narrow opening. The passage walls were raw rock; Derek knew little of geology, but the passageway didn't strike him as a natural formation. He walked now—according to Juliet's geoscans—in a space of excessive density, too dense to be a tunnel. After twenty feet or so it veered to the right, just as reported by Liebowicz. They took the turn and found the way strewn now with huge boulders and fallen slabs of rock.

"Must've been the quake," the marine said. "It sure wasn't like this before."

Derek directed his lantern into the rubble. "That looks like a passage through," he said. He tested the stability of the slab in front of him, then climbed cautiously over it. Past the obstruction, deeper exploration appeared possible; adjusted to a tight beam, the lantern's light cut a good hundred feet into the darkness. "I thought this was supposed to be a short tunnel."

"It was," the marine said. "The quake must've cut it deeper. You'd better let me go first, sir." The man sounded nervous to Derek, but he climbed over the slab and moved ahead, picking through the boulders. Derek followed; he felt too excited to feel foolhardy; after all the cerebral mysteries and trials of the past days, having something physical like this before him had a rejuvenating effect, as if, full of mental and physical fatigue, he'd dived into a pool of cool blue water. The stone here was granite; in his lantern's light it glistened and sparkled with a raw brilliance, illuminating something in the human soul, in memory—man's visceral affinity with the rock of the earth and the human urge to realize it, to sculpt it and bring out the images hidden deep within. Here, at last, the mystery was physical.

Through the rubble, the passage continued unobstructed a short distance, then opened up into a vast room. The lantern revealed desks and banks of electronics and computers—more defunct Sov science. Derek looked around and activated his comm device. "Juliet—are you there?"

"Awaiting your command, Dr. Soul."

"Pinpoint my location and match it with those geoscan holos."

"You are within solid rock," the computer said after a moment.

"Doesn't look that way from here," he said. "That's matched to a scan since the earthquake?"

"Affirmative, Dr. Soul. Two scans since the geological event."

"Thank you," he said. He approached the Sov equipment; some apparently detected his presence and, though abandoned perhaps for decades, powered on in a sudden show of lights. Holofield monitors activated—words in dead Cyrillic letters, but the icon-driven interfaces and associated pointing hardware looked familiar enough and inviting. Derek toyed with one, finding on first try a massive database of cryptic text and formulae. He pulled back the menu and made a second choice, this effort rewarded more visually with vidfootage of something he immediately recognized—star elves. "Jesus!" he said under his breath; he'd found without trying that which had eluded the entire Moscow operation for the past several years. Looking around, he found it hard to imagine that Paul Kramer had known of this place—it *must* have been laid open by the earthquake; however paranoid the man was, he wouldn't have kept this from Philadelphia—this was why he was really here. This discovery would have made Paul a hero, the success relegating any other potential concerns over his capabilities to insignificance. Derek felt a twinge of guilt: Paul had likely been on the brink of this discovery; had Derek's mission been delayed a few days, his ex-wife's husband might himself have stumbled upon this, and Holly's disappearance and Linda's death—the entire sequence of events of the past two days—might have been averted. Instead, Paul was in the viaduct to Berlin, headed for a fate at the hands of CI psychtechs that Derek preferred not to think about.

The star elves in the vid appeared to inhabit a small artificial environment—that meant a vacuum if he correctly recalled what he'd heard of their requirements. The chamber was bare, lined with rough-hewn rock and lit by a pair of solar strips in the ceiling. The creatures themselves—there were two—didn't do much; they lazed on the rocks. When they moved they were liquid, and in appearance they were much the same, gelatinous with large protuberances on their heads, resembling something between chimpanzees and rabbits. Derek watched a while, then skipped forward a few times before realizing he'd found archival research vid—to be measured not in hours or days, but in years. Sighing, he stood and stretched—the environmental chamber would be somewhere nearby; his lantern revealed a few passageways off the main chamber. "What do you think?" he idly asked the marine.

"More old Sov science," the marine said. "I suppose it means something to somebody."

Derek had almost imagined he still had Holly with him; the marine's response jolted him back to reality. He told the man to scout the perimeter and make note of each side passage. What really puzzled him was the excessive density—the geoscan's inability to map out this chamber which was obviously very real. He guessed some previously unknown trick of Sov technology was responsible— a trick that might have succeeded indefinitely but for the unpredictable violence of the Earth itself. Still, the idea didn't totally fit—if the Sovs could hide this part of the complex from satellite geoscan technology, why hadn't they hidden the entire Moscow underground? Or had they done just that in a more sublime way? Perhaps this chamber and the star elves experiments weren't the end, but just the beginning; perhaps all important research had been conducted in protected complexes such as this one, and he'd revealed only the tip of the iceberg.

So where did all this leave his own mission? Paul's desertion theory gained plausibility, at least on the surface. With significant portions of the Moscow complex hidden, perhaps some workers had stumbled upon them, maybe not deserting, maybe just getting lost. He hadn't made any great progress, but he had a strong feeling that what he'd learned played a part in the disappearances. Until he knew more, he decided it best not to speculate; if all the important Sov work was indeed hidden, a number of less benign theories could come quickly back into play—monsters and Sov death droids included. He reactivated comm with Juliet; "There's a Sov system here," he told the computer. "What do you need to tap in from remote?"

"That depends on the hardware—if it's typical, the interfaces are fairly plentiful near your location. I will require a human operator."

"Will a marine do? There are two men still outside."

The computer went silent a moment. "I am directing one

to the nearest interface on your orders. Is that all, Dr. Soul?''

''No,'' he said. ''Find me the best local geologist in the files and get him down here—I want an expert opinion on the geoscan failures.'' He directed the beam of his lantern around the room; the long shadows cast by the desks and equipment made him feel like a burglar. ''Get me some lights as well—use my marines, and don't let any of these instructions, or any future ones, be overheard; let's keep this discreet for the time being.''

''Understood, Dr. Soul.''

His marine escort returned briefly and reported four exits from the large room before Derek sent him scouting off once again into the darkness. Another man came in through the tunnel a moment later, carrying a device the size of a small briefcase; Derek listened to Juliet direct him to the banks of computers and instruct him on connecting the interface; her patient words would have been understood by a child, and Derek might have found the scene comical in less serious circumstances. Once the man had finally established a link to Juliet's satisfaction, Derek sent him back out to escort the others he hoped would soon arrive. While he waited, the first marine came back. ''You'd better come look at this, sir,'' he said.

''What is it?''

The man had a bewildered look in his eyes. ''I don't know,'' he said. ''Maybe you can tell me.''

Derek got up and followed the marine to one of the room's exits. The hall took a turn after a short distance; immediately beyond that, a thin wedge of light came through a half-open doorway. Derek moved forward and looked through the crack; the sight within made him gasp— a vast open space stretched out and down from the lip of the doorway. He recovered after a moment—this *had* to be a hologram; disconnected images floated in the space: pieces of equipment, men and women in Sov uniforms, articles of clothing—sensible things in the midst of abstract shapes and whirlpools of color; it was like the monstrous canvas of a surrealist vid director, stretching out to infinity in all directions.

"Well?" asked the marine.

"It must be a hologram," Derek said, "though it doesn't make a lot of sense."

The other man took a coin from his pocket and tossed it through the doorway; the coin arced and fell, meeting no resistance, quickly disappearing into the distance below them. "It's no hologram," he said.

"Jesus," Derek whispered. He started to reach for his comm device to summon Juliet when the floor beneath them shook violently. The marine was pitched forward, sailing into the open space with a scream while Derek was thrown shoulder first against the wall of the hallway; the impact left him dazed, granting the event a sheen of unreality, like a weird but natural twist in a dream.

A deep rumble filled the air, and the earthquake progressed, punctuated by loud cracks as bedrock gave way under pressure. Perilously nearby, a large chunk of ceiling crashed to the floor, jolting Derek into action. He hesitated only a moment, thinking of the marine, before turning back to fight the unsteady floor in an effort to get clear of the corridor. In the main chamber, however, matters were worse; the air was cloudy with the dust of pulverized rock, cutting visibility to little more than a few feet. He panted for breath, frantically casting about with the beam of his lantern, trying and failing to remember with certainty the direction of the exit. A shower of dust and small rocks came down on his head, propelling his legs forward aimlessly; he crashed into the banks of computers, then slipped on the floor made slick by fine dust, falling violently on his side. Pain seared up his arm as the sharp edge of a rock sliced the length of his forearm. Meanwhile, the rumble in the earth grew to deafening volume.

Derek shouted for help—futilely; he could scarcely hear his own pleading voice. He tried to stand, but his legs refused to cooperate, and he finally fell face forward onto the floor, covering the back of his head with his hands. Even if he could find it, the room's exit would almost certainly be sealed off, and for all he knew the situation outside could be worse. . . . Rocks pounded down around him on all sides, and something wet dripped onto his face—blood from his slashed forearm. It struck him obliquely and suddenly that these moments could well be the last of his life—any second, the raging earth might indiscriminately drop a ton of granite on his head. He tried to direct his thoughts elsewhere, to pleasant times—his first week with Linda, Holly's breakfast in bed—but these shadows of the past faded as quickly as they came, unable to compete with the mind-numbing demands of rock shattering against rock, the fury of the earth asserting its timelessness over man's short and fragile life.

He began to cry out with each new crash; he lifted his head—the world was a dark cloud of impenetrable dust now, all noise and blindness. The light of his lantern came in from the side in feeble shafts, mere shadowy flickers in the haze. He imagined hints of other lights at the edges of his vision—reds and blues and yellows—the death lights of the Sov machines, brief fires and transient bursts of electronic blue. A sudden thought of Juliet came to his mind—what percentage of the system's knowledge, he wondered, had she succeeded in spiriting away, or did the Sov system still fight on bravely as he did, an injured electronic entity struggling to pass on the accumulated data of its life while the light of its intelligence grew more dim with each moment? Then a small hand reached forward through the dust.

At first the hand seemed a disembodied thing, its owner nonexistent, not hiding somewhere beyond, in the clouded air. It was a child's hand, brushing lightly over his forehead, down his cheek to his lips and on to his chin. The roar of the earthquake lessened—not diminishing, but receding into an aural distance; the hand seemed to separate him from it, drawing a protective boundary to shelter his life from the earth's fury. Effortlessly, he reached out to touch it, drawing the little girl nearer until she towered above him like a miniature goddess. The blue pools of her eyes opened up like windows, engulfing him with ready arms and transforming his world. The earth fell away, yet something more solid replaced it, and he stood, eyes darting about in all directions to find only himself, alone, in the blue haze. He realized slowly that the roar of the earth had completely gone silent.

Was this death? he wondered. Ripples and swirls filled the blue, as if it had substance, like water or the ether of early physics. Was this his mind's final dream, his broken body now pinned to the floor by the unkind Earth? The little girl came back to him now, her eyes become true windows into the blue beyond. "Do you remember me?" she asked; she was whole again, with a tongue—just as in the dream of his childhood.

"Yes," he said. The ripples in the ether smudged the lines of her small figure, making it waver. She seemed to be going transparent.

"My brother is waking," she said, "and this is his pain. You must calm him and make him safe, for he remains much too weak to travel."

"Who are you?"

The girl's shape was liquid. "I am what you think I am—what your people came here to find. I am Kasi'yn; my brother was once called Gul'th."

Star elves? he thought incredulously. "But you're dead."

"No," she said. "The science that once ruled this place lied."

"Why?"

"It did not understand us."

Neither do I, Derek thought.

"I will show you," she said, reading his mind. Her form melted into the blue ether, wiped from his vision, and the blue gradually turned to black. Stars came out in the distant void, and he could feel them looking at him—no, beaming at him, rays of happiness and joy. He was twirling in a slow dance, basking in the light of the universe. He had no arms, but a million fingers—through them he felt the wind brushing over high, snow-crested peaks, water falling in cascades over cliffs, a slow steady sea rubbing coolly against him like an elemental lover. He had a sun whose warmth was always near, pouring down in gentle waves, teasing the air that teased his fingers. Above him, on a barren moon, his children played, awaiting their turns. . . . The vision shifted and time peeled away; now he became his child. A needle ship came from the distant void with men who landed and played with them, then put them in a gray cage to float under the stars—they still shone on him, but then time passed and he was removed from their sight, buried under rock by the men who'd torn him from the heart of his father. Within him, the command was *Wait!*— so he did. The men prodded and cut into him, tying him into their machines, flooding his mind with unnatural power. They twisted his world and bent him, then a final, irrevocable twist came, and the universe exploded in a shower of sparks and agony as man's science pushed him to grow into what his consciousness was not yet prepared to become. His liquid limbs seeped into the rock, and the maternal hand of sleep swept down to close his eyes and remove him, for a time, from the pain.

"Dr. Soul!" came a concerned voice from somewhere beyond. The weird, black vision fled into memory and Derek again felt the hard rock of the earth beneath him. "Dr. Soul?" the voice repeated.

He opened his eyes; he was in a corridor he didn't recognize. "Where the hell am I?"

The man bending over him was a marine, one of Morris's men. "The ramp between three and four, sir," he said. "We were just on our way down with the lights you wanted."

Derek pushed himself up to a sitting position. There were three marines with three t-bugs, the passenger areas loaded with lighting gear. He glanced at his forearm; wet blood covered it from elbow to fingertip, but when he probed with his other hand he could find no wound underneath. "Thanks," he said absently, unsteadily gaining his feet.

"Do you still need the lights, sir?"

"What?"

"The lights," the marine repeated.

Derek looked at the man, trying to gauge the situation. How the hell had he gotten here? His head felt light, as if the strain of recent events had stripped him of any ability to reason. "I don't know," he finally said. "Do we have any readings on that last quake?"

"What quake, sir?"

"The last ten, fifteen minutes! Didn't you feel it?"

"No," the marine answered. He looked genuinely perplexed.

Derek closed his eyes and rubbed his fingers against his temples. How could an earthquake like that not have rocked the entire complex? Then again, why was there blood on his arm, and no cut underneath? And to repeat—how the hell had he gotten here? "Dump some of those lights," he told the man. "I need a ride." He guided them back to the security post outside the tunnel; the two marine guards remained there, accompanied by a third man—the geologist, Derek assumed. The first marine—the one Juliet had used to establish the link with the Sov system—looked visibly shaken when Derek jumped from the t-bug and asked him what was going on.

"I don't really know, sir," the man said. "I just tried to take Mr. Anders here in, but the tunnel's not there anymore."

"What do you mean? Did the quake collapse the roof?"

"What quake?" Anders asked.

"You didn't feel it here either?"

"No. Listen, Inspector General—I've got better things to do with my time than chase after—"

Derek turned away from them, grabbing a lantern and moving into the crack in the tunnel wall. As before, it went in about twenty feet, then turned. After the bend, however, was a blank, rough wall—no sign of the passage he'd used before, not even a hint that any had ever been there. Gone were the fallen rocks and the corridor to the room beyond. . . . He went back out and spoke with Juliet's marine, confirming that the Sov laboratory hadn't resided solely in his imagination. The man said something about a Private McCoy—the one who'd first went with him, the one who'd disappeared into the weird, infinite room of floating people and shapes when the quake had struck—he'd been *very* real. Derek didn't know what to tell the man about his friend; at this point he wasn't sure about anything. All he had to vouch for his own sanity was this one marine; Derek had him describe in detail what he'd done and seen when entering the tunnel on Juliet's command—unless they'd ex-

perienced a mutual hallucination, a good part of what Derek
remembered had been real. He thanked the marines and told
Anders to explore the tunnel for anything unusual and file
a report with Juliet, then he left to go back to his own
chambers.

On the way, Derek brooded; just when things had almost
made sense, the world had turned upside down. What had
happened to McCoy? And what was he to make of the
earthquake and the little girl and her visions? How could
he now differentiate between reality and illusion?

Lieutenant Morris reported success in both tasks Derek
had assigned him; Derek thanked him, then sought the se-
clusion of the work lounge. "Juliet," he said once alone,
"did you get the data from that system?"

"Partial affirmative, Dr. Soul. Data transmission was interrupted after approximately five minutes, thirty-one seconds."

"Summarize please."

"I have data concerning the non-Terran life form from
Alpha Centauri commonly called star elves, spanning a period from July 2046 to September 2049. Data includes written, speculative information only—hard research statistics
and experimental results were never received."

"Anything our people didn't already know?"

"Much, Dr. Soul. I estimate a human time value of one
hundred or more hours to provide a verbal report on your
request."

"Skip it, then," he said. He thought of the names spoken
by the little girl during the earthquake that might or might
not have happened—Kasi'yn and Gul'th. "Did they ever
determine a capacity for language?"

"Negative," Juliet said. "However, the lead scientist
wrote several times of his suspicion that the creatures could
indeed communicate—perhaps mentally—but were unin-
terested in responding to human attempts to establish com-
munications on other levels."

So he couldn't verify the names. . . . "How did it end?"

"That's uncertain."

"Might the official reports of death be false?"

"Very possible, Dr. Soul. The Sovs went to great lengths

in their attempts to communicate with the Alpha Centaurans, wiring one subject into an advanced psych monitor and
control system. Biotech data reports indicate nervous processes occurred on a molecular, rather than cellular, level.
The subject was stimulated chemically and electrically over
long periods of time as its mental patterns were mapped
and analyzed by cryptographic systems—all without apparent success. In July 2049, the experiment yielded unexpected results, and operations were temporarily brought
to a halt—"

"Wait," he interrupted her. "Do you have a specific
report on that event?"

"Yes," Juliet said.

"Begin verbatim translation."

"Incident summary by team leader Vladimir Koontz,
number two-seven-dash-fourteen—quote: 'Today the bio
team added a new synthetic silicate into the chemical trans-
fusion mix. I supervised the operation, observing events
from the main view portal of the isolation chamber; when
the mix was robotically injected, the subject convulsed, and
the containing room appeared to lose substance. I experienced a brief hallucination—of being in the heart of an
erupting volcano, only without pain. The event consumed
perhaps one-half minute, then ended. Three independent
observers reported not similar, but *identical* hallucinations,
and I conclude this may only be judged as a true telepathic
event—the first true progress in understanding the alien's
mind.' End report."

"Thanks," Derek said. "What happened next?"

"Experiments resumed in late August, stimulation of the
alien increasing incrementally after a review of the chemical compounds involved in precipitating the previous
event."

"And then?"

"Nothing. Reports cease on September 4, 2049."

"You mean that's all the data you had when transmission
ceased."

"No," Juliet said. "That category of file in the Sov system extended only until that date, and not beyond. I'd be-

gun to receive visual data files when transmission was interrupted.''

"Well," Derek said, shaking his head and rubbing his eyes. "Ship what you got to Philadelphia for further analysis—send to the direct attention of the secretary; that ought to keep him busy a while."

"Yes, Dr. Soul."

Derek sighed and got up, going to his bathroom to wash the drying blood from his arm. With his arm clean, he thought he could see the faint hint of a scar. . . . What was he to make of all this? The hallucination in the Sov laboratory. . . . What if that wasn't it—what if it had been real? Could he really leap far across the gulf of reason and suppose what he'd experienced to have been not mental, but an authentic distortion of reality itself? The room of floating people—not a hologram? The little girl—not human, but alien, her "brother" the tortured creature subjected to Sov experimental agonies to a breaking point beyond human understanding—Derek's own vision of that very event valid, the alien somehow absorbed into the earth? And if the reports had simply stopped then, within the warped logic of the puzzle could he imagine that the people floating in the infinite, nonholographic room were the human debris of the project?

Perhaps that had been when the room was sealed away, the moment of the birth of the geoscan system's excessive density. It was all a tremendous stretch, but as a whole, it seemed no less plausible than the simple, blatant reality of an entire area of the complex appearing from nowhere, then disappearing as mysteriously as it had arrived—of that he had the confirming proof of another man's word as well as the real data Juliet had obviously received. And the earthquake—only a distortion of reality could explain how something that violent could *not* be felt by others in an adjacent corridor.

Derek wished he had Holly with him again; ideas such as these were her territory, not his. At every step, he couldn't help questioning his sanity. . . . He'd already assumed the little girl's appearance during the quake to be real, so what of her hallucination and her words? Had he truly communed in some way with an alien? Had she shown him her vision, at the same time transporting him to safety several hundred yards from where he'd begun? And for what—to save her "brother"? This strange entity, twisted by Sov researchers, sucked into the earth—the girl implied the raging earth to be his pain—how could all this be possible, and how on earth could he do what she asked?

On that thought Derek's runaway reasoning snagged; given all this being strange but true, how could he begin to contact, never mind assist, a creature he no longer had any idea of how to reach? He'd found it through a tunnel that now was apparently gone—was he supposed to await another earthquake—an *external* one that everybody could feel—for the earth again to crack and the alien again to be revealed? Or perhaps he should explore Paul's other tunnels; if he remembered correctly there were six or seven other accesses to the area of excessive density. That thought sent all energy fleeing from his limbs; it took all his mental stamina to hold the current puzzle precariously in place—he needed physical rest before injecting another mind-fucking experience into the equation. Assuming he could expect that to happen—somehow it didn't *feel* right; an insistent, rational element of his consciousness spoke sagely: *If you believe all this, Derek, then believe in the little girl. Holly would say she's the thing in the system— the one that brought you here with Linda, sent you away to keep you from danger, then brought you back here now. Holly would say she chose you, and that she intercepted the CIS memo and escorted you to your room in the form of Sheila Lorenz, and if you could tell Holly of your recent dream of your youth, Holly would point at it and call it proof—as far back as then, hadn't she "known" the computer? Holly would say all this was why you are here, and she would say to trust the little girl. When the time comes, the little girl will come back to you and tell you what to do—after everything else, she wouldn't now expect you to manage alone. . . .*

No, Derek thought. Holly would be right. In fact, if he should be doing anything, it should be hunting for her. If distortions of reality were possible, the disappeared—Holly

Linn included—might have somehow been shifted out of this one. They might all yet be alive, floating suspended somewhere akin to the nonholographic, infinite room. . . . How could he approach that problem? In a sudden flash of intuition, he recalled how Holly had located Tom Liebowicz by analyzing patterns of demands on the human maintenance systems. "Juliet," he said excitedly. "Did we ever look at the system log of the room Paul Kramer locked Holly in?"

"No, Dr. Soul, but I've anticipated your request."

"You what? Never mind, just tell me."

"She asked repeatedly for an external vidconnect, but requests were denied."

"Were any requests of any kind granted."

"Yes," Juliet said. "She played a vidholo—titled *The Shining Wall*."

Derek swallowed; he'd wanted desperately to avoid another mind-fuck, but here one was, thrust suddenly in front of him. His index finger traced the hard outline of Sheila Lorenz's vidchip in his pocket—could he imagine the proximity of this particular vidholo to two disappearances to be mere coincidence? "Did Holly ever ask you for a thorough analysis of that particular vid?"

"It's an animation."

"What?"

"I have analyzed a previously retrieved copy. The underlying equations are digitally smooth and lacking the spatial approximations typical of data converted from analog."

Derek frowned; though what he remembered was unreal, the idea that the cobblestones and fog were wholly computer-generated had never crossed his mind; they were simply too real in a visual sense. "Why didn't Holly tell me?"

"I don't think she knew," Juliet said. "I initiated analysis in Berlin; by your conversation there with Dr. Linn, I anticipated the request. The systems she tapped for her initial analysis weren't capable of reaching my conclusion; the artificial nature of the vidholo data is only apparent after reconciling extreme resolutions of the equations at multiple points. Standard animation techniques, even those used for virtual reality modeling, are less accurate by a factor of about one hundred.''

''So what are you telling me?''

''That the vidholo was built from scratch, using no visually recorded data, and no known catalog of animation icons or tools.''

Jesus, Derek thought. That sounded impossible, and made everything weirder still. Then again . . . ''How many of the others?'' he asked. ''How many others who disappeared watched that vid as their last recorded request.''

''Five,'' Juliet answered.

That was about ten percent. But, Derek realized, Sheila Lorenz wasn't on the list; she hadn't requested the vid per se, she'd just played a chip. Her room hadn't been equipped with projection vid; she'd had a manual system to compensate, and Derek guessed that was probably the rule, rather than the exception. Nervously, he drew Sheila's vidchip from his pocket and pushed it into Juliet's external interface, activating it manually. The black clouds filled Juliet's holofield, rolling toward him in waves; this time the effect was inescapable—visually and mentally, Derek entered the unreal world, losing all sense of the computer and the work lounge, and after a moment forgetting them entirely. The black, smoky fog and its cobblestone bed became everything; it swirled up, around and through him, dancing and folding into seeming infinity, surfaces like the rippled bellies of distant thunderheads, dark and aligned against the wind, only right before his eyes.

He stepped forward, and his foot touched the stones. Something ahead was calling him, and behind that, he could sense pain. *Gul'th,* came a thought to his mind. Small fingers curled around his hand; the little girl smiled up at him, working her tongueless mouth: ''My brother,'' she said, growing translucent, the fog moving through her, coiling into spirals behind the blue pools of her eyes. The cobblestones exhaled, filling her form with their black breath, retaking her space beside him, the black ghosts of her fingers peeling away from his hand and moving ahead like eddies through a murky sea that folded, back and forth, over its glistening bed of stones.

Another step, and the sound of his footfall echoed, coming first a wet slap, then a whisper, then at last the splash of a falling tear. His senses reached out from his mind like whole appendages, independent of physical nature and location; he thought he could hear the heartbeat of the world, the sound of waves lapping against distant island shores. His skin was a sea of grass, bristling with life, brushed by a wind that passed over his own lips. And before his eyes, the fog refracted and folded again before exploding in a shower of color.

Something pulled him back, and he sank through the cobblestones into the pain. *Gul'th*, he thought, the name echoing up from deep, deep within. The pain shattered the rising thought, but he fought against it; he could feel the little girl now in his mind, guiding his descent, her heart desperate, he both her vehicle and her only hope. He was there to heal. Visions came again, belching volcanoes and rivers of hot, molten blood. Giant needles and probes descended from above, stabbing into the earth, held by the fingers of men—an alien memory of torture. *No.* . . . In his hands he shaped his childhood and sent the boy across the lava plain to pull the needles from the wounds.

But men are evil! It came as more feeling than thought, but it was external, whole and comprehensible. . . . "No!" Derek insisted, his voice the first flowering wave of spring. *Ignorance and innocence*—men are *unwise*.

The visions crashed down, wave upon wave: Feral warriors stalked gore-soaked plains, their weapons dripping with the blood of children; factories dug themselves like leeches into the earth, sucking out the lifeblood of the stone, pulverizing it, spitting it out in clouds of poison that fell on trees that withered, streams that ran from water into lifeless, vile mud. Hordes of men lined up under banners raised from metal beasts with feet like spikes and guns spitting hellfire, bursting shells blossoming over tortured, melting earth. . . . Great forests bowed sadly before ruthless scythes, cradling the stolen lives of thousands while still more factories came, more metal beasts emerged, and more guns shouted their passionless, pointless invectives under bleak and sunless skies. Nearby, skeletal children starved silently; food was the privilege of the lords of steel.

"I know," Derek said with his tears. *I know*. . . . But there was more: There were still the children, human too. There were the small men pushed aside, then eaten by the factories—men without guns. He gathered them in his mind and pushed them into the pain, a parade of men, women, and children, faces marked by hope and sorrow, lightened by simple pleasures. This was man as well: A boy at a zoo, crying because they wouldn't let him set the elephants free; a girl patiently nursing a fallen bird, tending its wounds until it could rise up again to soar through the clouds; a man in the factory, giving his life without complaint to keep food in the mouths of those he loved, clothes on their backs, warmth in their home. Guns and metal meant nothing here. . . .

Through the pain now ran ripples, waves of calm. He moved into the calm, seeking the alien's heart. "There *can* be peace," he said. Men, even many among the lords of steel, were but children without guidance. *Unwise*, even the torturers and scientists—especially the scientists, for they above all feared what they could not understand. The calm was like a new universe, a silver world where the little girl came back. "He must grow," she said, then the universe turned inside out, and Derek plunged into bright, sunny void. His mind spread out and expanded, like leaves on a lake, a sensitive web of perception. The alien moved through him in a wash of starlight; for brief moments they were one, and he knew—everything: the elemental language of stars, the source of life and love, one and the same, secrets so rare that philosophers had never imagined them. Just a moment, then a thought formed and exploded in the starry void—*She is too near!* The communion was broken, Derek sent reeling through a bleak, gray expanse of shadows.

The fall was brief, but it felt eternal; when it ended, he was back where he'd begun—he could feel the fabric of the chair beneath him, smell the lingering scent of Holly's perfume in their work lounge. "Juliet," he said breathlessly, opening his eyes, seeing then that all was *not* the same: The room was bent, twisted somehow. *The Shining*

Wall had played out, and a matrix of orange-and-yellow lights had grown out of Juliet's holofield, enveloping the computer, grown up to touch the ceiling and spread out over the walls.

"Yes, Dr. Soul," she answered calmly.

"What—what is happening?"

"Here?" she asked. "That is a difficult concept."

"Try," he insisted. The lights about her moved and seemed alive.

"I have lost all contact with Philadelphia and the rest of the world," she said. "My limited analysis suggests highly improbable causes."

"Such as?"

"What an imaginative human might describe as a dimensional shift, a folding of reality along spatial lines. My connections with local systems have been unaffected."

"So why the lights?" They were like gentle snakes coiling around her—snakes or fingers. . . .

"My integrity is violated; I have concluded I'm being examined."

"By whom?"

"I've not been given a name."

Derek, however, knew; at least he thought he did. Reality had slipped sideways into the surreal; the wall blocking off his bedchamber had melted and sagged, and what was left had gone translucent, like parchment held up to a light. "Are you in danger?"

"I do not suspect it," the computer answered.

He stood up; things were still changing—he could almost see the details of his rustic hologram through the paper-thin wall. He started toward it, then a sound came from behind.

"Derek!"

It was Holly's voice. As he turned, she emerged from her own bedroom, her hair tousled and her clothes ragged, but otherwise whole and healthy. The sight of her abolished any lingering doubts in the back of his mind—her appearance heralded the end of a mystery; if it also meant the beginning of a new one, then he would not be alone to face it.

"I've just had this crazy dream," Holly said. "I mean,

I thought it was real—actually, I thought I was dead—but it was about Paul and Tom Liebowicz. Paul beat me and broke my arm. . . . Christ, Derek! You're already up and over your concussion—how long have I been out? And what's wrong with Juliet?''

At first he said nothing—just smiled at her. Finally, he moved forward and hugged her. "What's this?" she asked.

"Nothing," he whispered. He moved back and brushed the tangled hair from her face. "You weren't dreaming," he said softly.

"What? Derek, I said Paul broke my arm—look at it, it's fine now!"

"It's beautiful," he said. "You disappeared, Holly. Paul locked you in a room, and you watched a vidholo—remember that?"

Her eyes grew distant, the past coming back to her like a dream. "Actually, yes. Your little girl came and showed it to me. . . ."

"What happened next?"

"*The Shining Wall*—I went into it, beyond that I just remember being very warm."

"You disappeared, just like the others. At least I hope so," he added thoughtfully. "I think we should go out and look for them." He started to turn away.

"*Derek!*" she demanded in exasperation. "What on earth have I missed?"

"I'll tell you in the t-bug."

The work lounge's door opened directly into the outer corridor. Lieutenant Morris and his marines were nowhere to be found; in fact, their rooms themselves had vanished. Their guns, Derek realized. The lords of steel had been left behind.

"This isn't right," Holly said.

"It's okay," he assured her. "It's just different."

"Derek!"

"Come on," he said, taking the driver's side of the t-bug. Holly got in next to him, and he nudged the hovercraft forward at a snail's pace. "The worst news," he said, "is Linda died saving my life." He went on, detailing the frantic hours since he'd wakened—how he'd found her, Linda's fate and that of her husband, his exploration of Paul's mystery tunnels and the star elves archives, and finally his own experience with *The Shining Wall*.

XXXVI

ARESH WAS KISSING HIM, HER LIPS AND TONGUE SWEET
wine pouring into his mind from the future world while the
past, behind it, played on:

Holly Linn grabbed for Derek as their old hovercraft
rounded a bend, finding not the corridor she expected, but
a vast open chamber full of confused, disoriented people,
some from her notepad, but many more she didn't immediately recognize—Sovs, Americans, Japanese. . . . There
were hundreds of them. "*Jesus,*" she gasped. "*I wasn't
even sure I believed you!*"

Derek stopped the t-bug and hopped out. "*I wasn't sure
I believed myself until now*," he said. Was this the floating
room from Paul's tunnel, spilled out into the heart of this
new world? He raised his arms to gain their attention: "*My
name is Soul!*" he called out. "*There has been a—change
of some kind here. I can explain, but first you must wait
while I search for others!*" Among the crowd, awareness
flickered dully behind cloudy eyes. "*Did they hear me?*"
he asked, climbing back into the t-bug.

"*I don't know,*" Holly answered; among the people, she
picked out the faces of Sheila Lorenz and Shane Crawley—

it was like her most fervent dream come true, yet weird enough to demand contemplation of her own sanity for believing it.

"*They'll snap out of it*," Derek said, turning the hovercraft to explore the remaining corridors of the new unknown.

Aresh still kissed Orfei, drawing him back into *Dragon Dance*. "It is nearly complete," he said, opening his eyes. "I have seen the birth of Novyraj at last."

She lay down next to him; while he'd been with Soul, they'd moved him to a bed—crystal, in a crystal chamber in the queen's crystal palace. "What was it like?" she whispered.

He didn't answer for a long time; how could he describe it? "Like love," he said at last. "Lord He-who-knows was right—Goliath is very much alive, and he wants my help."

"For what?"

"I think to end all this. I've been inside his mind—very difficult to understand, but I think that's what he wants."

Aresh hugged him, pressing her body along the length of his. He expected her to ask how he might do such a thing, but she didn't; perhaps she thought he knew and that was all that mattered, or perhaps she knew he didn't know, making the question pointless. . . . In the silence, Soul and Novyraj drifted back to the forefront of his mind; Derek and Holly returned to their rooms, or rather, what their rooms had become—the web of light surrounding Juliet had grown thick, filling the larger portion of the work lounge. "*I have been reprogrammed*," the computer said when Derek asked what had happened. "*I am no longer certain I can fulfill your requests in my present state.*"

"*That's okay*," Derek told her. "*We may not have any more.*" When they left the room, the door dissolved, and the corridor wall grew a vivid green. Before they moved on, a voice came from above them:

"*I have been corrected*," the voice said; it was deep and resonant—no longer Juliet's voice. "*My purpose remains to serve you, Derek Soul. No matter where you are, you have but to speak, and I will hear you.*"

And that, Orfei realized, was the birth of Goliath; the alien Gul'th had taken the artificial intelligence Juliet and made her his voice. . . . All he'd known and understood in his life began here. . . .

The visions of the past commenced to rush forward through time: During Gul'th's transformation, the alien had moved sideways away from the world, keeping within him a spectral template—an afterimage—of the reality he'd abandoned; beyond him, the Moscow complex remained— in turmoil Derek discovered once he had Juliet/Gul'th— Goliath—reestablish unobtrusive links with the outside world.

Those left under the old Moscow could perceive no difference between Derek's disappearance and that of those who'd gone missing before him. But with Derek gone, Linda dead, and Paul Kramer out of the picture, no convincing figures of authority remained, and the workers he'd idled rebelled. As the chaos unfolded, a group of hundreds rushed in concert for the viaduct terminals; heedless of security, and contrary to standing orders, the marines at the checkpoints let them through. After that, the issue was no longer could they leave, but who among them could leave first.

From his haven in the heart of the alien, Derek looked on, fearing the marines would get high-level orders to commence shooting, but such orders never came. Philadelphia—and Secretary Collier by direct extension—had given up. Then, before the Reconstruction Department could renew its exploration of subsurface Moscow with a new project and a new team, the final devastating war came, settling the matter on a permanent basis.

As the Americans abandoned Moscow, life within Gul'th went on. Derek brought the people together, organized them, and formed the First Council. It struck him as strange, but none of the people of this early Novyraj ever expressed any desire to leave, even before the final war. The Sovs among them—from the time of the experiments more than half a century earlier—had nothing left of their homeland now but a nuclear wasteland, and the Americans brought in through *The Shining Wall* were all filled with a

sense of wonder of the new world akin to Derek's own.
Though Derek never knew for certain, he suspected that in
taking each of them, Gul'th had actually been looking for
him, for what he could give him to break the chains of his
past torture. Either that, or the presence of the others had
been the doing of Gul'th's sister, the little girl; Derek never
knew, and Goliath could never tell him. Gul'th had established his link with Juliet and withdrawn shortly thereafter,
leaving her—Goliath now—with much of his power but
little of his knowledge; she had become a part of him without access to the whole, like a conscious mind oblivious to
the subconscious guiding it.

With Aresh in his arms, Orfei witnessed all this, and his
visions of the distant past sped ahead, the years now peeling
away. Derek and Holly built the society of Novyraj, grew
happily old together, and died, taking many of Gul'th's
secrets with them. Two centuries later, the Second Council
twisted a part of Goliath back into the old world and
punched the lift shaft through to the surface, sending two
expeditions into unknown danger and death before deciding
to leave the surface to the radiation and mutated life dom-
inating the bleak environment; Novyraj would keep the
children of Soul safe for eternity—after all, in one or more
of the ancient tongues, had it not meant *New Paradise?*
Hundreds and hundreds of years after that, Orfei Agamon
was born.

In the far future beyond that, Orfei opened his eyes. At
long last, he had seen all Goliath had to show him; now
nothing was left but for him to act. Slowly, he rose. Beyond
his crystal chamber, the realm of *Dragon Dance* stretched
off to the horizon.

His creation. His light-opera brought to life.

Now, he knew, it was his task to destroy the world that
Dragon Dance had become, to separate its reality of light
from the physical nature granted it by Clystra so long before in the Hall of Meeting.

The age of the gateworlds had to pass, and only Orfei
could bring it to an end and usher in the next age, whatever
that might entail. Only Orfei could bring down the gate-

worlds and the prison they imposed on Gul'th's heart. Toward this purpose he'd been propelled, from the moment he'd stepped over the threshold into the Room of the Fourth, and the mind-bytes had entered his head.

"*You will both restore and end the world,*" the queen of Dragon Dance had told him.

Now it was time.

XXXVII

He walked out across a vast crystal plain, leaving the towers of the queen behind him, his eyes intent on the mountains rising slowly in the distance. Aresh walked next to him, and Keriktik glided silently through the air above. The queen and all of her people followed twenty paces behind. None of them spoke, or if they did, Orfei did not hear; his walk was a meditation, each step forward a mantric incantation bringing him closer and closer to the heart of the mystery he explored. With each step he could feel Goliath beneath him, and the air was thick with tension and yearning, as if he walked not only through his own creation, but into the mind of Goliath, the heart of Gul'th.

Orfei stepped, and the crystal earth shook. He stamped on the ground, and it cracked, a long chasm shooting out from his toes to stretch off toward the distant mountains. He stamped again and the earth spit fire. "I made you!" he sang. A slab of earth twisted, then became a feathery wing that pushed upward. He stepped back and demanded the dragon rise. A great beast came up through the crack, looked at Orfei with unreadable eyes, then shot high into the sky above. *That is the beginning*, Orfei thought. *The dragon is reborn.* He moved forward into the chasm, Aresh, then the queen, behind him.

In all directions the world glittered, like a valley of ice. He moved deeper and pushed the walls away. When he reached the bottom he sang again. This was *his* world, *his* creation—now he would bring it to an end. Orfei sang the themes of his light-opera, the theme of the dragon and the theme of the queen, the sad theme of the people and the horrible theme of war; his voice a searing blade slicing through to the source of time itself, he brought the disparate melodies together into a single strand, a heaving, harsh whip of dissonance. Around him, the crystal, holographic world melted and cracked, and still he sang on. Every detail he'd so carefully designed, he now destroyed. He sang, each line gaining new life as it echoed through the chasm. Mountains dissolved in the wake of cataclysmic harmonies—he could see it all in his mind, the queen's palace sinking into the featureless crystal plain, then sliding into the chasm that grew deeper and wider with each moment. Then, beneath him, he sensed Goliath's heart; it reached up to him with warm arms and embraced him, the mind-bytes buzzing frantically, then breaking free. They left his mind, and he sank to his knees.

Around him, through the chasm, his song echoed on. The walls began to melt and sink. He looked on with exhausted eyes, barely noting the weight of Aresh's hand on his shoulder. The walls grew misty, then came shattering down; he realized dully he'd returned them to where it had begun, the great chamber of Novyraj where Lysis and Clystra had tapped the power of Goliath and transformed *Dragon Dance* into the first of the gateworlds. Now *Dragon Dance* was no more. . . . The Hall of Meeting echoed with his song and the confused voices of men; Aresh held him close as new shapes took form in the air above them, vague shapes of buildings and harsh landscapes, crowds of people gathering along the edges of isolated realities—without the substance of the first gateworld to support them, the remaining gateworlds were closing in.

"Is it real?" Orfei whispered, looking at Aresh. "Am I dreaming?"

"No," she said softly. "You have begun the ending of which the queen spoke."

"You are truly the creator," Keriktik added.

"No," Orfei said. "It's only what he wanted—the mindbytes have left me now."

Aresh smiled at him and held him close. Long blades of color slashed through the air around them as the gateworlds converged, all spilling their human inhabitants into the great chamber. Beneath him, Orfei could feel the very fabric of reality stretch as the chamber grew to accommodate the growing sea of humanity, all that man had created over hundreds of thousands of years coming to an abrupt and sudden end. Eternity passed in an instant, then the great chamber's roof opened up to reveal a white, infinite sky.

"The end," Orfei whispered. The dragon of his creation swooped in from the expansive sky and shone like a brilliant constellation above them. The memory of Soul welled up within him—Soul within *The Shining Wall,* moving through the ancient, unfinished halls of Novyraj. "*She is too near!*"

The great dragon of *Dragon Dance* hovered over the heart of Novyraj while an object, the Earth's moon, came through the white of the high sky. The moon grew clear and the sky black, then the dragon shot toward it, a pillar of flame stabbing into the pocked, cratered surface.

Tides of fire washed over the gray world, then reality lurched and inverted in a blinding flash. When vision returned, they gazed up—not at the moon but at its mother Earth, rising now over the horizon of a new, living planet.

XXXVIII

Here ends the tale of the second genesis, the birth of history on our second Earth when Gul'th, the beast, became N'Gaia, the new moon, and the infinity within turned outward, in harmony, at last, with its universe. In other histories, the daughters of Aresh have cataloged the facets and evolution of N'Gaia, yet this is the heart of it all, the rememberer's heart—the truest song, that of Soul and Orfei. Rememberers since have lived nothing to rival it.

In the halls of enlightenment below the palace of Linn, the daughters of Aresh keep the mysteries alive and invite all to come and gaze in wonder at the last work of Orfei Agamon, the gossamer sculpture called Novyraj, its human form and honeycombed heart. It is supposed that N'Gaia resides in it, as he/she resides in all living things, yet on this the observer must decide, to allow the infinity without to reflect off the infinity within until the truth is revealed. The lessons of Orfei are legion, though all must know that some mysteries must remain.

Among the greatest mysteries of the catalog of Aresh is that of Gul'th's pain and final healing, his metamorphosis into N'Gaia on this new Earth so near yet so distant from that which gave birth to mankind. This exodus to the Earth's moon—what purpose did it serve? From the tale of Soul, we have, perhaps, the most telling clue: *The alien moved through him like a wash of starlight; for brief moments they were one, and he knew—everything: the elemental language of stars, the source of life and love, one and the same, secrets so rare that philosophers had never imagined them. Just a moment, then a thought formed and exploded in the starry void*—She is too near! *The communion was broken, Derek sent reeling through a bleak, gray expanse of shadows.* Such was the scene immediately preceding the birth of Novyraj on Earth, and one of the few times the *heart* of Gul'th came to Soul or Orfei in human words.

Who was this *She?* the daughters of Aresh have often asked, and why such pain? Was this Gul'th's insanity, a mere, final reflection of the tortures inflicted upon him by Sov science before Soul completed his healing? It is a thought upon which to reflect. . . . In his final address before his death, from his home in N'Gaia Fall (where the palace of Linn now stands), Orfei Agamon had this to say of it:

> . . . *of this last question (the exodus), I can only imagine that if sense can be made of it, the greatest of the old questions might finally have answers. "She is too near!" I heard Gul'th scream into the heart of Soul. I think perhaps that she might have been Gaia— Earth's Gaia—another of Gul'th's kind, the one, perhaps, that had reached Earth and reached maturity there in the ever-distant past, the one that had given birth to life on Old Earth just as most of us have seen it birthed here on the moon, before our eyes.*
>
> *How else might we understand how we have come here? How are we to know the laws that govern life itself? Might one such law be that only a single creature such as Gul'th may mature in any given space, on any given planet? Might another be that life may not happen at all without the presence of such a creature? These laws, if they exist, might explain much, but the questions cannot end here. Gul'th has thus*

far lived in four forms: The first the strange little vacuum-dwelling creature scarcely larger than a human child; the second the substance, space, and internal, contiguous infinity we knew as the first Novyraj; the third the fragmented infinity Novyraj became under the manipulations of the ancient Fourth Council; and the fourth this—the biosphere within which we now dwell. I have described this last form as "maturing," but how can I truly know when three of four metamorphoses thus far have been followed by another? What of further forms—fifth, sixth, seventh forms? Might they happen? And what might they be like?

What indeed? Much has followed these final propositions of Orfei Agamon—much, our historians tell us, to parallel the follies of the Old Earth. The Monks of the Third Soulistic Order have proclaimed the Fifth Manifestation a holocaust, while the Extended N'Gaia Institute argues with equal vehemence for a paradise at the end of things as we know them, when our sun itself explodes four or five billion years hence. Others say there can be no Fifth Manifestation as N'Gaia has reached perfection and will either die or remain constant until the universe itself comes to an end.

It is against such speculations that this chronicle is recorded, lest the controversies grow great enough to tear yet another world of men asunder, even as the wreckage of the old humanity's past passes daily through our skies. We are the children of Novyraj, yet in three generations we have become more akin to those of Earth before Novyraj was dreamed. We have learned anew the ways of a living planet, how to carve dwellings of the rocks and till soil—soil that did not even exist a scant hundred years ago. We know the value of sun and rain, the fury of lightning, and the pleasures of the seasons—to us, those who dwelled in Novyraj and knew none of this, though they be our fathers, seem like children. We have grown again, but let us not grow apart—let us not battle or divide ourselves on opposite sides, for or against some proposed or imagined truth. The dangers of such divisions far outweigh the temporary comfort of supposed knowledge.

No—let the truth be the truth and let mysteries remain, like the simple wonder to be felt in gazing out at the same stars known to our ever most distant ancestors. What is told here is all that is known and important of the genesis of our world; it is as real as a rememberer might make it— all that Orfei told Aresh over the last years of his life, all that she later conferred upon Keriktik, the dragon/eagle. The mysteries in this we must cherish for what they are, as we all continue to cherish Keriktik, the companion of Orfei and Aresh who yet lives, his crystal wings teasing the air of the palace of Linn, his wise voice and eyes known to us all.

No, let us not forget the lessons of the past, as we do not forget Keriktik, Orfei's own creation freed by Lord He-who-knows and who helped Orfei free N'Gaia from the false clutches of men. He who remains proof that all this is true, and he who, through the mystery of his nature, has offered me the honor to be. . . .

Artemis Drak
First Rememberer to Orfei and Aresh

THE CONTINUATION
OF THE FABULOUS
INCARNATIONS OF IMMORTALITY
SERIES

PIERS ANTHONY

FOR LOVE OF EVIL
75285-9/ $5.99 US/ $7.99 Can

AND ETERNITY
75286-7/ $5.99 US/ $7.99 Can